The Child of Two Worlds

M. E. Megahee

ISBN: 1494314800
ISBN-13: 978-1494314804

DEDICATION

This book is dedicated to my family who have always been there for me when I needed them, filled with nothing but love and support.

ACKNOWLEDGMENTS

I would like to thank David Skinner and Lisa Love for doing a great job on the cover. I would like to thank the AWC Writing Collective for all the things I learned from them. And I would like to thank my dad most of all for supporting my writing and doing everything he could to make me a better author. I would like to thank the rest of my family for their support and my best friends for loving my writing as much as they do.

CHAPTER 1
NEWCOMER

"Run, Schuyler," my aunt hissed, her voice only slightly louder than the splatter of raindrops.

"Why?" I asked.

"He's figured it out."

The man ahead of us had stopped walking with his head tilted in our direction, his nostrils flaring. He took a step toward us, and Aunt Lenore shoved me in the opposite direction. My feet moved of their own volition as I took off down a back alley, the water rolling off my leather pants. I glanced back and saw my aunt right behind me.

Sewage and other noxious odors bombarded my nose, but it wouldn't disguise my scent from the vampire following us. As he grew closer, Aunt Lenore whirled around. He lunged, but she sidestepped and kicked him against the brick wall. He collapsed on the pavement.

"Keep going, Schuyler," she said.

"Not without you."

The vampire surged to his feet, baring his fangs, and leapt into the air. He landed on the fire escape above us, sneering. I blinked uncontrollably against the rain that battered my eyes.

"We can't let him get back to his coven, now that he knows about you." Aunt Lenore looked back at me as the vampire ascended. "You know what you have to do."

"I hate this." I drew my short sword from the sheath strapped to my back.

We jumped onto the fire escape ten feet over our heads and gave chase. If he got back to his coven and told them about me, then the hunt would begin. I was a first in their world: a vampire/werewolf hybrid. The vampires and werewolves have been at war for over two thousand years and a co-mingling of the bloodlines was forbidden. To them, I was an abomination.

We leapt from roof to roof. The vampire was fast, but I was faster. Even though I was a barely into my immortality, being of both breeds made me stronger. When I was a few feet away, the sediment crunched beneath his feet as he turned to face me.

"So you think you can kill me," he said, but I saw fear in his eyes.

"I have no choice. Either you die or I do," I said. "It's nothing personal."

"Just let me go."

"I'm sorry."

In a flash, he knocked my sword from my hand and took me to the ground. He leaned over me, his fangs extending and his eyes turning black. As he lowered his head, my hands moved to push him back and he was catapulted across the roof, without my ever touching him. When he landed, Aunt Lenore removed his head with one fluid motion of her sword.

Aunt Lenore made her way to me as I got to my feet, staring at my hands without comprehension. She grabbed my forearm and jerked me closer.

"What did I tell you about hesitating?" she asked. Her stormy gray eyes looked worried. "They will not hesitate with you."

"I know. I'm sorry."

She sighed and pulled me into a hug. "Let's get rid of the body and get out of town."

We placed the body in an old rusted drum and lit a match. The fire consumed it in seconds. I looked at my aunt, so confident and strong, her white-blonde hair soaked to the skin with her ears poking out from the sides. Her brows were drawn and she was thinking hard on something. I pulled my leather trench coat tighter. But all I could think about was how I had thrown that vampire across the roof. That wasn't a normal trait for either a vampire or a werewolf.

****

The dismissal bell jerked me from my daydream. The students gathered their things and shoved them into their bags. The smell of old textbooks and new school supplies permeated the air. My sensitive hearing picked up the taps of raindrops on the roof of the trailer we were in. The girl walking out in front of me slipped on a wet spot and fell down the last two steps, her books and supplies going everywhere.

"What a loser," a kid from our class said, and other students laughed.

The girl on the ground blushed with embarrassment. The others walked away as I set my bag on the steps and bent down to help her gather her things. She glanced up at me and gave a small smile.

"Thanks," she said softly.

The wind blew some of her papers, and I rushed to grab them. "They're jerks. This is just high school. If you can make it through this, then you can make it through anything."

"They make fun of me every day."

"Let them. Besides, high school will probably be the peak of their life."

"I'm Laurel." She held out her hand.

"Schuyler."

We shook hands and stood before I handed her stuff back. As she left, I picked up my bag and headed for second period Astronomy.

In Astronomy class, I took a seat near the back and pulled out my notebook to doodle on as other students filed in. One of my favorite things to do on each first day of school was watch who chose certain electives. There were the jocks who thought this class would be a breeze, and then there were the "nerds" who thought we were all in a *Star Trek* movie. Sometimes I wished we were.

An intoxicating scent caught my attention and my hand froze mid-doodle. It was a scent I had never come across before. The scent's owner walked by me and sat down a few rows ahead and one row over. He had raven, black hair, chiseled features, and the physique of a god. But I couldn't look away from his face. He was talking to a blonde-haired guy sitting next to him. I had never seen either of them before.

The black-haired guy's nostrils twitched, and his head rotated in my direction only to stop when he saw me. Whoa! He eyes were beautiful, an ice blue color that had me mesmerized.

"Good morning, everyone," Mr. Matthews said as he strolled in, jerking me out of my trance, and went to the front of the class. He took his roster in hand and looked around the room. "Please raise your hand when I call your name."

The A's and B's passed, and I raised my hand when he called "Schuyler Chase". The blonde was Caleb Farell and the black-haired guy was Zachary Warner.

"Let's get started." Matthews clapped his hands together, and gestured for a student to turn out the lights.

Matthews fired up the Power-Point and we watched slides of astronomical phenomena. Seeing all those stars lulled me into a different daydream of my mother putting me to bed at daylight, my father humming a soft lullaby I heard only in my dreams. Five minutes before the bell, I put my things away and looked up to find Zachary staring at me.

In third period History, Caleb wound up sitting next to me.

"Hello," he said.

His voice was deep, but soft, soothing. My muscles relaxed. "Hi."

"I'm new here. My name is Caleb."

"Schuyler."

Caleb had the brownest eyes I had ever seen. "So. What do you do for fun around here?"

Well, there was running through the woods at night, hand-to-hand combat, and sword fighting. But I couldn't really tell him that.

"To be honest, not much. You kinda have to make your own fun," I said.

Caleb leaned closer in a conspiratorial manner. "It's a good thing I know how to have fun."

The teacher, Ms. Hawkins, handed out the syllabus after roll call. In a monotone, she began to recite the syllabus word for word.

"I hate it when they read the syllabus to us," I mumbled.

"It's like they think we can't read," Caleb said and smiled, making him appear even more handsome.

Syllabus reading was very annoying to me. This was my twelfth time going through senior year of high school. Since I was a hybrid, it wasn't safe for me to live in a coven or pack. So my aunt decided it was best to immerse me in the human population and move to a different state each time I graduated. I had to admit it was a good idea. Who would think to look for a sixty year old immortal in a high school? But that also meant I had to be absent for picture day, not to mention the fact that Aunt Lenore continuously ran a hacking program that deleted any pictures of me that surfaced on the internet if anyone took a picture of me without my knowledge.

"Would you want to hang out after school?" Caleb asked.

For a second, I almost said yes. I sat up straighter and cleared my throat. "I can't. My aunt's very strict." That wasn't true, but teenagers found it easier to blame everything on their parents.

"That's too bad."

The conversation paused as Ms. Hawkins droned on.

"Are you friends with Zac?" I asked.

"Yeah. I've known him since I was a baby," Caleb said.

"Why was he staring at me?"

"You caught that, huh?" Caleb chuckled and shrugged. "I guess he likes you."

"Great."

"What? Is there something wrong about him liking you?"

"I don't do so well with guys."

"Did you just get out of a bad relationship?"

I rubbed my forehead. "Never been in one."

Caleb's eyebrows shot up. "Really?"

"Really."

"That's hard to believe considering how beautiful you are."

There was no way for me to have any kind of relationship. Humans were forbidden to know of our existence, and a vampire and a werewolf would kill me on sight. That left me with zero options for suitors.

Caleb walked me to my locker once class was over, and then I headed to Anatomy. Zac caught my eye when I first entered the room. From the doorway, I could pick up his delicious scent, and my back straightened even more, the relaxed feeling I had with Caleb leaving me in a second. With a shake of my head, I cleared my thoughts and made for a table on the opposite side of the room. My training ensured I was always alert and ready for anything, but I found myself studying Zac.

His muscles bulged against his tight shirt and his dark blue jeans hugged his narrow hips. He had the body of a god. As I eyed him, he turned to look at me, and every nerve in my body tingled. Someone tapped me on the shoulder and I jumped.

"Sorry girl. I called your name twice but you were zoned out," a friend said as he sat next to me.

I gave him a smile. "Hi, Dante."

"How is my beautiful vixen doing today?"

I glanced at him and saw a big smile on his face. "I'm good. I'm assuming you have a new line you wanna try?"

"Yes. I practiced this one in the mirror this morning." He cleared his throat. "I've got a thirst, baby, and you look like my kinda Gatorade."

I laughed. "I haven't heard that one yet. I'll have to write it down." And I had heard a lot of lines.

Mr. McCoy was sitting at his desk, and once everyone was seated, he read roll call and then pulled out a sheet of paper. "I imagine everyone is sitting next to their best friends, but I know you won't pay attention. So I've made a seating chart and paired you up. There were an uneven number of girls and boys so a few of you will be paired with the opposite sex. Try not to lose your minds." He held up the sheet of paper. "Amerson and Garner, Banks and Davis, Thurman and Hoskins, Warner and Chase…"

Once my name was called, I quit paying attention. Dante groaned and made a face.

"How come I never get to be your partner?" he asked.

"You'll have to ask Fate about that one," I said.

McCoy finished and everyone found their partners and settled in. I took a seat next to the window since Zac hadn't moved. He watched every move I made while the two girls behind him pouted at the fact that I was his partner.

His scent increased in intensity being closer to him. Caleb had a powerful scent as well but it didn't affect me the way Zac's did. My throat went dry and my thirst begged to be sated.

"How has your day been?" Zac asked in a deep voice, making my stomach flutter.

"It's been good," I said.

"I'm new here."

"I know. I have third period with Caleb."

"Cool," he said as McCoy passed out the syllabus and a piece of paper for us to sign when we got our textbooks. "Your friend is staring at us." Zac nodded at Dante, who narrowed his eyes.

"That's Dante. He's harmless."

"He doesn't seem too happy you're over here."

We quit speaking as McCoy dropped off two books. Zac and I signed for them.

"He'll get over it," I said.

"I can see why he stares." Zac leaned against the table. "You're very beautiful."

My face grew hot, and I looked down to avoid his gaze. "Thanks. So where did you move from?"

"England."

"Really? Where's your accent?"

Zac had been flipping through his book when his hand slowed. Had I said something wrong? "I thought it would be easier to blend in."

"Yeah." I nodded. "Heaven forbid you do anything else to make you more attractive." Zac looked confused until he realized I was making fun of him. He smiled and my heart skipped a beat. "What made you come to the ass crack of nowhere?"

"I needed to get away from things at home, and this place just felt right."

Get away from things? Zac stared at the whiteboard, but I saw sadness in his eyes. "What was happening at home that you had to get away?"

"Just a lot of arguments between me and my parents."

I leaned forward with my elbows on the table. "About what?"

"They aren't the most tolerant people."

"That sucks. My parents died when I was three. If there's any advice I can give you, it's to cherish every moment you have with them, whether they're good or bad."

"I'm sorry about your parents. Maybe someday it'll work out with mine." Zac sighed. "But for now it's a breath of fresh air being away from them."

"Well, that's good."

"All right class. Settle down. Let's get started," McCoy said.

Our conversation stopped for a moment as McCoy went over what our learning schedule would be. Zac appeared to have tuned out the teacher as he stared at me.

After a moment, he leaned closer and lowered his voice. "I don't mean to be rude, but how old are you?"

"Eighteen."

"You look young for your age."

I chuckled under my breath. "You have no idea."

"What was that?"

"How old are you?" I asked, trying to get his mind going in a different direction.

"Eighteen."

"You look older than eighteen." I studied him for a while. "I've got it." For some reason, Zac held his breath. "You're an undercover cop doing a drug bust."

Zac laughed and everyone looked at us.

"Is there something you wanna share with the rest of the class, Mr. Warner?" McCoy asked.

"No, sir," he said, and everybody looked away. He turned to me again. "Do you really believe that?"

"It's happened before. A junior was selling to freshman. The junior went to jail and all of the freshmen were suspended."

"That's sad," Zac said, and we both laughed, making McCoy glance at the two of us again.

Theater was my fifth period, and after Zac followed me to my locker, he made every turn I did. What was he doing? I whirled around and he stopped short.

"Why are you following me?" I asked.

He gave an amused expression. "Other people have Theater besides you."

"How'd you know I had Theater?"

Zac took a step closer and I took a step back. His eyes narrowed, like he was readying to tell me that magic gave him the answer. "Your class schedule was on the desk."

"Oh." Embarrassed, I turned around and continued to the theater.

Normally, I wasn't a rude person but there was something odd about him. In the theater, once I took my seat, Zac sat next to me, resting his foot against the seat in front of him.

"What made you choose Theater?" he asked.

I suppressed an annoyed sigh. "In a play, you can be someone else. There are so many possibilities. For a moment, you can forget your life and all your troubles."

Zac had a look on his face I couldn't decipher. The teacher, Mrs. Thornton, came in and placed us in alphabetical order, and then handed out scenes. Somehow Zac and I ended up as partners again.

"Awesome," I muttered to myself. "Stick me with the one person whose blood makes me wanna get to the center of the Tootsie Pop." Even now, I could smell it.

Zac walked over to where I was sitting with the scene paper in his hand. "Come on, I know a place where we can do our scene."

Panic suffused me, even as my blood rushed at the thought. I couldn't be alone with him. "Why can't we do it here?"

"It's too crowded."

Out of excuses and with his eyes pulling me in, the thirst claimed the forefront of my mind and I got to my feet. Zac smiled as I followed him onto the stage, and behind the theater next to the prop shed.

"What's our scene about?" I asked.

"It's a romantic scene." Zac handed me the script.

Great. Not only was romance a subject I had no experience with, but it meant I would have to get close to Zac and that could spell disaster for the both of us. I leaned against the shed and stared at my feet, trying to control my thirst. Breathe in. Breathe out. Breathe in. The cool wind lifted my hair and the fragrance of fall greeted me. Zac stood in front of me, and his scent overshadowed all others.

"Are you okay?" he asked, and placed both of his hands on the shed beside my head.

What a bad idea. "I'm fine."

Zac leaned even closer and his lips parted, as if he was going to kiss me. "Schuyler?"

My eyes focused on his neck, where I could see his vein throbbing, begging for my bite. My pulse raced and my fangs descended, my lips opening to give them free reign. His scent was exhilarating and my body and mind craved to taste him. All it would take was for me to enthrall him with my vampire traits and lead him into the woods.

"I have to go." I bolted away from him into the theater, grabbing my purse as I passed my seat, and ran to the bathroom.

The fire in my throat was stronger than it had ever been, and once I was locked in a stall, I pulled a bag of blood from a hidden section of my purse. Aunt Lenore got me the bagged blood, though I never knew how she obtained it. In all honesty, I didn't really *want* to know.

The bag of blood sated the more intense thirst, but some of it lingered. The moment I exited the bathroom, Zac was there with his hands on my waist.

"Are you sure you're okay?" he whispered.

When he was so close, it felt as if I hadn't drank any blood at all. "We can't be like this, Zac."

"Why not?"

"We just can't."

He seemed confused as we went back to practicing our scene, and then I went to sixth period Spanish, which flew by. At my locker, I grabbed all the different sheets that needed to be signed and headed to the parking lot.

There was a loud commotion and people were huddled around two guys fighting. I placed my stuff in my car and approached the large group. One of the fighters was Brock, a football player, and the other was Zac. Brock threw a hard punch, but Zac evaded it and blocked the second punch aimed for his head. Zac got both of Brock's arms in his grasp. Since his arms were bound, Brock knocked his forehead into Zac's, but Zac shook off the blow. Brock collapsed.

Brock's friends rushed in all at once, and I feared Zac would get his ass handed to him. Zac took each blow as if a child was hitting him, but oddly he never struck back. Why were they fighting? There were no teachers in sight. Somebody had to do something. And I was stronger than all of them.

Brock rejoined the fight, and he looked like he wanted to kill Zac. "You gonna regret that."

I grabbed Brock's arm and he spun around and hit me in the face. It didn't really hurt, but when I looked at Zac his expression changed from one of focus to one of fury. This time when someone attacked, he laid them flat. He grabbed Brock around the throat.

Caleb appeared out of nowhere and pried Zac's hand from Brock's throat. "Calm down, Zac. You need to calm down."

Caleb's muscles bulged as he pulled Zac away, and I was glad someone had taken control before Zac could hurt Brock. Zac looked at me and took a step closer. My hand covered my cheek and I stepped back, my body tight with tension again.

Caleb came closer instead and stroked my cheek with his thumb. "Are you okay, Skye?"

His voice calmed me. "I'm fine. He just grazed me." With a last look at Zac, I walked away.

My Jeep wasn't far away, and before I knew it I was home. There wasn't any homework so I found a book to occupy my brain until my aunt got home from work. After dinner, I did the dishes, and Aunt Lenore grabbed her purse.

"I need to run the perimeter," she said. "I'll be late so don't wait up."

"Okay."

Every few days, Aunt Lenore would drive a few miles away from the house and run in a circle. She used her werewolf senses to make sure no werewolves or vampires were hunting near us or establishing a new coven or pack. It usually took her a couple of hours, and even though I worried about her, I knew she could take care of herself. An hour later, I heard a car pull in the driveway and two doors open and close. I looked at the clock. It was too early for my aunt to be home.

CHAPTER 2
LOVE SCENE

Most of the lights were off, so I switched off the TV before hiding in a dark corner. I heard a metallic clicking noise as the lock was picked, and then the door swung open with a creak. Two different scents reached me; the intruders were human, and male. Their attempts at a silent entry were laughable. My sensitive hearing picked up the slightest moves they made.

The first man entered the kitchen and squinted in the darkness. He wore black clothing underneath a black cloak that hid most of his face. His hands twitched, and the light from the hallway glinted off the knife in his hand. They chose the wrong house. Foolish humans. The man had no time to react when I shoved him against the wall, grabbed his neck, and lifted him up. He kicked at me, so I tightened my grip. He raised his knife to stab me, but I caught his arm and wrestled it from him.

The hood covering his face fell off to reveal a shaved head. Movement out of the corner of my eye caught my attention. The other man had pulled his cloak off, his biceps bulging as they increased in size. How was that possible? He was human. I released the man I was holding and was next to the other in a flash. He moved faster than a human should and threw me against the wall. The drywall crumbled and then I collapsed on the ground.

The strong man sent a kick to my stomach and I flew into the wall again. In a flash, I was on my feet with fangs descended. He seemed shocked to see the fangs, and that gave me the opening to attack. My claws slashed his side open and he dropped to one knee. So he was strong, but he couldn't take the hit like a werewolf or vampire could. And that meant I was hurting a human. That was something I never wanted to do.

Distracted by my thoughts, the other man jammed a second knife between my ribs, all the way to thc hilt. Flesh squelched, bone crunched, and blood poured. I backhanded the one that stabbed me and his neck snapped. Ripping the knife free of my body, I stabbed the other one in the heart, and only pulled it out when I heard the last beat.

Once he was dead, I stared at him. How was he so strong? As I was staring, I saw a black mark on his neck. With the knife, I moved his shirt aside and saw a black tattoo in the shape of four slash marks across a crescent moon. I had never seen that symbol before. Suddenly, the reality of what I had done sank in. The knife slipped from my fingers and clattered on the wood floor. I stepped back until my back touched the wall and slid to the bottom.

Hours passed without me moving. The door opened and Aunt Lenore froze in her tracks. "Schuyler!" She rushed over to me. "What happened?"

"They broke in. I thought they were human, but they were too strong. I had no choice but to kill them."

She checked my wound. "I'm sorry you had to."

"How were they so strong?"

Aunt Lenore went over to one of them and sniffed him. "He's been injecting himself with werewolf blood."

"What?"

"Some humans know about us. They're from the Lupine Order. They work for werewolves in the hopes that we'll turn them. Some give them their blood to pacify them until they die. It makes them stronger without turning them."

"I killed them." I started to cry.

Aunt Lenore grabbed my face. "I know. But it was either them or you. And I'm glad it wasn't you."

"What are we going to do with them?"

"I'll take care of it. You should get cleaned up."

Nodding absently, I got to my feet and went into the bathroom. My brain was still trying to wrap itself around what had happened as I washed all the blood off in the shower. I drank a bag of blood to kick-start the healing process and went to bed.

****

At school the next day, when I entered my Literature class, Laurel waved at me. I sat in the seat next to her.

"What's up?" Laurel asked.

Last night I killed two humans. "Not much. How was your first day?"

"It was okay. It's high school after all." She shrugged and pulled out her Literature book.

Once everyone was sitting, the teacher handed out poetry books and told us to choose one from the book and write down what we thought it meant. The teacher went back to her seat and Laurel shifted her desk closer to mine.

"Did you know there's a rumor going around about you?" Laurel whispered.

"What?" Her question surprised me and the word came out louder than I intended.

"Girls," the teacher interrupted. "Quiet down and finish your work."

"Sorry," Laurel said.

I waited for a second. "What are people saying?"

"Well, the girls are all jealous that the new guy, Zac, likes you."

"How do they know he likes me?"

"I heard he stares at you a lot. If you ask me, that's kinda creepy."

Maybe I wasn't the only one getting a weird vibe from Zac. "He's certainly different."

"His friend Caleb's in my class. Now *he's* hot. And really nice."

Caleb's and Zac's friendship confused me; they seemed to be on opposite ends of the personality spectrum. Laurel chattered on about other pieces of gossip as we finished choosing our poems. Before I knew it, I was walking through the door to my Astronomy class.

Zac sat in the desk next to me and Caleb took the one in front of him. When Zac looked at me, his ice blue eyes snared me. After closer inspection, I realized there were flecks of lavender in the ice blue, softening the harsh color.

"How's your cheek?" Zac asked.

His question reminded me of his brutality when he fought yesterday. "I'm fine."

There was a pause as I couldn't find anything to say. Caleb rotated in his seat so he was facing the two of us.

"Did you hear about the break-ins happening around town?" Caleb asked.

My head snapped up to look at Caleb, which caught Zac's attention since he was always staring at me.

"Yeah, I did hear about that," I said. "I guess we should be careful."

Zac's brow furrowed, and then Mr. Matthews entered the room. As Mr. Matthews spoke, a note landed on my desk. I opened it and saw it was from Zac.

You look beautiful today.

It brought a smile to my face but I didn't continue the conversation. Zac looked disappointed when I didn't write back.

After third period, Caleb approached me at my locker with a big smile. "What's up?"

"Literally nothing has happened since one minute ago when the bell rang," I said. Two teenagers ran by, yelling at each other. "Can I ask you a question?" Caleb nodded. "Why was Zac fighting with Brock yesterday?"

Caleb took a deep breath. "I don't know, but I don't think he started it."

"Well, he sure finished it. He could've seriously hurt them."

Human lives were minute compared to an immortal's, and yet some lived richer and fuller lives than me. They were born into an unforgiving world and I hated that immortals only made their lives harder.

"You seem a little distracted." Caleb interrupted my thoughts.

"I'm just tired."

Caleb walked with me part of the way to fourth period, and then I was faced with a whole period sitting next to Zac.

"Hi," Zac said when I set my stuff down.

"Hi back."

"I've noticed something about you since yesterday."

My gut tightened. "And what is that?"

"Pretty much every guy in this school stares at you whenever you pass."

That was it?

"Hmm. I never noticed," I lied with a shrug. "It seems all the girls only have eyes for you."

"They can look all they want. No one else holds my gaze the way you do."

My face felt hot and I looked away from Zac. "You're just wasting your time. I can't give you what you want."

"But you don't know what I want."

"Well, I can guess."

Zac leaned closer with his arm resting on the table, a smirk appearing in the corner of his lips. "And you'd probably be wrong."

I made it through Theater unscathed and then Spanish and the drive home. At home, I switched on the news. It was an everyday ritual because sometimes we could find clues as to whether vampires or werewolves were near. When dead bodies or murders made the lead story, I could use the details to determine whether it was done by an immortal.

"We give you the top stories in the first five minutes," the anchor said. "First off, we have the most recent abductions. We go to Elaina Marshall for the update."

A beautiful black woman with perfect almond skin appeared. "There's been an increase in abductions in the Gwinnett county area," Elaina said. "The police are investigating the missing people but have nothing to go on. You can find a list of people that have gone missing and photos on our website. If you know anything, please call the toll-free number on the screen."

This wasn't good. Disappearances so close together in one area could mean vampires were over-feeding or establishing a new coven. But now was not the time to make rash decisions. I would wait and see what happened.

After that news, I attempted to read a book, but all I managed to do was sit with it in my lap as I stared at the page. My aunt found me like that when she came home from work.

"Are you all right, sweetheart?" she asked as she set her purse down.

"Do you ever get lonely?"

"No. I have my beautiful niece to keep me company."

I put my book on the coffee table and scooted forward. "Do you ever miss the life you had before I was born?"

Aunt Lenore was quiet for so long I thought she would never answer me. She sat beside me, her gray eyes showing the turmoil in her mind.

"Yes," she said. My heart felt heavy, as if it had turned to lead. Tears welled and my throat constricted. "I was happy with my life." She put her hand on mine. "But that life was lacking something."

"What?"

She smiled. "You."

"You just said you were happy with your old life."

"I was. But it wasn't until you came along that I learned I could be happier than that," she said. "One day you won't have to hide."

"But not yet. There have been many disappearances in our county. I think vampires are establishing a new coven."

She listened as I told her about the disappearances and deaths on the news.

"I don't think vampires are establishing a new coven," she said. "Vampires don't normally take humans and they very rarely kill when they feed. This is something different."

Saturday night I pulled into the parking lot of the Barnes and Noble bookstore. The area around the bookstore was packed with cars so I was forced to park in the darkened area at the back of the store. I got out of the car and was putting my keys in my purse when I heard something in the dark trees. My eyes scanned the darkness and my breath hitched as two men materialized. Their scent was human but I had a feeling they were going to be just as strong as the last ones.

CHAPTER 3
A NEW FRIEND

"Leave me alone," I said to them. "I don't want to have to hurt you."

They also wore hooded cloaks like the ones before them that swayed in the wind as they came toward me. Neither of them said anything so when the first one came at me, I ducked his swing, went around him, and kicked him in the back. He dropped to the ground as the second man grabbed my arm and flung me against the side of the building. Rushing to my feet, I punched the second man and he coughed up blood.

The first man pulled a knife from his belt and tried to stab me, but only managed to graze my side. The second man made contact with my face and the flesh throbbed and began to swell. I dropped to the ground. In my mind, there was mental battle between self-preservation and the fear of killing more humans. The first man brought the knife down, about to cut me open, when someone grabbed his hand.

A girl with blonde hair and bright blue eyes pulled him to his feet. She ripped the knife from him and knocked her head into his. He staggered backwards as the second man ran at her. She evaded his attack with more grace than an ice skater, and laid him flat with one punch. The two men got to their feet and made to attack the girl together, but they stopped mid-stride, their eyes widening, and then they bowed their heads and fled.

She turned around and held a hand out for me. "Are you okay?"

"I'm fine," I said, taking her hand and getting to my feet.

"Your cheek looks swollen."

"It'll be fine by morning. Thanks." I paused. "I'm Schuyler."

Her expression was pensive and then her eyes widened. "You're Schuyler?"

"You know me?"

"I'm Sarah, Caleb's sister."

"I didn't know he had a sister."

"What can I say? He's a guy." She frowned when I grabbed on my side. "Did he hurt you more than your cheek?"

"He just grazed my side."

Sarah took my arm and pulled me closer to inspect the wound. "That doesn't look fine."

"It'll be okay."

"Let's go inside. I'll help you clean it up."

We went by her car where she grabbed a small bag and headed into the bookstore and into the bathroom. Sarah locked the door behind her and opened the small bag that had medical supplies. Lifting my shirt, I watched her as she bandaged my wound.

"Why did those guys attack you?" Sarah asked.

"I don't know." I winced when she cleaned the wound. "You took them down with like, two hits. Where did you learn to fight like that?"

"I do have a brother," she said with a chuckle.

"How did you know who I was?"

"Zac hangs out at our house all the time. So I hear the two of them talking about you a lot."

She cleaned up the supplies and closed the bag. We exited the bathroom and sat at one of the tables in the café section.

"They talk about me?" I asked.

"Oh yeah. Zac can't stop thinking about you."

The same went for me but that was because of his blood. The way I felt towards him was purely a thirst issue. Nothing else.

"Awesome."

Sarah's brow furrowed. "Is that not a good thing?"

"He confuses me."

"You know if you ever get tired of the boys you could come and hang out with me."

It had been so long since I had a really close relationship with someone, and I missed it. And Sarah seemed cool, especially after helping me out when those men had attacked me. Her intervention took the decision of killing them out of my hands.

"That sounds really good right about now," I said.

Sarah smiled. "Perfect."

Sarah and I talked for an hour at the bookstore and she successfully kept my mind off the humans dosing themselves with werewolf blood. But when I got home, my adrenaline left and I crashed. I was lying on my bed when a thought occurred to me. If I had trouble fighting against the Lupine Order, then how did Sarah send them packing with only two hits?

CHAPTER 4
ANATOMY

Monday rolled around, and I was in Literature, sitting next to Laurel. The moment I entered the room, her face lit up, and she beckoned for me to hurry to my seat.

"Guess what?" Laurel asked.

"What?"

"I met someone."

"That's cool. Where'd you meet?"

"We met at the mall."

I smiled. "What's his name?"

"Aaron. He's gorgeous with an Irish accent. He invited me to dinner tonight." Laurel was bouncing in her seat.

"He sounds really nice."

Laurel pulled out her homework. "I wish I'd a picture of him. I'll get one tonight."

"Okay." My mind circled back to the disappearances. "But be careful. There have been a lot of disappearances lately."

Laurel grinned. "I will."

In Astronomy, we watched a Power-Point about different constellations. A note touched my hand and I looked over at Zac, who winked. I opened the note and read:

You look beautiful today.

"You said that last time," I said.

"I know," Zac said.

In History, Caleb watched me as I pulled out my History book and homework.

"My sister said she met you last night," Caleb said.

"Yeah. It was quite a surprise. I didn't even know you had a sister."

Ms. Hawkins stood and handed out worksheets.

"Are you doing okay?" Caleb asked.

"Yeah, why would you ask that?"

"Sarah told me what happened."

I closed my eyes. "You didn't tell Zac, did you?"

"Not unless you want someone to die," Caleb said.

"Why would someone die if you told him?"

"Please work on your worksheets," Ms. Hawkins interrupted.

Caleb leaned closer. "He feels very protective of you. It's hard to explain."

"Some people like a little mystery in their lives, but every time Zac is mentioned, it's followed by the sentence, 'It's hard to explain,' or, 'you wouldn't understand'. That's way too much mystery for me."

"Are you sure you're okay?"

"They didn't hurt me that bad. It's just a bruise," I said, and gave him a stern look so he would drop the subject.

I entered Anatomy and sat next to Zac. He smirked at me, which caused me to sit harder in my chair than I meant to.

"How was your weekend?"

"I met Sarah at Barnes and Noble."

"Yeah, she said you did," he said, and then McCoy came in through the door, shutting it behind him.

"Good morning, everyone. Today we're labeling the parts of the body." McCoy called out groups.

Zac and I were given the muscular system. McCoy handed out the worksheets as I turned to the page with a diagram of the muscles on it.

"This is gonna be easy," Zac said. "Do you need any help memorizing it?"

"I've already memorized it."

"Really?" Zac smiled. "Prove it."

"Ok, we'll start with the head." I placed my hand against his forehead, and heard his heart stutter in his chest. "We have Occipitofrontalis which wrinkles the forehead." Zac's eyes followed me as I moved to his temple. "Temporalis is for chewing. Orbicularis oculi closes the eye." I grazed his eyelids before my fingers went to his nose. "Nasalis flares your nostrils." Zac made his nostrils flare, and I gave him a look as I went to his jaw. "Masseter and buccinator are for chewing." I went above his lips. "Orbicularis oris closes the mouth."

Zac's eyes closed when I touched his lips. My fingers went from just above his lips to the side of his neck. "Sternocleidomastoid turns the head." I went down to the right and touched his shoulder blade. Then I pulled his arm out and continued naming muscles on the front. "Biceps rotate and bend the forearm. Flexor digitorum superficialis bends the fingers." I slid my fingers between his and felt a tingling in my stomach. "Flexor pollicis brevis bends the thumb. Lumbricals control the fine movements of the hands."

Finished, I lowered his arm and touched his chest as it rose and fell with each breath. "Pectoralis major moves the shoulder and is involved with deep breathing." Then I touched his abdomen. As my fingers grazed each toned muscle, it would tense in response. I liked the way his body felt beneath my fingers and had the sudden urge to tear his shirt apart. When I looked up, Zac was giving me a heated look with his lips parted. "Rectus abdominis strengthens the abdominal wall." I reached down to the rim of his pants. "External oblique is part of the abdominal wall." When I got to his back, the enticing heat from his body lured me closer. He sucked in a breath when I balanced myself with a hand against his abdomen. The heat of his body drugged me and I leaned closer to him, wanting to press my body along his.

Once I was done with his back, I brought my hand around his side and over his hip bone to rest just below the belt line of his pants. "Gluteus medius helps you walk." I reached back and tapped my fingers against butt. "Gluteus maximus is for standing up and climbing." I made my way down to his hamstring on the back of his thigh. "Hamstrings move the hips and the knees." I went down further. "Soleus is for standing. And the Gastrocnemius is for walking and jumping." I touched right behind his ankle. "And the Achilles tendon also helps you walk, so you are S-O-L when it is cut."

I labeled the muscles up the front of his leg and stopped on the inside of his thigh. He inhaled sharply. "And last, but not least, Gracilis which bends and twists the leg."

I sat back down on my chair, and watched as Zac slowly regained his composure. My hands were shaking a little and my heart was pounding in my chest. I had no idea that I would get so flustered just by touching him. He wore a confused expression, but it looked like he didn't care. Zac took a second before he could sit down. Once everything was labeled on the worksheet, we filled in the blanks on the other systems as each pair labeled a blank diagram on the overhead projector.

The dismissal bell rang, and I gathered my things. When I reached for my book, Zac snatched it off the table, his fingers brushing over mine. At my locker, he handed me the book back, and I exchanged it for my Theater notebook, as if we did that every day. Zac stayed with me until we split to go to our assigned seats.

My heightened senses felt his eyes on me. When I turned around to check, he winked at me. I blushed scarlet and slid down into my seat. Mrs. Thornton came down the aisle and counted the students to see who was absent. Then she announced that we were watching a video, and walked back up the aisle to her office. Zac dropped into the seat next to me, the screen was lowered from the ceiling, and the movie started. When the lights went out, my senses sharpened and the electricity between us increased. Out of the corner of my eye, I saw as Zac moved closer to me.

I rested my hand on the armrest and tried to calm my nerves. Zac's arm moved, and he placed his hand on mine. There was a rush of sensation that flowed through my body and I knew that I should move my hand but I couldn't make myself do it. During sixth period, I stared at my hand, remembering the way his skin felt against mine. Before I knew it, the bell rang for the end of school.

"Hey, Skye," Sarah said, as she skipped over to my locker.

"Hey. What's up?" I asked.

"You feeling better?"

"Much better. Thanks."

"Do you wanna hang out at my house?"

I shifted my books to my other arm. "Yeah. That sounds great. Can you pick me up?"

"Sure." Sarah waited as I wrote down my address.

At home it took a few seconds to do my homework—gotta love eidetic memory—and then there was a honk from the driveway. I grabbed my purse and headed out the door.

"Did you have any trouble finding the house?" I asked, after I got in the car.

"Nope. You don't live that far from me." She backed out of my driveway, and turned onto the street. She drove a dark blue four-door compact car full of discarded garments, a few text books, and loose paper. It felt so…normal.

"Cool. So what're we going to do?"

"Well, I have a pool so we can go swimming if you want, or we could watch a movie in my room."

"I like the sound of a movie." I glanced at her and she smiled. "What?"

"Just so you know, Zac will be at my house. But we'll beat him there and you won't have to see him."

It took a few minutes to get to Sarah and Caleb's place. Her house was about how big mine was, painted a pale yellow, with a driveway leading to a two car garage. There was another car in the driveway, which I assumed belonged to Caleb. When I walked in the house, Caleb was sitting on the couch, flipping through the channels.

He looked up when we came in; his eyes went from Sarah, to me, and back to Sarah. "Hey, Skye. I didn't know you were coming over."

"I invited her after school." Sarah closed the front door behind me.

"And why didn't you tell me?"

"Last time I checked, you weren't my father. I do what I want." She stuck her tongue out at him. He made a face back at her. We started to head upstairs when she turned around. "And when Zac comes over, you won't tell him Skye's here. Or you will pay."

Caleb held his hands up in surrender. "My lips are sealed." He motioned like he was zipping his mouth shut.

We went upstairs to Sarah's room, and closed the door behind us. Her walls were a lilac color, matching the drapes and the comforter on her bed. She had a flat screen television sitting on a chest, and rows upon rows of DVDs next to it, lining the walls.

"So what would you like to watch?" Sarah asked.

"I don't care. You can pick whatever."

Sarah settled on the movie *Van Helsing*, which made me laugh. Here I was, a vampire/werewolf hybrid, watching a movie about vampires and werewolves, and a man who killed both. But I wasn't complaining, because, come on, it's Hugh Jackman. Need I say more? Too bad he wasn't a real werewolf. And too bad he was already married.

Downstairs, the front door creaked open, and I heard muffled voices. Zac must have arrived. There was an urge telling me I should be downstairs where Zac was, like he was the sun, and gravity was pulling me closer.

"What do you have to eat?" I asked.

"I'll show you."

Sarah led the way back downstairs and showed me where the kitchen was. I looked through the pantry as Sarah rifled through the fridge. A noise came from the back yard. Curious, I went to the window and peeked through the screen to see outside. Zac was sitting on one of the pool chairs, his back facing the window, with his shoes off to the side.

When he stood up and started unbuttoning his shirt, my heart pounded in my chest and I sucked in a mouthful of air. Zac froze and tilted his head to the side. I didn't move a muscle. Sarah started singing as she made herself something to eat, so Zac went back to undressing. The first thing I saw when he pulled off his shirt was the rigid muscles of his back.

The sight of his bare skin excited the bloodlust in me. I had had two bags of blood at lunch earlier, yet I was still feeling the call of his pulse. Then he turned around. His chest and abdomen looked as if they had been chiseled from stone. My eyes snagged on a dark mark on his left pectoral muscle. It was the angled claw marks across a crescent moon, like the tattoos the men who attacked me had.

My palms began to sweat as I backed away from the window. How could he have the same tattoo? The air left my lungs and my heart slammed against my ribs. Sarah wasn't paying attention as I backed out of the room.

When I turned the corner, I slammed into a naked chest.

"Zac!" I squeaked. "You can't sneak up on people like that."

"I'm sorry. I didn't mean to surprise you, even though I didn't know you were here. Speaking of sneaking, maybe you can tell me why you were spying on me taking off my shirt."

"I don't know what you're talking about."

Zac placed his hand against the wall, and then the other one on the other side of my head, caging me in. It brought the tattoo closer, but the aching in my mouth as my fangs readied for his blood distracted me.

"I know you were watching me, Skye. You can lie to yourself all you want, but you can't lie to me."

My eyelids drooped, the call of his blood almost taking control. Looking away from his chest, I peered up into his eyes. I opened my mouth to say something, but closed it when I realized I didn't have anything to say. Zac leaned in with his head tilted to the side, his lips millimeters from mine. My mouth mimicked his and I exhaled.

"Just admit you're attracted to me, Skye. Admit you wanna be with me as much as I wanna be with you," he said, his breath washing across my face. My legs shuddered, and my nails dug into the soft plaster of the wall.

"I can't." He could be the reason those men kept coming after me. The fact that they had the same tattoo couldn't be a coincidence.

One of his hands came down to touch my cheek, and I closed my eyes at the contact, leaning into his hand. That single touch made me want to forget any connection he might have with those men.

"Why can't you?" He was holding his breath.

"Zachary Warner," Sarah called, and stomped over to where we were. "What do you think you're doing?" Zac straightened up, and Sarah grabbed my hand and led me away.

Once he pulled back, I could think again. Zac had something to do with those men. I needed to figure out the connection between them. Back in Sarah's room, my cell phone was ringing. After a second of rummaging, I pulled the phone from my purse.

"Aunt Lenore?" I asked.

"Where are you?"

My eyes shot to the digital clock on Sarah's nightstand. Aunt Lenore had gotten home earlier than usual. "I went for a walk. You're home early."

"Get your ass home now."

"I'm on my way," I said, and snapped my phone shut. "I have to go."

Sarah got to her feet. "I heard. Do you need me to drive you?"

"It'll be faster if I run. I know a shortcut." I grabbed my purse. "See you tomorrow."

Zac was next to me when I came downstairs. "What's wrong?"

I edged away from him. "My aunt's pissed. I've gotta go."

"Let me drive you."

"No!" I cleared my throat. "I mean, I don't need one." Zac looked dejected. "I'll see you tomorrow."

Zac managed a small smile, and watched me as I walked out the door. When I hit the woods, I ran at full speed, and made it to my house in under a minute. Aunt Lenore was waiting for me, her foot tapping on the tile floor.

"Where have you been?" she asked.

"Walking," I said.

"With your purse?"

"Yeah." That sounded weak but I wasn't in the mood to explain.

Her expression told me she knew I wasn't saying something. "You need to be more careful."

"I will." I paused and some of her anger abated. "Why are you home so early? Is something wrong?"

"I had a bad feeling. But it's gone now."

Aunt Lenore walked into the kitchen and I stayed near the front door, unsure of what to do. My thoughts were rushing in different directions. A chill crept up my spine and I spun around and peered out the window. I scanned every inch of the woods on the other side of my house but I couldn't see anything. Even though I didn't find anything, I couldn't rid myself of the feeling that I was being watched. It felt like someone's eyes were on me at this very moment.

CHAPTER 5
BAD LIAR

Early the next morning, in the cafeteria, Sarah took a seat opposite of me at the table. She looked tired, and I figured she wasn't used to getting up this early.

"Hey, not that I mind, I'm just curious, but what are you doing here this early?" I asked.

"I wanted to make sure I didn't get you in trouble with your aunt."

"No, I forgot to leave her a note telling her where I was going. It was nothing you did. Besides, I'm used to it. It's always the same argument anyways."

Sarah pulled out her breakfast and took a big bite. "So your excuse was you were out walking. Is that why you didn't want me to drive you home?"

"Yes," I said. "I didn't want her to be mad that I was at a friend's house without leaving a note, so I'm gonna wait for her anger to abate."

Sarah's brows went up, her lips scrunched to the side, and she shrugged. I watched as she devoured her food, like she hadn't eaten in days.

"Do you eat that much all the time?" There was enough food for two. "Please tell me you're not eating for two."

"I'm not eating for two, and yes, I always eat this much."

"Do you eat that much for every meal?"

"Yep. I love me some food." She smiled as she finished. I looked at her arms, and then under the table at her legs and the rest of her torso. "What are you looking for?" Her head joined mine under the table.

"I'm looking for where the food goes." We straightened back up at the same time. "How do you keep your shape and still eat like an entire wrestling team?"

"I have a fast metabolism."

"Yeah, the metabolism of an Olympic athlete."

The bell rang, and Sarah and I split up to go to our first period. Today we were reciting our poems to the class. Students filed into the trailer but Laurel was nowhere to be seen. Usually she beat me to class. As each student recited their poem, I grew more and more distracted as I thought about Laurel.

I jumped when the bell rang. Before Zac even entered second period, I could feel his presence. He strode in and sat next to me. His eyes scrutinized me, like I was his prey.

"Did you get in trouble with your aunt?" Zac asked.

"No. She was just mad that I didn't leave her a note," I said.

"All right, all right, everyone settle down," Matthews said. "This is a list of different constellations. Everyone needs to find a partner and pick a constellation."

"Do you wanna be partners, Skye?" Zac asked.

My sensible half was saying I shouldn't, but there was another, unfamiliar part of me that wanted to be near him. It wasn't like I couldn't protect myself: from humans and immortals alike. At least this time I would be prepared.

"Okay," I said. "How about you go and pick a constellation?"

"Sure." He signed for a constellation, and came back.

Once everyone had picked one, Matthews stood before the class. "This project will be ongoing, and will be worth half your final grade. One night of each week, you'll need to observe the night sky and record the movement of your constellation. You'll need a compass and a GPS unit. If you don't have one or both of those, please see me after class."

I had to spend one night of the week alone with Zac. This was going to be interesting.

Third period ended, and I was walking with Zac toward my locker. A delicious scent blossomed beneath my nose, spilling over my taste buds, driving me crazy. Without drawing Zac's attention, I skimmed my hand along the side of my purse, and it felt wet. Blood.

"I have to go," I said, and ran into the nearest bathroom.

The last thing I saw was Zac's perplexed expression. I went into the biggest stall and yanked my purse off my shoulder, sorting through it until I found the concealed compartment. The bag of blood had somehow burst and spread throughout my purse. My wallet and keys remained unscathed and I was thankful for that. After checking the coast was clear, I left the stall and, using a paper towel, dug through some of the trash to place my purse at the bottom, so no one would find it full of blood.

After straightening my clothes, I was getting ready to leave when I spotted a dark stain on the side of my jacket. Damn. The blood had leaked through that, too. With jerking movements, I tugged off my jacket and shoved it under the trash along with the purse. I raised my arm and checked the side of my top, making sure it didn't leak onto that as well.

No one was in the hall as I ran to my locker, making it to history before the late bell. Once I was sitting, Caleb gave me a what-happened-to-you look. I shrugged at him, trying not to appear frazzled, and pulled out my homework. We were taking a test, so there was no chance for him to talk to me, even when we both finished early.

The moment Zac's scent hit me when I entered Anatomy, my gut tightened and I took a deep breath. Zac looked up when he saw me come in. My feet felt heavy as lead as I made my way to my seat. Zac monitored me in a circumspect manner, like he was worried I would explode.

"What?" I asked when he didn't look away.

"Where are your purse and jacket?"

Of course, he would notice that.

"I was hot, and I put my purse in my locker."

As if Fate were playing with me, I shivered. Zac didn't say anything about it, but I knew he saw it. McCoy stood and asked one of the students to turn off the lights. We were scheduled to watch a medical video, talking about the human anatomy and the different types of jobs in that field. Everyone moved around to get situated, laying their heads on the table or propping their feet up. I held in a surprised shriek when my chair jerked and was dragged backwards, the metal legs squeaking along the linoleum floor.

I turned around to glare at Zac, but he just raised an eyebrow, daring me to object. The stool didn't stop until I felt it bump against the rim of his, his legs spread out on either side of me. I wanted to scoot forward, away from the heat of his body, but he placed his hand against my hip.

When the class was immersed in darkness, Zac leaned forward with his mouth next to my ear, tickling the sensitive lobe. "Don't act like you're not cold. I'm just keeping you warm, is all. Nothing more than that."

My head turned as his scent drew me in. It was like something from a cartoon where the steam from a cooling pie on the window sill turned into a hand that beckoned the main character to eat the pie. My eyelids drooped as his scent grew stronger. The warmth from Zac's body pulled me in and my back arched to fit along his stomach and chest. His hand was hot against my hip before it slid down my leg. His hot breath fanned across my neck and his scent exploded until that was all I could think about. Part of my brain registered when his hand went to my other leg and his arm wrapped around my waist, enveloping me in his heat.

The bell cut into the middle of the video, causing me to jolt in surprise and leap from my stool. Zac chuckled at my reaction, stood, and gathered his things. I refused to look at him. How had I let myself be so careless with him? Since I had said that I left my things in my locker, I couldn't open it. At the last second, I continued past it.

"Don't you need to get your notebook from your locker?" Zac asked, catching up.

"I left it at home."

Zac kept his mouth shut as we made our way to the theater. After Mrs. Thornton did a head count, Zac and I headed onto the stage. He took my hand and pulled me into the darkened wing off stage. I had already lost myself with him once. I couldn't do it again.

"What's wrong? Are you okay?" Zac asked.

"I'm fine."

My eyes found the vein in his neck in seconds. Since the bag of blood had burst, my thirst increased tenfold, and being so close to Zac made it worse. I shook my head when I realized that I was closing the distance between us, leaning closer to his neck.

"Something's bothering you. Why can't you tell me what's going on?"

This time I met his gaze. "I just can't."

"Then tell me something else." He moved closer, and I stepped back until I came into contact with the wall. Zac was in dangerous territory, tempting the animal instinct in me to bite and feed. "Why do you shy away from my touch?"

"I don't do that."

The corner of his lips drew back into his familiar smirk. "Then you won't stop me from kissing you."

He leaned closer, surrounding me with heat and his scent. My legs started shaking and my heart raced. His lips were about to touch mine when another student, came into the wings. Zac pushed away from me, and I took that moment to escape. Zac didn't say anything for the rest of the period. The rest of school was a blur and at home I turned on the news. I didn't pay much attention to it until Elaina came on.

"There have been more disappearances since last week. The most recent disappearance is Laurel Albright from Lilburn. Her parents say she went out Tuesday night and never came home. If anyone has any information, they're asked to call the Lilburn Police Department," Elaina said.

It felt like all the oxygen had been sucked from the room, and I gasped for air. Laurel had been abducted? When the shock passed, I decided on a plan of action. Aunt Lenore wasn't home, so I wrote her a note, hopped into my Jeep, and left. Laurel said she had met an Irish guy named Aaron at the mall. And that's where I was going to start. For all I knew, Aaron could be behind all of the abductions. If I went to the mall, there was a chance I could find her scent and follow it to find her.

It was late on a school night, so there weren't many people hanging around the mall. I parked and got out of my Jeep. There were traces of human scents everywhere, so it would take a while to isolate Laurel's.

"Where are you, Laurel?" I said to myself. "Help me find you."

I walked around the parking lot as I searched for a hint of Laurel. The few people still at the mall watched me warily as I meandered.

"I must look crazy walking around, sniffing the air like a hound dog."

When I felt like I wasn't going to find anything, I caught a flash of her scent and followed it until it got stronger. On the ground was a strand of her hair. There was a very strong scent near the strand of hair, and I followed it. The scent led me to the edge of the parking lot. There was a steep hill covered in ivy, but it was effortless for me to jump to the bottom. I walked through the trees until I came to the road. The scent vanished.

"Where are you Laurel?"

Turning back to the hill, I sank to my knees. I felt like such a failure. Anger filled me and I surged to my feet, striking the trees with my claws as I passed.

My anger built within me, and the trees groaned and bent away from me. A thunderous crack sounded as one tree collapsed. I was so surprised the tree had toppled over that it overcame my anger. How did that happen? Trees didn't fall over willy-nilly. I looked at my hands. Something was wrong with me.

****

Literature class felt empty without Laurel, and I found myself glancing at her seat, as if she would appear out of thin air. It killed me that I couldn't protect her. I had all of this power but I couldn't do anything with it. When I was a child, I had a human friend named Jaime. She wasn't allowed to see that I wasn't aging, so when we graduated high school, I left without a word. Laurel getting abducted felt like I was repeating that horrible part of my past.

"Are you okay?" Zac asked when he sat down in Astronomy.

"No," I said. "Laurel Albright went missing Tuesday night. She was in my Literature class."

"I'm sorry, Skye."

"She's got to be so scared. She's a good girl. She doesn't deserve this."

Zac looked worried, too, but there wasn't much he could say to make me feel better. Laurel wasn't coming back, and common sense told me she was already dead.

I was glad when sixth period ended and I was heading to my locker. When I rounded the corner, I saw Sarah waiting for me. She looked worried, but she didn't say anything until I got to my locker.

"I heard about Laurel," Sarah said.

"I feel so useless. I don't know what to do."

"There's nothing we can do. We'll just have to pray the cops can find her."

"The day before she went missing she told me she'd met a guy named Aaron. I know he has something to do with it." I closed my locker.

"Where'd they meet?"

"The mall. And that was where she was meeting him for their date."

A mischievous glint appeared in her eyes. "Why don't we go to the mall and figure this out for ourselves?"

"And how are we going to do that exactly?"

"We'll think of something."

I made a face at her. "You have no idea, do you?"

"Nope."

We laughed, and that eased my tension somewhat. Even though I had already followed her scent and found nothing, I felt more productive being active. Sarah rode with me and used her cellphone to pull up a picture of Laurel. In the mall, we showed each store employee Laurel's picture, but none of them had seen her.

"I thought at least one of them would've seen her," I said as we sat at a table in the food court.

"I don't know where to go from here," Sarah said.

I sighed and the feeling of defeat weighed down on me. "I guess we should get going then."

"Yeah."

The sun was shining in the cloudless sky, reflecting off the cars' windshields and chrome rims. Sarah's cell phone started ringing.

Sarah answered it with a droll, "Hi this is Helga, how much can I do ya for?" Her raspy cigarettes-and-curlers voice made me laugh. "What's up, Caleb?" She paused while he spoke. "I went to the mall with Skye. We're leaving now, so I should be home in…"

A loud bang interrupted her. Sarah and I crouched down, darting behind a car. Adrenaline pumped through my veins, making me dizzy and draining me of energy. Caleb was yelling so loud I could hear him on the other side of the line.

"Sarah? What the hell is going on?" he asked.

She shoved the phone up against her ear. "I don't know. There was a loud bang. We ducked behind a car, so I didn't see anything." Sarah poked her head around the car.

My shirt felt like it was plastered to my skin. I raked my eyes down my front, and what I saw didn't quite register at first. When my head ceased spinning, I saw fresh blood, still warm and oozing from a spot on my abdomen. Then came the pain. I pressed a hand against the wound, which made it scream at me, but I had to stop the bleeding. If I lost too much blood, then my instincts would take over, and I would bite someone. I couldn't let it get to the point where I might hurt Sarah. I would never forgive myself for that.

"What did it sound like? Can you describe it?"

"I have no idea what happened," Sarah yelled into the phone, and glanced around the car again.

"It was a gun," I said.

Sarah went silent, and turned around. She took one glimpse of my pale face, and the blood seeping between my fingers.

"Shit," she said, and Caleb stopped talking.

"What is it? What's wrong?" he asked a second later.

"Skye's been shot."

"What?"

"We're heading back." She hung up. "We need to get you to the hospital." She helped me stand up, and supported me as we walked.

"No hospitals. Take me to my house." Blood gushed through my fingers as I moved. The wind blew a scent toward me, and the hair on the back of my neck stood up. It was still a human scent but it was one that I was becoming vastly familiar with. "We need to leave now."

"Why?" Sarah asked.

"Just do it."

Sarah sped up, holding most of my weight, as we hurried to my Jeep. She helped me into the passenger seat, and then jumped into the driver seat and started the car. She floored it out of the parking lot, and then we were speeding toward my house. Or at least I thought we were. When we got close, we blazed right past it.

"Why didn't you stop at my house?" I asked.

"I figured you wouldn't want Zac knowing where you lived, so I'm taking you to my house. Zac and Caleb will meet us there."

When we arrived at her house, they were there, Zac looking very worried, waiting in the driveway. Sarah slammed on the brakes right in front of them, and Zac ran and opened my door for me. I was about to step down, but he looped an arm under my legs and the other around my waist, and lifted me into his arms. He strode through the front door, and held me while Sarah and Caleb covered the couch with towels. Zac set me down, and moved the hand covering my wound. He pulled up my shirt and winced at the wound.

"Caleb, get some bandages and antibacterial ointment. Sarah, get some clean towels and hot water," Zac said, and the other two ran to do as he bid.

They returned seconds later, but I just thought it was my mind making everything hazy, and I was losing more time than I realized.

Zac looked at me and I could see the pain in his eyes. Why was he in pain? "I'm going to make the pain go away," he said.

My teeth were clenched so hard I couldn't speak. Zac took one of the towels and wet it in the hot water, then cleaned the blood from around the wound. I watched his face the entire time. He nodded at Sarah, and she left and came back with a brown bottle. What was that? The fierce aroma of alcohol assailed my nostrils before pain attacked my lower abdomen.

"Ahhh!" I arched off the couch in pain.

Zac pushed my abdomen back down, and looked into my eyes. "I'm sorry, Skye. I need to do it again." He gently pushed some stray hairs behind my ear. "I'm sorry."

When the stinging abated, the pain went back to what it was before. Zac applied something wet to my skin, and then there was a small pinprick. There was a tugging sensation as Zac concentrated hard, his brow furrowing as he frowned at something. There was a small metallic clink, and Zac's look of concentration melted away.

"Did you pull out the bullet?" I asked.

"Yeah, you're going to be okay. I'm bandaging it up now." He put antibiotic ointment on the wound, and I heard medical tape as he tore it off the roll, taping the bandage to my skin.

Sarah and Caleb cleaned up, while Zac stayed by my side. My mouth was dry, and the pain was coming back with a vengeance. The pulse at Zac's neck throbbed, tempting me to bite and take the blood I needed to heal. It rushed through his veins as his heartbeat increased. I needed to leave while I still could.

"I'm thirsty," I said. My throat burned like it was on fire.

"I'll get you some water." He squeezed my hand before he hurried off to the kitchen.

Ugh. Water. My mouth only watered for his blood. His pace was slow, so I had a few seconds before he would be back. I tensed and hobbled off the couch, grabbing my keys where Sarah had left them, and made it out the front door before Zac caught up with me.

"What do you think you're doing?" he asked.

"I need to go home," I said, and kept walking. Well, limping was more like it.

"You need to rest. Sarah said you wouldn't go to the hospital, why can't you stay here?"

"I can't explain it to you. I have to get home."

I opened my car door, but Zac put a hand against it, closing it.

When I turned to glare at him, my legs collapsed and I sank against the car. Zac caught me, but as soon as I was standing, I pushed him away from me. I needed to leave, and having him support me was just making it harder.

"Skye, let me help you. Please."

"Just let me go, Zac. Just let me go." My fangs sliced into my tongue when they descended.

"I can't. You don't understand. I can't let you go."

Zac grasped my wrist to yank me to him, and I snapped. The pain made my temper short, and I was tired of being pushed around by Zac, even if he had my best interests at heart.

"Let go or I'll make you let go." He still pulled me closer. Closer to his neck that was begging for my bite.

I reared my hand back, and hit him in the sternum with my palm. There was the crack of a bone breaking before he lost his grip on my wrist, and stumbled backwards to land on the hard concrete.

CHAPTER 6
UNDER THE STARS

He was so stunned, he didn't move from where he was sitting, so I utilized that time to scramble into my car and back out of the driveway.

The trip to my house was agonizing and slow. I parked in the driveway and got out of the car with no trouble, but was careful to hide the blood on my shirt in case my aunt was home. Her car wasn't in the garage. Thank God. Like an old woman, I tottered through the kitchen, using everything I passed as a crutch, grabbed a bag of blood from the fridge, and made my way up the stairs. Just walking winded me, and I had to stop a few times on the steps when I got dizzy and shook so hard I had to sit down. In my room, I peeled off my ruined shirt and tossed it in the trash can. Then I tore into the bag and drank the blood down in three gulps.

Hours passed, and I had gone through three bags. My aunt still hadn't come home from work, so I went into the bathroom and stripped the tape and bandage from my skin. It had been two and a half hours since I had been shot, and the wound was almost healed. One more bag before I went to sleep would finish the job.

My phone beeped, and I went to see who had left me a message.

<*I'll be home late.*> The text was from Aunt Lenore.

<*I'm tired, so I'm going to bed early.*>

As I lay down, I was left with more questions about Zac. I was left with several questions: how did Zac know how to remove a bullet, why did Sarah and Caleb have the supplies for such an eventuality, and why no one suggested calling an ambulance.

There hadn't been any news on Laurel's whereabouts, and I grew more anxious as each day passed. My nerves were taut as piano wire, and it didn't get any better when I entered Astronomy the next day. Zac was already there, watching me.

"You look like you're feeling better," Zac said.

I had been pretending I was still healing after being shot, but the charade was wearing thin.

"Yeah." I took a deep breath. "We need to find a place to get our project started."

"Do we?"

My annoyance level went from simmering to boiling. "It's a project. Stop being a jerk and help me out."

An amused smile appeared. "Okay, what do you want to do?"

"Do you know of any open places where we can watch the sky?"

"I know of a place. But it will be a while before we can get started. Do you wanna go to the football game first?"

A football game was a safe place to be with him, since there would be so many people there.

"I don't see why not," I said.

Matthews came in, and started writing on the board.

"So how are you? Seriously," Zac whispered.

"You know, sometimes I just don't get you."

Zac chuckled. "I have a condition for tonight."

Great. A condition. Like I needed anything else to worry about.

"What is it?" I asked.

"You have to answer some questions, and you have to answer them honestly." I gave him a look, and he said, "Sarah told me not to be so pushy about getting my questions answered, and I know I'm hard to deal with sometimes. If the conversation goes in that direction, then you just tell me we can't talk about it."

"Fine. As long as you promise not to corner me when I don't answer."

"I promise." He crossed his heart for emphasis.

At the end of school, I saw Sarah waiting for me at my locker again. She was hopping up and down, making her blonde hair bounce.

"Are you going to the football game with us?" Sarah asked.

"I am."

"Yes. This is going to be so much fun."

"I wanted to ask you if it would be all right if I spent the night tonight."

"Of course you can," Sarah said.

When I got home, I prepared what I was going to say to my aunt. After the fiasco with Jaime, I hadn't gotten close to any other humans. So I wasn't sure how she would take it.

Aunt Lenore got home around five-thirty. She came through the garage door, throwing a "hi" at me as she entered the kitchen.

"Aunt Lenore?" I asked.

"Yes, honey?"

"I wanted to know if it would be okay if I spent the night at a friend's house."

"Sure. You're definitely of age to do what you want. I just like to know where you are."

"Okay," I said with a smile. "We're going to the football game tonight."

"Football," Aunt Lenore said with a sigh.

Werewolves had many wolfish traits, even in their human form, and playing anything involving a ball was an absolute must. I laughed at her as she daydreamed for a second about chasing the ball.

At seven, I drove over to Sarah's house and hopped into her car and went to the school. Not many people had arrived yet, but the few that had were tailgating with hot dogs, hamburgers, and soda.

Things like cookouts and tailgating were tricky for me. Since I drank blood for sustenance, I had no need for food. Some people tended to notice when you were the only one not eating or drinking anything. We parked the cars next to each other and walked toward the field.

"Hey, Skye. Come over here." Dante waved at us.

"Hey, Dante, how are you?" I asked.

"Much better now that my sexy lady is here."

"Well, thank you." I turned to Sarah. "I don't know if the two of you have met. This is Sarah." Zac and Caleb stepped closer. "This is her brother Caleb and you already know Zac."

"'Sup, Zac," Dante said. "It's nice to meet you Caleb and an extra nice to meet you, my golden goddess."

Sarah raised an eyebrow. "Finally. A man who sees my true potential."

Caleb rolled his eyes at Sarah. "Do you think we have a chance at beating Brookwood?"

Dante scoffed. "Parkview always wins."

Caleb and Dante went off into a detailed conversation about football, and which teams were the best. I was more of a soccer fan than football.

"Do you want something to eat or drink, Skye?" Sarah asked.

"No, thanks, I'm fine."

Sarah started a conversation with Lindsay, another student, as my eyes went to Zac. He was like a magnet to me, and I had no choice but to be pulled to him. As I watched him, Scott, a small statured guy with thick glasses, came up to him.

"Hey, Zac," Scott said. Zac turned around and they shook hands. "I wanted to thank you again for last week. Brock hasn't messed with me since."

"No problem, man. In a couple years, you'll probably be his boss," Zac said. Scott walked away, and Zac looked back and noticed me staring at him. "What?"

"What was he talking about?" I asked.

"Last week, in the parking lot, Brock was messing with Scott. He shoved him and Scott hit his head on a car door. So I confronted him."

"Is that why the two of you were fighting?"

"Yeah. I tried to just block his hits."

"Then why did you start hitting back? Even against all of his friends, you were winning."

"Because he hit you."

Zac sounded like that was obvious and I shouldn't question it. Part of me wanted to believe he was a good guy, but I knew he was somehow connected to those immortal-blood-juicing-humans.

People arrived at a steady pace, and the parking lot grew crowded and louder with raucous cheers. The excitement was infectious as the four of us headed to the stands. The drum line was tapping out a well-known beat that pumped up the crowd.

Most of the people around us were wearing Parkview's orange and white school colors, while Brookwood's fans sported maroon and gold. Our panther mascot ran along the edge of the field, followed by another student waving Parkview's flag. The crowd cheered even harder when "Eye of the Tiger" blasted over the sound system. Sarah and I sang along at the top of our lungs, while Zac and Caleb made up their own lyrics.

"I'm glad you're having fun," Zac said in my ear when the song was over.

His deep voice made me shiver. "Me too. It's nice you stood up for Scott."

"He didn't deserve to be treated like he was inferior."

This was a side of Zac I hadn't seen, and it made it harder to remember that he could be dangerous to me. The game started and we were absorbed in it. As I watched, I got this feeling that something was going to happen so I gazed around. My immortal eyesight made it easy for me to see details on faces hundreds of feet away. I scanned the crowd and saw the dark brown hair and brown eyes belonging to Laurel. She was here.

"I'll be right back," I said to Sarah.

"Are you okay?" Zac looked worried.

"I just have to go to the bathroom," I said.

The other spectators paid me no heed as I shoved past them with a murmured excuse. My eyes were intent on Laurel as I sped down the stairs and wound around people. As I got closer, I could see Laurel's eyes following the people passing around her.

Her brown eyes were even darker, and I saw a familiar hunger that made them glow. My breath hitched as my eyes went to her mouth to spy her new glistening fangs. She was a newborn vampire, and the football game was too much temptation. I had to get her away from all of these humans before she killed someone.

Someone must have scored because the crowd erupted. Their eyes were occupied so I moved faster than humans could see and was next to her in a millisecond. She was so focused on a teenage girl cheering for the team, she didn't see me coming. I grabbed her arm and dragged her away from the crowd. Even though she had the strength of a vampire, she didn't resist me.

In the parking lot, I pulled her further into the shadows of the trees. When we stopped, Laurel took a deep breath.

"Laurel, who did this to you?" I asked.

"It was Aaron. I met him at the mall and he…I don't know why, but I followed him into the woods."

"He was enthralling you. It's a vampire trait. It makes it so humans don't fight back. I see he turned you."

"He made me a monster. Whenever someone's close, I can hear their heart beating and I want to bite them. They smell so good." She unconsciously leaned in the direction of the field, but then clenched her fists in anger. "You smell different from them. And how do you know so much?"

Listening for others, I checked our surroundings to make sure no one was near us. "I'm like you, but I'm different."

Laurel's eyes widened and I knew she was close to losing it. I took her face between my hands and forced her to look at me.

"Where's Aaron? He's your creator. He's supposed to teach you how to survive."

Laurel shook her head vehemently. "He's not a good guy. He's been killing humans all over this county."

"Sometimes vampires kill when they feed, even though they don't have to."

"No. He killed them on purpose. He told me that was what they were supposed to do. He said the only reason he didn't kill me was because he liked me."

My stomach churned. "There's more than one?"

"There are four of them." Her head turned toward the field again when the crowd cheered.

"Laurel, listen to me. You need to get as far away from humans as you can."

"Can't I just go home?"

"I'm sorry, Laurel. You can never go home. Humans aren't allowed to know we exist."

Tears streamed down her cheeks, and my heart broke for her. She had been plunged into a world she didn't understand, and she had no one to help her.

"I don't wanna live anymore."

"It gets better once you get past the thirst."

"It's too much. I can't stop it."

"Go into the woods and feed on an animal. It won't taste very good, but it'll satisfy your thirst and help you learn control. And you'll need to find a place to take shelter from the sun." The sound of footsteps approaching caught my attention. Dark figures stalked between the trees. The Lupine Order had returned. "Laurel, you need to run as fast as you can."

Laurel pulled me closer for a hug, her lips next to my ear. "He smells different, too."

She took off before I could ask who she was talking about, and was gone in a second. The figures came closer as I emerged into the parking lot. They were getting desperate if they were risking exposure by coming after me with so many humans around. Then a thought struck me. Had Zac told them I would be here? Was this all a setup? Two of them attacked together and I eluded their grasp. One punched me in the abdomen and the other one tripped me. I fell to my back and kicked the man that followed in the gut, sending him through the air.

When I got to my feet, a third man snatched my arm and slammed me onto a car, denting the hood. He grabbed me around the throat and raised a knife. Man, that was going to hurt. A hand caught his wrist as it descended and we were both surprised to see Zac. The ferocity on his face was frightening and the knife slipped from the man's hand. Zac hit the man in the face so hard that he hit the floor, unconscious. His friends picked him up and carried him away. Once they were out of sight, Zac pulled me into his arms. For some reason, I couldn't stop shaking.

"Skye, are you okay?" Zac asked.

"What the fuck was that about?"

"They work for my father. He's looking for me."

"If he was looking for you, then why did they go after me? That makes no sense." I pushed away from him a little. If Zac truly was working with them, then he would have let them take me and not have interfered. Not to mention the anger that consumed him when the man was about to stab me. "How did you know I was out here anyway?"

"I was watching you." He said it so casually.

"Why?"

"Just to make sure you're okay."

"Make sure I'm okay? Did you think something like that was going to happen to me?"

"No. I just had a bad feeling."

"That sounds like more than just a coincidence. And I get the feeling it has something to do with the tattoo on your chest. " My anger made me careless but I needed to figure out whether or not Zac was a danger to me.

"We can talk after the game," Zac said.

This wasn't the time to talk about it so I turned around and Zac followed me as I walked back to our seats. As the game went on, I prayed Laurel would be okay on her own. When the game was over, Zac and I took one of the cars and headed to a place where we could watch the stars. Minutes later, he parked the car and we got out, the cold wind blowing. I wrapped my arms around me and looked to Zac. He rounded the car and halted at the trunk, pulling out the telescope we borrowed from the school and a thick blanket. At least he had been thinking ahead. I forgot we would be sitting on the ground.

Zac led the way through the woods at a leisurely pace, since I was "injured", and I followed his tracks so I wouldn't trip over anything. Not that I *would* trip over anything, seeing as I had great night vision.

I saw a clearing in the woods ahead of us. Zac broke through the woods first and smiled back at me. Even though the sky was dark, I could see every blade of dark, blue-green grass. We continued to the middle of the clearing and set down our stuff. Zac spread out the blanket, and then set the telescope up so it was facing Orion's Belt. We both sat on the blanket, Zac being a little closer than I was accustomed to, and gazed up at the sky.

The stars twinkled down at us from above, and I felt a longing as I gazed up at them. Stars were fascinating. They were billions of light years away, yet their light reached our tiny blue and green planet.

"It's so beautiful," I said.

"Yes, it is."

When I looked over at Zac, I saw he had been staring at me. My face felt hot, but I didn't look away from him. A slight breeze circled the clearing and wafted his scent toward me. I allowed myself to breathe it in, hoping that overexposure would lessen its hold over me.

"So I'm thinking we should check the position every ten minutes to get an accurate reading." I checked the time on my phone. "It'll be ten in seventeen minutes. You wanna start right at ten?"

"Sounds good to me."

I turned away from him and flipped to a blank page in my notebook, proceeding to make a chart for the data we would collect. His intake of breath sounded impatient, so I looked at him. His incredible light blue eyes seemed lighter than usual, in a luminescent way, the way cat's eyes did when the light caught them, except it was doing that without a light source. I blinked, thinking I was hallucinating, but the glowing was still there.

"I assume you want to ask me your questions," I said.

He was quiet for a second. How many questions did he have? "What's your favorite color?"

That wasn't a question I had been expecting. "What?"

"You promised you'd answer honestly."

"I know. I was just expecting a more complicated question. Well, I guess my favorite color would have to be between light blue and lavender."

"Why those two colors?"

I exhaled in a rush. When I said I would answer honestly, I meant it. If anything, I was true to my word. "Because those are the colors in your eyes."

He smirked. Damn him.

"What's your favorite movie?"

"*Highlander*."

His smile got bigger as he leaned back on his elbow. "Why?"

"There's just something about an immortal warrior that draws me in."

Zac nodded in agreement. "Swords are awesome."

"Yeah. But who wants to live forever?"

"I've always thought if you found the right person, eternity wouldn't be long enough."

When he said that, I could almost feel the strength of his conviction, like eternity with him would be worth fighting for.

"Are you happy with your life?" he asked.

"I guess so. I mean, this isn't the life I would have chosen, but it's the only life I know. It's better than no life at all." Since he was asking questions, then so could I. It would be good to learn more about him. "Are you happy with your life?"

Zac thought for a moment. "I used to be. But something changed, and then there was nothing but arguing between me and my parents. Then I moved here. The moment I saw you, I felt like all the puzzle pieces had fallen into place."

"Why do you seem so certain about me?"

"There's this feeling that guides me."

My aunt had described something like that once before. She had said when a certain person entered our lives everything was forever changed.

"If you could have anything in the world, what would it be?" Zac asked.

There was only one thing I ever wanted. "I'd want to have my parents back."

I turned away from Zac so he couldn't see the tears welling in my eyes. Zac scooted closer to me. I sensed his hand hovering over my shoulder.

"Next question, please," I said.

"Um, ok." He was quiet for a second. "Why don't you like me touching you?"

"It's not that I don't like you touching me, it's that I like it too much."

Zac thought about that for a moment. "How are you so strong?"

Shifting uncomfortably, I forced myself to look him in the eye. "What do you mean?"

"When you shoved me yesterday, you knocked me off my feet. Not to brag, but I'm strong."

"I guess I had an adrenaline rush." I thought back. It *had* taken a lot of strength to get him to release me.

"I guess."

We needed to get off this line of questioning, and I knew which question would do the trick. "Those men that attacked me each had the same tattoo. When I was at Sarah's house that day and I saw you—"

"You mean spied on me."

I sighed heavily. "When I was *spying* on you, I saw that you had the same tattoo on your chest."

That wiped the smile off his face. "It's a popular tattoo."

"Maybe. I just find it a little odd that I've come across it so many times in one week."

"Are you saying those men attacked before?"

"Not them. But they have friends. The night I met Sarah, she saved me from two of them."

Zac's brow furrowed and his jaw clenched. "She didn't tell me that."

"Why should she tell you anything?"

"If I had known that someone was following you, then I wouldn't have let you go off on your own."

"It's not your job to protect me, Zac."

"What if I want it to be my job?"

Neither of us said anything for a long time. When it was time to check our constellation, Zac leaned forward and peered through the telescope and then started writing stuff down. As he wrote, he began to hum a soft tune that brought back the memory of my father humming my favorite lullaby as he put me to bed. My eyes flashed open. A shiver crept down my spine as the melody flowed through me. Everything went cold. It *was* the lullaby that my father used to sing to me. Zac finished writing, looked at me, and the tune stopped.

"Sorry," he said. "I didn't realize I was humming."

"Where did you learn that song?" My mind was in a flurry.

"I didn't learn it."

"What do you mean?"

"I made it up."

That made no sense. "Just now?"

He shook his head. "No. I wrote it. I play the piano."

"That's not possible."

"What's not possible?"

"That was the lullaby my father hummed when I was a little girl. Every night before I went to sleep."

Zac raised an eyebrow. "That's weird."

"After my parents died, I searched everywhere for that song. My father said he'd heard it long before I was born, so I figured someone had written it. I thought I'd never hear it again."

Zac smirked and began to hum again, and I knew it was because it made me happy. But my mind was reeling over my new discovery. I hadn't been lying when I said my father heard that lullaby long before I was born, and that was at least sixty years ago. Zac was only eighteen.

CHAPTER 7
DISCOVERY

By the time I entered Sarah's room, I hadn't come to any conclusions. Sarah perked up when I came in, but frowned when she saw my face.

"Are you okay?" she asked.

I sat on the end of her bed. "You've known Zac since you were little, right?"

"Yeah."

"Does he ever lie about anything?"

"Does he lie—what?"

"I don't know." I put my head in my hands. "I'm so confused."

"Why don't you tell me what happened?"

"While we were star gazing, Zac started humming. It was the same tune as the lullaby my father hummed for me at bed time. I've never heard it anywhere else so I asked where he learned it. He said he wrote it—"

"Yeah, he plays piano. He writes a lot of music," Sarah said, though I could tell she didn't know where the conversation was headed.

"My father told me he heard it before I was born, so how could Zac have written it?"

"Your parents died when you were young. Maybe you heard wrong."

Heard wrong my sixty year old hybrid ass. I could feel Sarah's eyes on me and I looked at her.

"I asked Zac about that tune once," Sarah said. "He was always working on it, trying to perfect it, and he was so excited when he finished. He told me it was the most important song he ever wrote."

"Why is it important?"

"He said it was meant for her." She made quotation marks with her fingers on the last word.

"'Her'?"

"The one he was meant to be with forever."

When we went to bed, the lullaby played in my head. But instead of my father, I dreamed Zac humming was the lullaby as I slept in his arms.

****

This was a dream. I was sure of it. I was in Sarah's bedroom, but I was the only occupant. The room was too dark for even my immortal eyesight, but that was the way of dreams. I twisted around and saw the silhouette of a man lurking in the shadows.

He opened his eyes. They were ice blue and cold. He took a step forward into the moonlight, and my eyes were drawn from his to take in the scar trailing from his temple to his jaw. The guy was built like two men. He was tall and muscular, and when he stopped in front of me, his monstrous frame towered over me.

"Who are you?" I peered up at the giant.

He remained silent, which annoyed me.

"What do you want?" I asked.

He pointed a finger at me.

"Me? Why do you want me?"

"I've been looking for you," he said, and stepped closer.

His long, black hair hung in his face, concealing part of the scar on his cheek, and brushed the tops of his shoulders. He kept coming toward me as I shrank back in fear.

Before I could do anything, his hand was around my throat, constricting my air way. My neck felt like it was being crushed, and I didn't doubt that he could kill me. I struggled with all my might, but it was useless against his strength. Everything felt so real in this dream. It felt like his arms were actually around me.

"Since you're both going to the same place, give Zac my regards," the man said.

My vision blurred, and black spots appeared. Then I heard something in the distance, like someone calling my name.

"Skye." It sounded like it was coming from far away, down a tunnel.

The voice sounded like Zac's. I struggled anew against the hand. After the stranger killed me, Zac would be next. And a human wouldn't last very long. I had to warn Zac that someone dangerous was in the house.

My limbs were still flailing when my eyes flashed open, and I was back in Sarah's room with the fan light on and Sarah, Caleb, and Zac standing over me with worried faces. Zac was clutching my shoulders, as if he had been shaking me awake. Zac's hands went from my shoulders to cupping my face. He looked so concerned. And I had never been so relieved to see him.

Without a thought, I flung my arms around his neck, and pulled myself against his chest. His heart was pounding against his rib cage, and I was comforted by the sound of it. He pulled me back to look at me.

"Skye, are you all right? What's wrong?"

"What do you mean what's wrong?"

"You were screaming. Sarah couldn't wake you, and when I tried you started struggling." He fixated on my eyes, like he was searching for something.

That was when I noticed he wasn't wearing a shirt. And neither was Caleb. Zac's black hair was sleep rumpled and I smiled, embarrassed. "I guess I was having a nightmare."

"What was it about?" Caleb asked.

Option one: I could lie and say I couldn't remember it. But it disturbed me and I needed to talk about it. Option two: I could tell them part of it. Option two seemed the best route to go. "In my dream, someone was trying to kill me."

Zac glanced at the other two, licked his lips, and then edged closer to me. "What happened to me in your dream?"

Could he read minds or something? "How'd you know you were in my dream?"

Sarah came closer as well. "You kept screaming 'Not Zac! Not Zac!'."

Caleb crossed his arms. "Tell it to us from the beginning."

"I was in this room by myself, but when I turned around, someone was behind me. I couldn't see anything except his silhouette. He opened his eyes and they glowed in the moonlight even though it wasn't touching him." I caught the look the three of them shared. "Why did you three just look at each other when I said that?" It wasn't just my imagination. I wasn't the only one keeping secrets.

"I was looking at one of them to see if they thought that was as weird as I thought it was," Sarah said.

"Okay... Well, the guy grabbed me by the neck and started choking me. Right before my vision started going dark, the man said, 'Since you're going to the same place, give my regards to Zac.' I knew he was going to kill me, so when I heard your voice, I was afraid he was going to kill you, too."

"What did he look like?" Zac asked.

"He had black hair, blue eyes, and a huge scar that went from his temple to his jaw."

"Hold on a second." Zac straightened up off the bed and darted out of the room.

Perplexed, I looked at the others, but their eyes were downcast, a frown showing on their faces. Zac came back in the room with his wallet. He dug through it and pulled out a picture. The edges were yellowed and it looked very old.

"Is this what the guy looked like?" He handed me the picture. It was the picture of a man and woman with sable black hair, and the man had ice blue eyes and a scar on his face.

"Oh my God. That's him. Who is he?"

"It's my father." All three of us jumped when he threw his wallet across the room, where it collided with the wall, breaking the plaster. His muscles rippled, drawing my attention. He was built, but it was more so than a normal teenager could accomplish, even if they went to the gym every day.

I got to my feet next to him. "Zac, why would your father want to kill me?"

His brows were drawn and his eyes looked like he was a man haunted by his past. "I don't know."

"Didn't you say your parents weren't the most tolerant people? What kind of people do they not tolerate?"

"Trust me you're not one of them."

"I need some air." I headed out the door and downstairs to the backyard.

Zac followed me, but stayed a couple of feet away, while I stood staring at the sky. The wind blew and I shivered. Without fail, Zac's arms were around me, and I let him comfort me. Confusion clouded my judgment. In all my sixty years, I had never had a dream about someone I didn't know, much less them trying to kill me.

"Why would I dream about your father, Zac? Why would I dream about someone I've never met?" I rotated in his arms, and wrapped mine around his waist.

He looked down and I could see in his eyes that he was at a total loss. "I don't know. I don't know why you'd dream about him, or why he'd be trying to kill you." He touched the side of my face and caressed my cheek. "I could never let anyone hurt you."

"In my dream, I wasn't scared of dying. I was only scared when I heard your voice, because I couldn't live if *he* hurt *you*."

I hugged him tighter, but then he drew me back by the shoulders and clutched both of my wrists. He examined them and cursed under his breath.

"What is it?"

"I made you bruise. I had to pin you down pretty hard." He frowned. "You're strong for your size." He held up one of my wrists and kissed the underside of it.

My head swam for a second at the light contact of his lips. After Zac had saved me from the Lupine Order, I couldn't make myself believe that he had anything to do with them. He said they worked for his father, and my dream confirmed that his father was behind it. I just didn't know the reason why.

****

The next morning, I put everything in my car as I prepared to leave for school. When I got in, the passenger door opened, a backpack dropped to the floor and Zac climbed in. For a second, all I could do was stare.

"What are you doing?" I asked.

"I'm riding with you," Zac said.

"Why?"

"I don't feel right leaving you alone after your dream."

The moment we pulled out of the driveway, Zac rolled down his window.

"Are you hot? I can turn off the heat," I said.

"I'm fine."

He didn't look at me; his eyes scanned the side of the road. At a stoplight, I nudged him.

"You okay?" I asked.

"Yeah."

"Are you sure? You're acting like we're being followed."

Zac looked me square in the eye. "We are being followed."

My gut clenched and I whipped my head around. "We are?"

"Yeah. By Sarah and Caleb."

When I looked back at him, he was smiling. "Jerk."

At a table in the cafeteria, Zac sat with his back touching the table, facing outward. Sarah and Caleb came up and took seats around me as well, in a ring of protection.

"Okay, you guys, this is getting ridiculous. If, and I say if, my dream comes true, it won't happen at school. So stop with the bodyguard thing."

Sarah stood. "Skye, come to the bathroom with me."

Grateful for the distraction, I got to my feet to follow her and so did Zac. "Zac, the bathroom is five feet away. We'll be fine."

I led the way into the bathroom and went to look at my appearance in the mirror. Through the mirror, I watched as Sarah looked under all of the stalls and then went and locked the door.

"Why did you lock the door?" I asked.

"Skye, do you feel like you can trust me?" she asked.

At first I wanted to laugh, but her expression meant business. "Yeah."

"Now I don't want you to freak out, but I know what you are. At least, I have a theory about what you are."

Every once in a while, someone that was really perceptive would come to the conclusion that I was an alien or something, but it was always due to an overactive imagination. It was something I had dealt with before and it seemed like Sarah was one of those people.

"And what do you think I am?" I asked.

"When you had the dream last night, before you started screaming, I tried to wake you up, and your shirt slid up over where the gunshot wound should've been. It was completely healed with no scar. Only certain kinds of people can heal that fast. And I'm one of them."

I froze. If Sarah could heal that fast, then that could only mean one thing; Sarah was an immortal. And I had gotten careless around someone that could actually hurt me.

"Skye?" Sarah stepped closer to me.

The sound of breaking tile filled the air when I pinned her against the tile wall with my hand around her throat. My fangs descended and Sarah's eyes widened. She didn't struggle against me; her arms were hanging at her sides. My grip lessened a fraction.

"Why aren't you fighting back? Trying to kill me?"

Her eyes watered with emotion, like my question was offensive. "Because you're my friend."

"But your people want me dead. The three of you could easily turn me in."

"Skye, Zac and Caleb don't know what you are. I haven't told them."

My fangs receded. "And why haven't you?"

"It's not my secret to tell." I released her and took a step back. Sarah cleared her throat and adjusted her clothes. "Caleb and I left our pack, just like Zac, because we don't believe in the blood feud. We refused to kill vampires. Besides, if I wanted them to kill you, you'd already be dead."

"What do you mean?"

"I've suspected what you are for a while. It was just confirmed when I saw the healed wound, and not to mention now when you showed me your fangs."

I certainly didn't expect this, and I leaned against the cool tile wall. "Since you know what I am, then maybe you can clear some things up for me."

"Sure."

"Those men that attacked me when I was with you and when I was with Zac had the same tattoo of four slash marks across a crescent moon. My aunt said they were from the Lupine Order. Zac has the same tattoo. When I asked him, he told me that it was just a weird coincidence. I thought that maybe he was one of them. Since he's a werewolf, I now know that they were serving him." I paused and thought back to the football game. "But then he also stopped the one from slicing my stomach open. So do they work for him?"

"No, they work for his father, Craven. Craven is our pack leader. Zac's his son, hence the tattoo. Zac didn't want to kill vampires any more than we did, but there were times when he would go missing for hours or even days and have no memory of it. He said he couldn't trust his own mind, so the three of us left. I have no doubt that his father is sending the Lupine Order after him to bring him home."

"Then why attack me? Why not take him and leave me?"

"Because he cares about you. I wish it wasn't true, but Craven would do anything to hurt his son," Sarah said.

There was a sharp pain in my heart. "If Craven is watching him, then he'll be watching me. If Zac figures out what I am, then Craven might figure it out, too. And from what you told me, he loves killing vampires. Capturing me would be too tempting to give up."

"Zac is nothing like his father."

I shook my head. "He can't know, Sarah. He can't know what I am. Promise me you won't tell."

"I promise."

With that promise, I felt something I had never felt before. That pit of loneliness didn't seem so deep, like the vertical walls had begun to slope so I could climb out. Back at the table, I recalled the dream that now had a clear meaning. If the dream was real, then Craven was going to find me and kill me.

The first period bell rang and I headed to my locker. The dream hung like an ominous cloud above my head. My hand froze on a book in my locker. One thought going through my head. Zac was going to live forever. And I realized that I couldn't live forever without him.

A pair of arms slipped around me, and I closed my eyes as the anxiety melted away along with my train of thought.

"How was class?" Zac asked.

"Good. How was yours?"

"Boring without you in it." He took my books for me and closed my locker.

Two cheerleaders walked past, ogling Zac, but he didn't even spare them a glance. I adjusted my purse on my shoulder and his eyes darted to it. "New purse," I said.

"What was wrong with the old one?"

"I just felt like a change."

In the classroom, we set our things down and took our seats. When I looked at him, he seemed preoccupied. His eyes were shadowed by some feeling, as he gazed at the linoleum floor. I reached over and touched one of his hands.

"What's wrong?"

"I can't get that dream out of my head. I'm worried about you."

"He won't hurt me, Zac. He has no reason to." Well, that wasn't true, but I wasn't about to let him know he was right.

"Will you stay at my house after school?"

"Why?"

"When you aren't in my sight, I feel really anxious. There's this…" he paused as he thought of the right word, "instinct inside of me telling me, I need to protect you. It screams at me, telling me I'm not doing enough, that I need to be around you to make sure you're protected. And now that you've had that dream, it's gotten even worse. You have no idea how many times I was about to get up, and walk out of class to come and find you, just to know that you were safe."

Aunt Lenore had once described what it was like to have your instinct kick in, making you need to protect something to the point it was painful to ignore. Did Zac feel that pain when he couldn't do what his instincts wanted him to?

"You can't watch me forever."

"I can try." He looked at me, like he was staring into my soul. "Will you stay with me after school?"

"What about my aunt?"

"Tell her I'm your boyfriend."

"But I can't always stay at your house."

"Then just stay at my house until your aunt gets home. Please. It would put my discomfort at ease."

So it was causing him pain. "Okay. I'll stay at your house after school until my aunt gets home. But you can't loiter around my house when I leave. You have to trust that my aunt can protect me when you aren't around. She's protected me for my entire life. You have to promise me, Zac."

He leaned forward and pressed our foreheads together. "I promise, Skye."

When school was over, Zac directed me to his house, which was a block over from Sarah and Caleb's, and pulled into the driveway. The inside of the house was beautiful. There was enough furniture for an entire family, which made the house look cozy, and it was painted with soft colors that hinted at an antique design.

"Did you decorate the house yourself?" I asked, looking around.

"Yeah. Do you like it?" I nodded and he smiled, set down his stuff, and offered his hand. "Come. I want to show you something."

I took his hand and he led me toward the back of the house. He opened the door at the end of the hall and pulled me inside. The smell of fresh paint greeted me, and I looked around. The walls were a bright white with plastic covering the floor, cans of paint all around.

"What's this room going to be?"

He gazed at the wall, as if he was imagining its purpose right then. "I'm not sure."

"What color are you going to paint it?"

"Well, I was going to do the top half a gray blue, and then the bottom half a moss green."

"Why those two colors?"

"You aren't the only one whose favorite color is someone's eyes."

I blushed harder than ever. "Can I help you paint?"

"Sure." He took the wrapping off the new brushes before handing me one.

Zac started on the top half of the wall as I painted the bottom. Whenever I dipped my brush in the paint, I couldn't help but gaze at Zac. An idea formulated. I stuck my finger in the paint, and then stalked over to where he was standing. When he turned around, I swiped my finger down his cheek, leaving a stripe of gray blue in its wake. He stood there, stunned.

"Did you really just put paint on my face?" he asked.

I nodded and bit the inside of my cheek to keep from laughing.

"Oh, you're so going to get it."

He came at me with his brush, and I raised mine. I dodged his brush and swiped mine down the length of his forearm. He smeared paint on his hand and seized me with it; the paint was cool on my skin, making the hairs in my arm stand at attention. He yanked me closer and attempted to get paint on my face, but I brought my brush up in front of his, and pushed both of them back against his neck. He threw his brush away, and brought me to the ground. He endeavored to keep me there with his knees on either side of me, but I struggled against him, trying to get him with the brush again. We were both laughing and wrestling, when he held himself above me and pinned my arms to the ground; my paint brush lay forgotten. I wriggled beneath him, and he groaned.

"That's really not having the effect you intended," he said.

We both froze; his face was inches from mine, and my gaze dropped to his lips. My pulse raced as the hunger grew, waiting to be unleashed. My lips parted on a slow breath. Zac's gaze dipped to my mouth. He lowered his head and it felt like time had slowed, except my heart which pounded faster than a hummingbird's wings. After what felt like forever, his lips brushed against mine.

Heat surged through my body like wildfire. His lips were soft to the touch, yet firm when I pressed against him. His lips molded to mine and it felt like a piece of me that was out of whack had slid into place. My skin tingled each time his body grazed mine. He relaxed his grip on my arms, and I flung them around his neck to pull him closer. He chuckled against my mouth and pulled away from me.

"Why'd you stop?" I asked.

Zac leaned back up and pulled away from me. "I don't want to do anything you're not ready for."

Zac's eyes were intent on me as I rose up on my knees, cradled his face in my hands, and pulled him closer; his hands slid along my waist. Our lips touched, and his kiss made me dizzy with sensation. He deepened the kiss, giving me a taste of him. The moment I met Zac, I knew his taste was going to be addictive. But I was surprised to find that I didn't care.

"Did we miss the party?" Sarah asked from the doorway.

I broke away from Zac with a surprised gasp, but Zac looked half amused and half annoyed.

"Nice of you two to join us," Zac said. "You could've come a few minutes later." He got to his feet, and held his hand out to help me up.

Sarah and Caleb joined in on the painting, and we got into another paint fight when they teased us about our paint covered clothes. It was the most fun I had ever had in my life. I wished it would never end.

Zac gave me a tender kiss before I got into my car and drove home. The window was down as I drove home, and while I was stopped at a red light I caught the scent of more Lupine Order members. Trying not to be obvious about it, I looked around with my mirrors to see if I could see them. No one looked out of place. When the light turned green, I drove off, taking turns that led me in a big circle. All but one car took a different turn.

I turned into my neighborhood and then into my driveway. I got out of the car and stood in the driveway and waited for them to come. They pulled into the neighborhood and my heart raced. How many of them were there? They stopped in front of the house and we stared at each other. The man in the front seat opened his door and set one foot on the ground.

CHAPTER 8
THE BIG REVEAL

The man was about to stand up when the driver touched his arm. He looked through the back window, pulled his leg into the car, and they sped off. A few seconds later, Aunt Lenore pulled into our driveway.

"Hey, sweetheart how was school?" Aunt Lenore asked as she got out of her car.

"Good. Slow like usual, but good." I paused and took a deep breath, giving a mental prayer for luck. "Aunt Lenore, can I ask you a question?"

She came back into the living room and sat down. "What is it?" Her face went from a look of curiosity to concern when she saw the expression on my face. "Schuyler?"

"Have you ever had a dream that came true?"

"You mean prophetic dreams. Have you had one?" The look on my face must have said something because she moved to the edge of her seat. "Tell me everything about it."

I couldn't let her know that it was at Sarah's house or she would never let me go there ever again, and I couldn't tell her what the guy looked like since he was Zac's father, and one look at Zac would make her think it was him.

"Well, I don't know where or who it was because his face was in the shadows. He just walked up to me and started choking me to death."

"We need to get out of here." Aunt Lenore stood. My heart pounded against my rib cage and my throat felt like it was pinched shut.

"We can't jump to conclusions."

"We can't stay here if you dreamed about someone killing you."

"But I didn't dream any more than that. What if moving is what gets me killed? We don't have anything to go on and if we do something rash, we may be setting things into motion."

She sat down. She was silent for a while then looked at me. "You're probably right."

"If I have another dream like that one, then I promise I'll tell you everything."

She nodded. "I'll be in my room if you need me."

Even when I was younger, and Aunt Lenore wasn't sure what to do, I had never seen her look so defeated. It was as if she felt nothing she did worked and they would find us in some way. My aunt needed to be freed from her responsibilities. I flipped open my cell phone and dialed Sarah's number. She picked up on the first ring.

"What's up, Skye?" she asked.

"Can we hang out? I need to talk."

"Of course, where do you want to meet?"

"I'll see you in your room."

Opening the window, I jumped to the ground below, jogged to the woods near my house, and then ran as fast as I could to Sarah's—getting there in seconds. From the outside, I could see she had left the window open for me, and I jumped onto the ledge and stepped down into her room.

"What's up?" she asked.

"I asked my aunt about dreams that come true. She called them prophetic dreams. I couldn't tell her I'd dreamed of being in your room killed by Zac's father, so I just told her I didn't know where I was or what the guy looked like that tried to kill me."

"What did she say to that?"

"She immediately thought we should move and get out of here."

"That's not good."

"No kidding. I told her we didn't know anything about the dream and that if we moved, we might be setting the dream in motion. So, for now, everything's good."

Sarah studied me. "But that's not what's bothering you."

"When I said that, she looked defeated and I've never seen her like that. Keeping me a secret is slowly killing her. She needs her own life. It's about time I took care of myself and took the burden off her shoulders. She deserves that after looking out for me for sixty years."

Sarah's eyebrows shot into her hairline. "Wow. You're young."

"Young? How old are you?"

"Two hundred sixty-five."

My jaw dropped. "How old are Caleb and Zac?"

"Caleb's three hundred and twenty-two and Zac's three hundred and fifty-four."

Sarah waved her hand in front of my face when I got quiet. "Talk about robbing the cradle."

"Robbing the cradle? Talk about robbing the grave."

We both laughed at that. Once we settled down, I got serious again. "But I don't know what to do about it. I know she wouldn't let me go out alone while she was still alive, but she can't live like this anymore."

"I could go with you. I've had to survive on my own before. I could teach you the tricks of the trade, as it were."

I gave her a stern look. "I put anyone who has contact with me in danger. I couldn't do that to you anymore than I could let my aunt continue like this."

"Skye, I know what I'm getting into. If there's one thing I live for, it's fighting the good fight. You're my best friend, and I won't let a bunch of crackpot old fools with ancient beliefs try to kill you just because you're different. Wherever you go, I'm going with you."

It was the greatest feeling to have someone behind my back. I had never been able to vent my frustration before, and it was making me feel a lot better now that I wasn't the only one contemplating a solution to my problems. "You have no idea how much that means to me."

"You know Zac and Caleb would do the same thing."

The carpet in her room suddenly became very interesting. "I know. But know that I'd rather not get anyone in a position where they could be killed for helping me."

Sarah nodded in acknowledgment. She turned her head to the side and sniffed the air. "Zac's downstairs. Do you care if he knows you're here?"

"He'll be able to smell me either way." A thought presented itself. "Can you tell if someone is a werewolf just by their scent?"

"Yeah."

"Could you tell what I was by the way I smelled?"

Sarah pursed her lips. "You smelled familiar, but there was enough of a different smell I wasn't sure what you were. You smell nice. I guess what I'm trying to say is I couldn't tell just by smelling you."

"Aunt Lenore told me vampires and werewolves would be able to tell the difference between how I smelled compared to both races. That they'd be able to smell the others on me. How is it you can't even smell the difference?" I recalled all the times Aunt Lenore had made us go in a different direction because she caught the scent of a werewolf or vampire.

"I don't really know. How old is your aunt?"

"At least eight hundred years old."

"Maybe only older werewolves and vampires can do it. Or it might be a learned trait."

There was a soft knock at the door. Sarah bade them enter, and

Zac strolled in. He looked devilishly handsome. He had changed into a pair of jeans and his shirt was a dark blue button down, the sleeves rolled up to his elbows.

"Hey, I didn't know you were coming over," he said.

"I didn't know myself until a few minutes ago." He gave me a curious look, so I said, "I needed to talk to Sarah."

In his eyes, I could see disappointment. "Oh, ok. Is anything wrong?"

"Nope. Just girl talk."

He came over and kissed me on the lips. "Caleb and I are going to watch a movie downstairs if the two of you want to join."

"Sounds great." I texted my aunt to let her know where I was.

Moments later, I was sitting on the couch, reclining within Zac's warm embrace and breathing in sync with him. My arm was looped under and around his neck, playing with the curly hair at the back of his head. During the movie, he would brush his lips lightly against my earlobe and kiss along my neck. Every touch from his lips sent shivers down my spine and stirred the butterflies in my stomach. As I sat there, I thought about my life, never dreaming this was where I would be after sixty years.

Sarah said Caleb and Zac believed in the same ideals as her, and that they would be okay with what I was. The only problem with telling someone a secret was you couldn't un-tell them. My stomach was in knots over whether Zac would accept me.

There was something about Zac that made me cling to him, like I had never done to anyone else. Not to mention he had an underlying instinct to protect me to the death. But would that instinct hold up against the blood enemy his family had fought against for millennia?

****

A month later was the fourth week of our project, and it was back to stargazing. Zac spread out the blanket while I set up the telescope and pulled out my notebook. We sat down together, with me sitting between his legs, reclining against his chest. The more we had gotten to know each other, the more I thought about letting Zac in on the secret Sarah and I shared. We sat in silence, so I used that time to think of a way to tell him without him freaking out.

"Zac, what are you going to do when you leave school?" I asked.

"Go to college, I guess."

"What about after that?"

"Probably get a job." He brushed my hair off my shoulder and kissed my neck. Man, was he good at distracting me! But I couldn't let that happen.

"What about in fifty years when everyone around you ages and you look the same?"

His breath hitched and I heard his heart skip a beat. He pushed me away from him only to turn me to face him. His eyes searched my face, like he was trying to determine whether or not I was being serious.

"What are you talking about, Skye?"

"I just want to know what you'll do when you look the same age while everyone else gets older."

"Skye, I will age. Just like everyone else. Just like you."

"Well, if you're going to age just like me, then you won't age at all." He seemed even more baffled. I made an exasperated sound. "Zac, look at my eyes. What do you see?"

"Your eyes are beautiful."

"You aren't looking, Zac." I pushed away from him and stood. An idea went through my head, and I backed toward the dark forest. "Look at me as if you were hunting."

Zac still looked perplexed as he stood, but he put one foot in front of the other to follow me. I shrank back into the darkness and ran away as silent as the night itself. My acute hearing picked up Zac entering the tree line as he stalked after me. The fact he was hunting me excited me, and I smiled as I left my scent on the trees. The point was for him to find me, but I wasn't going to make it easy. After creating a false trail, I leapt as high as I could into the nearest tree, alighting on branch after branch going in a different direction.

I saw Zac stalking on the ground below me. Soundlessly, I dropped from my perch in the tree and followed Zac as he wound through the woods in search of me. When he was looking in the other direction, I jumped to tackle him. At the last second, he turned and caught me as my momentum took us to the ground. Zac took the impact on his back. When we skidded to a halt, and he saw the glowing in my eyes, his lips parted in disbelief.

The longer he was silent, the more anxious I became.

"Zac? Say something," I said.

His hands moved from around my waist to cupping my face. He brushed a stray hair behind my ear. "I knew you were strong but I never thought…I thought I was imagining it all. I thought I was imagining it because I wanted you so badly. I tried so hard to be gentle with you. I always stopped our kissing because I was afraid if I got lost in it, I'd hurt you."

"That's why you always stopped us from going too far? It wasn't because I couldn't control myself?"

"No. I'll always want you." He tugged my face down to kiss him.

Nothing felt as good as his lips against mine. The muscles of his abdomen tensed and relaxed beneath me, and I liked the way he felt. I gasped against his lips when he looped an arm around my waist and rolled over, so that he was angled over me. The instinct in me growled with pleasure. It liked the sweet pressure of his body on top of mine and, even though we were touching, I felt like I needed him closer. I wrapped my leg around his waist and he slid his knee up, locking it in place. He ran his hand down my thigh, squeezing my leg when he ground against me. My nerves got the better of me, and I was getting more embarrassed by the second.

When I could break away from his kiss, I was panting. "Zac, this is too fast."

He leaned up to look at me, breathing hard, too; his eyes were bright with unfulfilled lust. He rose up on his arms.

"Sorry. You just have no idea how you make me feel. And the fact that you tackled *me* pushed me over the edge," he said. We both got to our feet.

There was a brief, awkward silence. "We should probably check the telescope." I glanced at him before biting my lip. "Race you." I bolted towards the clearing.

Zac ran after me but, just as I thought, he was too slow.

"Damn, you're fast," he said, and I grinned.

We settled back on the blanket and my mind wandered back to our first visit to the clearing. Zac had hummed the lullaby my father had hummed for me as a baby. If Zac was three hundred and fifty four years old, then my father *had* heard it before I was born.

"You know, the fact you're a werewolf explains how my father heard that lullaby long before I was born," I told him.

"Yeah, that did seem a little hard to explain, and I had no idea how to make it work out logically." Zac's finger went under my chin and delicately turned my head to face him. "I finished that piece right after my hundredth birthday. Most of the oldest in our pack say young werewolves are still settling into the idea of an immortal life around their first century, so they tend to focus on something to pass the time and ease their mind. I decided to focus on finding the one I was meant to be with. The elders told me looking would do no good, that Fate would bring her to me when I needed her the most. But, of course, I still looked. After a few years, I realized they were right, but I didn't want to give up. So I composed a song that was just for her and I knew someday it would reach her. And it has."

His thumb stroked my cheek. I closed my eyes at the feeling. "But how do you know it reached the right person?"

"Trust me, I know." Zac leaned in closer with our lips almost touching; electricity sparked between us. "I've longed to know where you've been hidden from me. If I'd known where you were, then I would've searched endlessly for you."

His nearness intoxicated me and I felt drunk on his scent. "Well, it would've been pointless before 1952."

Zac reared back so suddenly you would have thought I had struck him. "Wait a second. Are you saying you're only sixty?"

"Yeah," I said, unsure of what he was thinking. "Is that a bad thing?"

Zac cupped my face with his hands. "No. It just means I haven't missed much."

He pressed his lips to mine, nothing like the all-consuming, fevered kisses from before, but the languid, sensuous kisses that made me feel like we had centuries to perfect the craft. Every touch of his awakened a deeper animal instinct and each slight reaction he gave taught me his likes and dislikes. And I was an apt pupil.

There was a rustling sound at the edge of the clearing. Zac jerked away from me, his eyes scouring in the area. I rose up on my elbows and looked from Zac to the woods. Zac sniffed the air and got to his feet.

"We need to leave," he said.

"What is it?" I asked as I gathered our things in a hurry.

"Lupine Order."

Those words got me moving and Zac led the way to the car. Shadows loomed on either side of us and when we got to the car, I could spot others nearby. We were surrounded. Zac shoved me behind him and wrapped an arm around me to keep me in place.

"You have two choices. You can leave and never return, or you can die," Zac said to the men.

The Lupine Order men didn't say anything. There was no sound or signal, but all of them charged at the same moment.

CHAPTER 9
SERIAL KILLER

Zac wouldn't be able to fight them all off, and the thought that he could get hurt overwhelmed me. Zac braced for the attack so I had the chance to slip out of his grasp and stepped in front of him.

"Skye, don't," Zac said.

Following my gut instinct, I raised my hands facing the men. Energy surged through me and erupted from my hands, hurling toward the men. They were thrown into the air and, when they hit the ground, they didn't get back up. Zac grabbed my hand and opened the passenger door for me. I got in as he rushed to the driver's side, and then we were speeding back to his house.

"What did you do back there?" Zac asked.

"I don't know." I looked behind us to make sure we weren't being followed. "What are we gonna do?"

"I want you to stay at my house tonight."

"But my aunt—"

"I need you to stay, Skye."

"Okay," I said.

Zac was still asleep when I got up. I wrote a note telling him I was going home to change and left through the window. I was changing clothes and my thoughts drifted back to the dream I had earlier. This time Sarah and Caleb were there. We were in a car Caleb was driving, and we were speeding, as if someone was chasing us. Caleb glanced back frantically and then the car was crushed on the left side, slamming us into the trees.

Sarah and I stumbled from the wreckage but Caleb wasn't moving. Just as I was about to pry him from the car, Sarah pulled me back and led me away. In the opposite direction.

"We have to save him, Sarah," I said, desperation coloring my tone. I peered back at the smoking, mangled mass of metal.

"He knew what he was doing. Zac told us to keep you safe. We all knew what we were getting into when we ran with you. It was our decision." She yanked at my arm a few more times before I obeyed her command.

Sarah and I ran into the concealing woods as someone crashed through the trees behind us. They were gaining more ground, and I knew they would catch us soon.

"Skye, you need to get out of here." Sarah stopped and was doubled over to catch her breath. "I'll hold them back. Just get as far away as you can."

"I'm not leaving you, Sarah."

Her eyes darkened, as well as her skin, and her nails elongated, becoming razor sharp. She shoved me and I lost my balance for a moment. "I'm not arguing with you." There was a large crash and the ground shuddered. She looked forward and then back at me with wide eyes. "Run, Schuyler. Run."

I sprinted away and when I glanced behind me, I saw them strike her down. With a single slash, they separated her head from her body. "Sarah," I screamed and dropped to my knees.

I pushed the dream to the back of my mind. I trudged downstairs and gathered my things for school.

At school, I stopped by my locker before going into the cafeteria to sit in my usual spot. Zac sat down first and gave me a lingering kiss, quelling the disquiet of my mind for a brief second, before Sarah and Caleb joined us on the opposite side. As soon as I saw Caleb and Sarah, the dream came rushing back like a tidal wave. And it hit me hard. Sarah noticed my sullen mood and opened her mouth to say something, but Zac preempted her question with one of his own.

"Guess what?" Zac said.

"What?" Caleb froze mid-bite, obviously not expecting a guessing game.

"It would seem that Skye is one of us."

Sarah looked shocked. Out of Zac's field of vision, I mouthed that I had told him.

Caleb set his food down. "I'm not sure I understand and I don't want to blurt out something stupid and then be completely off the subject you're talking about."

Zac smiled. "She's a werewolf."

Now it was my turn to be shocked. I glanced up at Sarah, who seemed to realize what he was saying as well.

"She's only…" Sarah began, but I kicked her in the shin. She held in a cry of surprise, but couldn't stop her eyes from watering.

Zac gave her a questioning look. "What were you about to say?"

"I thought she only told me," Sarah said.

Zac's smile faltered. "Oh, so you already knew?"

"I didn't tell her. She guessed," I said.

"Oh, okay then." His smile returned.

Great. So Zac had guessed I was an immortal being just like him, but he thought I was only a werewolf. It didn't seem likely for a werewolf to even consider the possibility of a hybrid. At some point, I would have to tell him and deal with his reaction, but for now, I was just fine with him thinking I was a werewolf.

Sarah eyed Zac for a second then looked to me. "Okay, now that that's out of the way. What's wrong, Skye?"

Zac set his fork down and examined my face more closely. Caleb stopped eating his breakfast long enough to glance at me. I would have to tell them. Maybe they could help me figure out what it was about.

"I had another dream," I said, and all three of them stilled. "This time Sarah and Caleb were with me. We were in a car and Caleb was driving and someone was chasing us. Then we crashed and Sarah and I managed to crawl out. Caleb was unconscious and I tried to get him out, but Sarah wouldn't let me. She kept pulling me away from the car."

"You left me in the car?" Caleb said.

"Shut up, Caleb. That's not the end of it," Sarah said, without looking away from me.

"We were running through the woods and we could hear people weaving through the trees behind us. Sarah told me to go ahead without her and we argued, but I left her behind and when I looked back…"

"What did you see?" Sarah whispered.

"You died."

Sarah couldn't hide the look of horror on her face. She was the only one that knew why someone would be chasing me and why they would kill her for getting in the way. Just being friends with Sarah put her life in danger. My heart hurt like a spike had been drilled through it. When I glanced up, Sarah was looking at me like she knew what I was thinking.

"I have to go," I said, and got up from the table and bolted out of the cafeteria. Everything inside of me was at the boiling point, and I felt like I was going to burst.

No one followed me and I was grateful for that. I couldn't let my friends get killed because of what I was, especially when two of them didn't even know what I was. It wasn't fair that I was putting them in that position. But more than anything, I was afraid that Zac would reject me.

I hurried to my locker and shoved my things back in. There was no way I could go to class today. My mind could think of nothing but the dream I had. There wasn't much to go on from my dream, so I didn't know if Caleb was going to be killed or just left in the car. Zac wasn't even in the dream and somehow that scared me more than the rest. We shared something, and I was connected to him in a way I couldn't understand.

After I left my locker, I continued to the parking lot, got into my Jeep, and fled from the school. It was still dark outside, so I drove a little way from the school where there was a small recreational park and pulled in. I went to one of the playgrounds in the park and sat on a swing.

If my dream came true, then I would have at least killed my best friend. Just the thought of never seeing Zac again made my heart feel like it was locked in a vise. Aunt Lenore said prophetic dreams always came true, if you did nothing to change them. But how could I change it if I didn't know when or where it was going to happen?

The wind blew, stirring my hair like invisible fairies at play. I watched the sun rise and the young children squealing with delight as they played in the sandbox, on the swings, and the jungle gym. The smell of flowers permeated the air. There was no hesitation when they ran to their mother's open arms, a smile on their face and happy peals of laughter. There was nothing I wouldn't give just to hear my parent's voices when they told me they loved me.

My phone started ringing and I dug it out of my purse; Sarah's number displayed on the screen.

"Hey, Sarah," I said.

"Where are you?"

"The park. Is Zac asking you to make sure I'm okay?"

"At the moment, Caleb's forcing him into the car and back to his house because I know you need space. He wants to know you're safe, but I'm making sure you're not thinking about doing something drastic, like leaving without telling anyone."

"Everything would be better if I just left."

"Trust me, it wouldn't. Besides, that would drive Zac crazy." Her voice came from my right.

I jerked my head to the right and saw her standing with her phone at her ear. She hung up and sat on the vacant swing next to me.

"I saw your face, Sarah. You couldn't hide that from me. My dream freaked you out. Hell, it freaked me out. You may know what I am and know the risk you take, but Caleb and Zac don't. Aunt Lenore told me prophetic dreams always come true—which means it is only a matter of time till they find me. If I leave, then none of that will come to pass. It's the only solution I can think of."

"Skye, I'm not going to stop being friends with you just because others want you dead. That's what friends are for. Friends are the people that stick around when everyone else runs. Friends are the people that go against the natural instinct to preserve their own skin. I'd fight for you because you're my best friend and I love you. I would die before I let anyone else hurt you because of what you are."

"I could never forgive myself if I got any of you killed."

"Don't worry about it." She swung for a second. "But there's one thing I'd like to know."

"What's that?"

"If you told Zac what you were, then why did he say you were just a werewolf? Did he think we wouldn't accept you if we knew you were a hybrid?"

"I think he just assumed what I was. I just showed him what made us alike, but I never outright told it to him. I didn't say the words 'half vampire and half werewolf'. It's only logical he'd think I was a werewolf, because I'm out during the day." My stomach felt a little queasy whenever I thought about Zac knowing the truth. "I'm afraid he won't react well to what I am."

"I promise you he won't care. I mean, that was the whole reason he left his family in the first place."

"People tend to react differently when the person in question is their girlfriend rather than just their friend. In all my sixty years, you're the only one that has accepted me for what I am," I said. "I'm lucky you don't have a problem with that. Most people react violently to what they don't like or understand."

"Skye, Zac would never do that to you. He's not a violent person unless he is protecting someone. I can't see him reacting violently towards you."

"Okay, well, none of that really matters because what we need to be worried about is *when* my dream comes true. It apparently happens once at least Caleb knows what I am. So I figure as long as Caleb is kept in the dark then we should be okay. I think."

"We should head back soon otherwise Caleb won't be able to keep Zac there without knocking him out."

Knocking him out? "Yeah, I guess I've played hooky for long enough."

We pulled up and the moment I entered the house, I was enfolded in Zac's comforting embrace. I slung my arms around his muscular waist and rested my forehead against his chest. The strong and perfect thumping of his heart was like music to me. It was proof he was real. Zac's hand curved along the back of my neck and head. When I looked up at him, he leaned down and kissed me.

"Are you all right?" he asked, and I knew he was worried that I had left school when the Lupine Order was after me.

"I'm fine."

"Do you want to talk about it?" He wanted me to be able to trust him as much as I trusted Sarah. But I couldn't let him know. There was the chance I would cause a second dream, one even worse than before if I told him.

"Not really. Someday. But not now."

The disappointment in his eyes made me feel guilty before he kissed me again, and then led me into the kitchen. I hopped up onto the counter as he pulled out the things he needed to make a sandwich.

"So you were in the park all day until Sarah came to get you?" he asked, and began assembling his sandwich.

"Pretty much. I hadn't even realized how much time had passed until Sarah called me."

Zac noticed me staring at his sandwich. "Are you hungry? I could make you one, too."

"I'm good, thanks."

"You know what?" He paused in what he was doing. "I've never seen you eat. Not once. And we have lunch together every day."

I almost choked in surprise, but Zac missed it when he took a bite. "I don't like school food."

"What about today? You said you've been at the park the whole day."

"I wasn't hungry."

Lies wearied me. Lies were my entire existence and I wanted to be rid of them.

"Well, I guess you miss out on my delicious sandwich," Zac said.

He went to town on the sandwich, like it was his last meal. "When I found out you were werewolves, it explained why Sarah ate so much and never gained a pound."

Zac laughed at that and Sarah yelled from the other room, "I heard that, you little punk. Laugh again and I'll make sure you can never reproduce, Zac."

Then I started laughing, and Zac almost choked on his sandwich. Caleb came in from the backyard and halted at the sight of us laughing so hard.

"All right, what did I miss?" Caleb asked.

Sarah came in from the other room. "Zac was just making fun of me, so I told him if he laughed at me again I'd make it so he couldn't reproduce."

The great thing about Caleb was he always took everything in stride. Nothing ever really fazed him, and he let things roll off his shoulder, like it didn't matter. But when things did matter, he always knew the right thing to do. If Caleb knew I was half vampire, I had a feeling he wouldn't care, and that he would pick up the sword and fight for me because that was what he thought was right.

Caleb shrugged, walked over to Zac, and snatched the last of his sandwich out of his hand, swallowing it in one bite.

"What the hell? That was mine," Zac said.

"You snooze you lose," Caleb said, with a big smile.

"I'll show you snoozing." Zac lunged at Caleb.

It was good I was sitting on the counter because Caleb collided with Zac and they crashed into the cabinet, fracturing the wooden doors. The violence of it should have shocked me but it felt strangely normal. Sarah jumped onto the counter with me and we watched the wrestling match.

"This would be better if we had some popcorn," Sarah said.

I cringed when more wood cracked. "Yeah. And tougher cabinets."

Caleb got Zac in a head lock, but he managed to scramble out of his arms and spun around to pull his arm at an awkward angle. Caleb jabbed him in the ribs until he let go, and then they were standing, grappling with their large forearms and butting heads.

I looked to Sarah. "Do they expect us to watch this all day?"

"They'll keep going for a good while," she said.

"So what else do you want to do?"

"Let's go and watch a movie."

"Sounds good to me." We edged our way around Caleb and Zac's wrestling limbs to the living room.

Sarah went to the shelves of movies to pick one to watch, while I flipped on the television. Sarah came over with a movie but I stopped her.

"Wait, Sarah. Take a look at this," I said.

Sarah sat down on the couch next to me and we both listened to the headline story.

"It's been two weeks and the police still have no leads pertaining to the many deaths that have occurred all over Gwinnett County. The victims of this serial killer have been found in different places with no connection between them, except that they have all been drained of blood. County officials believe the bodies are being disposed of away from the original crime scene. The police urge everyone to never go anywhere alone, and to only leave your homes when necessary. We hope to have more on this story in the days to come, but in the meantime, please stay safe."

Everything was quiet; Zac and Caleb had stopped fighting and come into the living room. We were silent at the grave reminder of the dream I had had, and for a while I was content to stay that way. Zac came over and sat down on the couch next to me, and pulled me closer. His strong heartbeat calmed me and I relaxed in his arms. I glanced at Sarah out of the corner of my eye, and her oh-shit-face told me she had drawn the same conclusion. Immortals were killing humans.

When I got home, I knew I would have to talk to Aunt Lenore about the deaths. It was most likely vampires since the bodies were drained of blood. The high number of deaths in the same area meant there were a lot of them. I clicked on my television to watch the news as I waited for Aunt Lenore to get home. She needed to know what was going on, even if I didn't want to tell her. Part of me wanted to keep it under wraps because I didn't want to leave this place. Now that I had Zac, I didn't want to lose him.

Aunt Lenore came in late, so I waited for her to eat dinner and settle down before I talked with her. When she finished dinner, I switched off the television and took a deep breath.

"Did you see the news today?" I asked.

"No. Did something happen?"

I summed up the story in as few words as possible and watched Aunt Lenore's reaction to each added detail.

She was silent for a long time. "I think we should wait and see what they do."

"You want to wait? I thought you'd demand we leave now." This wasn't the reaction I was expecting. "Wasn't this what you were afraid was going to happen?"

"I want to make certain they're after you before we just relocate and alert them to our presence by moving. It's a risk, but it's not like we weren't risking everything in the first place."

"Well, let's hope they're just all in the same place at the same time by accident."

Aunt Lenore was willing to wait it out, but something needed to be done.

CHAPTER 10
HUNTING

I was running as fast as I could. My throat burned; large bruises marred my cheek and temple, making my head pound. I had no idea what I was running from, but I knew I had to get away. Somehow something had gone wrong. There was nothing in my dream to indicate if someone was chasing me, or if I was just running. The cold air was like an ice pick scratching its way down my throat with each breath I took.

The tears streaming down my face blurred my vision. My heart had been ripped in two. I was crying so hard, I didn't see the car coming down the street as I was crossing it. My body was thrown across the street, and collided with a tree. The car that struck me didn't even stop. It increased its speed and was soon out of sight.

Even though it was painful, I forced myself to crawl into the woods, and when I was a good ways in, where I could no longer see anything but trees, I broke down and sobbed. Someone had broken my heart and it was an extreme shock to see myself so vulnerable. A shadow crossed my path and I whirled around to see who it was.

My eyes opened and I jerked upright in my bed, gasping for breath. The dream had felt so real. My skin was cold and clammy, my heart was racing, and the pain in my chest was almost unbearable. The red numbers on the clock read three in the morning. I changed my sheets before entering the bathroom and starting the shower.

My night shirt was plastered to my skin. I peeled it off followed by my shorts, tossing them to the floor, and then stepped under the stream of hot water. I let the water wash away my doubts and fears, and any other bad feelings from my dream.

I took my time in the shower, washing my hair, and scrubbing the dirty feeling from my body. My skin felt raw by the time I was satisfied that I was clean enough. The lights were still off in my room, so it was easy to see my phone, which had lit up with a text message. I picked up the phone, expecting it to be a note from Sarah, but it was from Zac. My brow furrowed as I clicked on the message.

<I don't know if you're sleeping, but I got a feeling you were uneasy. Text me back if you need to talk.>

I hesitated with my finger over the reply button. The hole in my chest got smaller whenever I heard his voice.

<I had another prophetic dream. No one else was in it this time. Just me. I was running from someone, but I don't know who.>

His answer was immediate.

<Do you want me to come over?>

Aunt Lenore would catch his scent in a second if he came over, and then she would kill him. *<Actually, could I come over to your house for a bit?>*

<Sure. I can come get you.>

<There's no need. I'll be there in a second.>

I combed through my wet hair, pulled some jeans on, and a long sleeved black shirt. Once I was dressed, I went out my window and ran to Zac's house. I needed his calming presence, I needed his strong arms around me, and I needed him to tell me I was safe. He would never let me be harmed as long as he didn't know what I was.

As I neared his house, I saw the window to his room had been left open. Leaping onto the sill, I climbed through the window and saw Zac sitting on the edge of his bed, waiting for me. When my feet touched the floor, he approached me and pulled me into his arms. He wore a concerned expression, but didn't say anything. After a minute, I pulled away, went to his bed, and sat down on the edge, the mattress sinking under my weight. Out of habit, I pulled off my shoes so I could sit cross-legged on the bed. Zac sat so he was facing me.

"What's up?" he asked.

I shrugged and made a face. "These prophetic dreams scare me. I'm the common denominator in all of them. I don't know which dream is going to happen first so I don't know what to prepare for. But the thing that scares me the most is I'm not the only one getting hurt in my dreams. I'm responsible for Sarah's death and possibly Caleb's. I don't know if I'd be able to take it if I dreamed of you dying."

"What other people do isn't your fault. I won't let anything happen to you. I'll protect you with my life. I don't want you to worry."

"I know, but it would still be my fault if others got killed."

Zac scooted closer and cradled my face between his hands. Gazing into his eyes made me want to cry even more. The ice blue and lavender flecks held me in a trance.

"Don't blame yourself."

He gently pulled my face towards him and kissed me, my eyelids fluttered closed. His skin was warm, soft, and inviting. I rose to my knees so my head was leaning over Zac's, breaking the kiss. He gazed up at me before pulling me flush against his abdomen, his arms around my waist.

His hand ran up along my back to the nape of my neck to pull my head back down to his. As we kissed, my fingers ran through his shiny, raven black hair and then down his back, where I grabbed onto the hem of his shirt and started to pull it off. He ceased kissing me long enough to yank his shirt off and toss it to the floor, and then his lips were kissing along my neck, making my body feel like it was floating. I sighed with pleasure as his lips grazed my neck, and I raked my nails across his bare back, making him growl low in his throat.

As we kissed, I rested on my knees with my legs parted around his hips. Suddenly Zac looped an arm around me and leaned forward so he was pressing me down onto his bed. Zac maneuvered himself on top of me, like he had in the woods, but this time it was so much more intimate. The hypnotic effect of his scent was even more powerful since his shirt was off, and I was reveling in his glorious skin and defined muscles. He kissed along my collar bone, sending me into a lustful frenzy, but then I started to get embarrassed again.

I tapped Zac on the shoulder and he reared back to look at me. A dazzling smile spread across his face. "Sorry. I can't seem to get enough of you."

He rolled over onto his back, and I rested my head on his chest with my arm and leg draped across his body. We laid together like that for a couple of hours, just content in our silence. After a while, I convinced myself I needed to get home. I sat up as he leaned up on his elbows to gaze at me.

"I need to get back. My aunt will freak if I'm not there when she wakes up," I said, and gave him a kiss, telling him I didn't really want to leave, before I jumped off the bed and headed toward the window. "Goodnight, Zac. Or, well, good morning."

"Night, Skye. Be safe." His expression looked like he was restraining from following me as I leapt out of the window.

In seconds, I was back in my room and under the covers when my aunt checked on me. After a few minutes, I got back out of bed and dried my hair before changing clothes. Something inside of me was pulling me back to Zac's—I even looked at the window a couple of times. Downstairs I turned on the television to the news channel.

The reporter looked tired. "Seven more bodies have been found in the Athens area. Police officials believe there may be multiple suspects, and that they are most likely killing at random. Police officers are working overtime to find the vicious killers, and there are volunteers manning the phones for the police tip hotline. The toll free number is at the bottom of your screen. Again, I urge everyone to travel in groups of three or more and to not go out after dark unless absolutely necessary. I'll have more updates for you as soon as possible, and please, stay safe."

The high number of deaths couldn't be a coven feeding a lot in one area. Even inexperienced vampires killing during feeding was rare. They had to be killing humans for a reason.

A theory went through my head and I clicked off the television, threw the remote onto the couch, and hopped into my car and sped to the school. While I was in the parking lot, I texted Sarah and told her to meet me earlier than the guys. Her reply announced she was on her way. My wait only lasted for a few minutes before Sarah sat down in front of me. Her hair was disheveled and her shirt was on backwards. I cleared my throat and pointed at her shirt, trying to hold back a smile.

"Dammit, I was in a hurry," she said, and pulled her arms back through the sleeves, and turned her shirt around with sharp, abrupt jerks. "So what's up that I had to get here before the guys, which is really hard by the way?"

"Did you happen to see the news this morning?"

She shook her head. "I don't usually watch television in the morning at all, much less the news. Why, what happened?"

I summed up everything that had happened on the news, and followed with my thoughts.

"So what part of this couldn't the guys hear? They know it's a vampire who's killing all of those humans."

"That's just it. I don't think they're looking for me."

"You've lost me."

"I know they want me. What I'm saying is I don't think they're *looking* for me. If they were looking for me, then we would have come across one of them by now. I don't know what you know, but vampires don't kill when they feed. The fact that there are so many bodies tells me they want me to know how many people they're killing."

"Where are you going with this?" She set her food down.

"I think they're killing so many people on purpose. I think they're using the deaths to make me panic and leave."

"They know you'll connect the deaths with vampires. And they're waiting for you to react to their presence by leaving, and then they'll know where you are."

"Exactly." I paused. "Those people are dying because of me."

"No, Skye. It's not your fault some evil vampires are looking for you and killing innocent people to do it. If you go looking for them, then your parents will have died in vain."

"I have to do something." There was no way I could stand by and do nothing.

"Skye, if you go looking for them, then I'll tell Zac everything. The consequences be damned." She went quiet when a student passed.

"Promise me you won't go looking for them."

"I promise." And I was going to keep my promise, even though I would rather turn myself in than let more people die for me.

We quit talking for a while as we waited for the guys to show up. They both came in twenty minutes later and sat with us after grabbing food from the lunch line. Zac sat next to me and Caleb sat across from him on the other side.

Caleb glanced up before eating and paused. "Skye, you're white as a ghost."

"Thanks for noticing."

"Are you okay?" Zac leaned in closer to my ear. "Are you still worried about the new dream?"

"You had another dream?" Sarah said loudly, and then cursed when Caleb elbowed her. "What happened this time?"

"I was by myself. I was running from someone, but I wasn't sure who. There wasn't much to it. Sorry."

"Were you thinking of something else? Something besides the dream?" Caleb glanced at Sarah and then back at me.

"I'm assuming neither one of you watched the news this morning either." Caleb and Zac looked at each other and shrugged. "It would seem our serial killer killed seven others last night."

Caleb and Zac both dropped their food to stare at me. I ignored the idle chatter of the rest of the students as they filed into the cafeteria.

In first period, the teacher had a moment of silence for the people that had been found dead last night, and then she gave everyone a chance to talk about the deaths and how it was making them feel.

At the bell, I headed to second period, my gut twisting and roiling. Mr. Matthews informed us we would all be going to the gymnasium for an announcement.

When it was time for our class to leave, Mr. Matthews came in and ordered everyone to leave the room in a single file line. As we walked down the hall, I spotted a man that towered over the students and teachers. Zac clutched my arm to pull me back just as I noticed the tattoo on his neck. The Lupine Order was here. What were they doing? The Order was forbidden to reveal our existence, too, unless they wanted to die.

Caleb came to my other side as the man reached behind his back. The man pulled out a gun and the humans screamed and ran for cover. In the chaos, Sarah crept behind the man.

A freshman stood frozen in fear, between the man and me. And I doubted the man would care if he killed a child. Ripping my arm from Zac's grasp, I charged the man. Like it was happening in slow motion, the trigger was pulled, the bullet left the chamber, and I shoved the kid out of the way. Hot metal pierced my abdomen, searing flesh and cutting bone. My legs gave way and I crashed to the floor.

Sarah snapped the man's neck a second before Zac screamed my name. He ran to my side and got on his knees next to me. He pressed hard against the wound to staunch the bleeding, and I cried out when the pain kicked in. Caleb knelt on the other side of me and put his jacket under my head.

"I'm really tired of being shot," I said.

"Someone call nine-one-one," a teacher said.

"There's no time." Zac knew I couldn't go to a real hospital because my blood wouldn't read human. Humans could never get access to immortal blood. "Caleb, get the car started."

Caleb and Sarah ran out of the building as Zac picked me up, and then hurried out of the school and toward the parking lot. Sarah and Caleb met us before we even got to the stairway and Zac jumped into the front seat with me in his lap. I would need blood to heal, but now that Zac thought I was a werewolf, he wouldn't understand why I couldn't stay with him when he had the supplies to take care of me. Sarah was sitting in the back seat, so I looked over Zac's shoulder and mouthed "blood".

She nodded her head, but I was having trouble keeping my eyes open. At Sarah's house, Zac carried me in and set me down on the couch. My mind was in a fog that wouldn't lift and everything was going slow. I could feel how fast Zac and Caleb worked as they took the bullet out, cleaned the wound, and bandaged it.

Sarah came down from upstairs and looked me over. "Zac, carry her upstairs to my bathroom."

"Why?"

"Look at her." She made a face like it was obvious. "She's covered in blood. I'm going to help her take a shower."

"I can help her with that."

"Zac, she just got shot. Give the girl a break and do what I say."

Zac carried me upstairs to Sarah's bathroom, setting me on the toilet. Zac left the room when Sarah came in and she locked the door behind her. She opened the towel she had in her hand. Cradled in the heart of the towel were three bags of blood. Sarah grabbed one and cut a hole in it with her fingernail and handed it to me.

"Drink up, Skye," she whispered.

After the first bag, the cold chill in my body disappeared, and then I was able to open the second one myself. Feeling was returning and the sharp pain diminished. By the time I was finished with the third one, I could stand straight and I had gained back most of my strength. It was an effort to climb into the shower and rinse off all of the excess blood from my skin. Sarah had also grabbed some of my clothes when she went to my house, so I had something to change into when I got out of the shower.

Thankfully Sarah had gotten me the blood I needed though I didn't know how.

"How did you get the blood out of the refrigerator? It has a code," I asked.

"I kinda broke it. Sorry."

As I scrubbed the blood from my body, I thought about Zac's reaction to my injury, and not wanting to be separated from me. "Why does Zac act so possessive when I'm injured?"

"It's not just when you're injured. He acts that way all the time. You should've seen how he was the first day after he met you. Caleb had to knock him out and watch over him the entire night to make sure he didn't go searching for you and scare the shit out of you."

"Really? Why?"

"Because you're his mate."

I moved the curtain to the side to give her a look. "What's a mate?"

"You don't know?"

"No."

"Every werewolf and vampire has a mate. Your mate is the match for your soul. It's like they're made for you. You know them by their scent, their voice, and their face. And you only get one. Forever. Zac gets very anxious when you're not around because he feels an almost painful need to make sure you're protected, and that you have everything you could want or need. Basically, you wouldn't want to get between a werewolf or vampire and their mate."

That explained a lot of Zac's actions, and why he had been trying to keep me at Sarah's house when I needed to get home. Every time I got shot was just making his anxiety worse. Not to mention there was that strange pull I felt toward him whenever we were apart. Was that why I felt such an intense attraction to him?

Once I was clean, I changed into the clothes Sarah had brought for me, and then she helped me back down the stairs. Progress was slow as I staggered over to the couch and laid on it. Zac knelt at the side of the couch, and moved the wet hair out of my face, leaving his palm resting along my cheek.

"How are you feeling?" he asked.

"Better," I murmured.

"What were you thinking?"

"That kid could've gotten killed."

"So what are we going to do now?" Caleb interrupted, and the three of them exchanged glances.

"My aunt has to be told," I said, and tried to sit up.

"Why do we have to tell her?" Zac pushed me back down.

"How many people do you think saw me get shot? The school will notify my aunt. She has to be told. But I think it would be best if she only knew one person knows about me. And that person should be Sarah."

Zac looked ready to argue but said nothing. That way I didn't have to mention Sarah was the only one who *really* knew what I was. No matter how close I got to Zac, I couldn't get the feeling out of my head that something bad would happen.

With my stomach full of blood, I felt drowsy. I turned my head to the side and fell asleep looking at Zac. When I woke back up, I was still on the couch, but Zac was gone. I peered around and realized I was in my house. Sarah must have taken me back while I slept. My aunt's face hovered above me. A small smile spread across her face.

"Hi, sweetie. How are you feeling?" Aunt Lenore asked, and helped me to a sitting position.

"I'm fine. Sarah?"

"I'm here," Sarah said, and walked into view. "Don't worry. I told her everything."

Aunt Lenore looked at her with an amused expression. "It was quite a surprise to come home to a werewolf in my house. Why didn't you just tell me, sweetheart?"

I gave her a skeptical look. "If I told you my friends were werewolves, what would you have thought?"

She chuckled. "We'd have moved. But that won't happen now. If anything, I think we're safer."

"But not everyone else."

"What do you mean?"

I filled Aunt Lenore in on all the disappearances and murders, and what I thought they were trying to accomplish.

"I told you that's not your fault," Sarah said.

"You think that's your fault, Schuyler?" Aunt Lenore asked, and I nodded in response. "I've told you they'll do anything to find you. You can't blame yourself for what others do. You can't save everyone."

I lifted up the hem of my shirt and checked the gunshot wound. It was almost healed. The skin was still raised and pink, but would be gone in an hour or so.

"I am curious though, about why Sarah is the only one that knows what you are. Why do Caleb and Zac only think you're a werewolf?"

"Well, I didn't flat out tell Zac. I wanted him to figure it out for himself, and at first I thought he had, but I didn't think it through. Now I get this feeling, well, more of a warning, telling me that he'll freak out if he knows what I really am," I said.

"He believes the same thing I do," Sarah said. "He believes the blood feud is pointless. That's why he left his family and his pack."

"I know he's a good guy. I just have a bad feeling."

"What kind of feeling?" Aunt Lenore asked.

I felt like a broken record as I repeated what I had told Sarah. "I don't want to feel that way, I just do. But we have to do something about the people dying. We can't ignore it any longer."

"I won't let you find them so they can kill you," Sarah said.

"I know. What I'm saying is we should find them and kill them first."

"What do you suggest we do?" Sarah asked.

"The last people they killed were in Athens. I say we go hunting."

"What about school?" Aunt Lenore asked.

"Do you really care?" I asked, and Aunt Lenore smiled.

"Have you ever been taught to fight?" Sarah asked.

"She's been taught by the best. I made sure of it." My aunt smiled and stood. "Come with me."

We followed my aunt into her bedroom and she went into her closet. To the untrained eye, it looked like a normal closet. But I recognized where the wall paper separated. Aunt Lenore thumped her fist against the wall and the whole thing trembled before it slid to the side, revealing a wall covered with weapons. There were swords, knives, and even a few throwing daggers.

"How are we going to explain to the guys why we're looking for the killers?" I asked.

"Leave that to me," Sarah said.

CHAPTER 11
ONE WITH THE DARKNESS

"So, we're going to do what, exactly?" Caleb asked, as Sarah and I strapped the weapons onto our bodies.

"We're going to find the one or ones killing those humans and kill *them*," I answered.

Zac stopped me in the middle of what I was doing. "Why are you doing this?"

"If there's something wrong, then those who have the ability to take action have the responsibility to take action," Sarah said.

"Thank you, Nicholas Cage," Caleb said, and Sarah gave him a grin.

"Then we're going with you." Zac began to set weapons aside.

"Okay," I said.

"Okay? I thought you'd be against us coming." Caleb twirled a dagger in his hand.

"We don't care if you come along. We just weren't going to let you stand in our way."

"Oh, okay." Caleb stuck a knife down into his boots. "Whoa. That's cold. Did your aunt keep these in the freezer?"

The black leather clothes I was wearing were engineered for fighting; they were the symbol of my strength and agelessness. My boots hugged my calves up to my knees with loops down the sides to hold knives. I was wearing slim, tight black leather pants with holsters on the sides. My long sleeved shirt was covered by a vest my aunt had made for me when I had frozen into my immortality. It was worn and supple leather covered with etchings of ancient Celtic runes. It was a reminder of my past, my training, and the sense of one thing that would remain like me:

unchangeable. There was a strap with a harness that slipped over my shoulders and tightened around my waist to keep it from moving. Last but not least, I grabbed the sword my aunt had taught me to fight with, and slid it into the slot between my shoulder blades where it hung across my back.

Sarah was wearing something similar though it looked a lot older than mine. As we waited, I pulled my hair back into a ponytail and Sarah braided her blonde hair into twin French braids on each side of her head. Caleb came back downstairs just as Zac came in the front door. Zac looked *good* in black; the dark shade went well with his raven hair and light blue eyes. The sword at his side brought images to mind of an immortal warrior who would protect me even if it cost him his life. He gave me a questioning look as I approached him and rose up on my toes to kiss him. It made me feel safe and protected to have such a strong immortal male crave me like he did.

"Can you guys save sucking face for later?" Caleb asked. The question would have been sarcastic and rhetorical from someone else, but he said it with such sincerity.

Zac and I broke apart, chuckling.

"What was that for?" Zac asked.

"No reason."

Sarah and I waited as the guys armed themselves. To kill the immortals committing all the murders, we would need to be swift and silent. When we were in the woods, we took off, silent like the sleeping world around us. The wind blew through my hair as I raced in a serpentine path through the dark tree trunks, over fallen logs, and around other debris. We traveled alongside Route 316 toward Athens. When I saw lights nearby, I slowed to a stop.

"You really are fast," Zac said, and the others nodded in agreement; they were all doubled over, trying to catch their breath.

I smiled at them and went back to scanning the area. The small downtown area of Athens was right next to the University of Georgia campus. It was called the "party town" for a good reason. There were young adults walking down the street after hours of carefree drinking, never thinking of the dangers lurking around them in the gloomy and oppressive night. They were easy prey for a vampire, and the fact that they were drunk made it a lot easier for vampires to feed without resistance.

Drinking blood from a source was said to be pleasurable for both parties, my mother had told me once, so the human would never put up a fight, but sometimes humans could resist the lure and that never turned out well. The oldest vampires were so powerful they could even enthrall another vampire.

Most werewolves considered it a shame to have the bite of a vampire on them. Those that were bitten were shunned and lived solitary lives. There were more werewolves who lived like that than even their own kind knew. I knew because I shared their bane—I, too, was shunned by both kinds, my very existence being the catalyst for their hate.

"If it's vampires killing humans, then I want you to be prepared. The murders have given the police nothing to go on, which means the deaths were clean and the victims didn't fight back. Otherwise, there'd be skin under their fingernails or some other sign there was a struggle. This leads me to believe the killer or killers are probably older vampires. We need to be on our guard because an old vampire could easily kill the four of us," I said.

"How's that?" Sarah asked.

"All vampires have the ability to enthrall their victims. Some humans can resist their ability to control them. They can make a human *want* to give them their blood. They'd walk to their death, which leaves no sign of resistance. A really old vampire could do that to us. It doesn't matter that we have stronger will power than humans. You need to be on your guard."

"Caleb will stay with Sarah and I'll stay with Skye. We'll protect each other," Zac said, and the others agreed.

"All right, I say we walk amongst the drunken idiots," Sarah said. "Maybe I'll pose as one." We all looked at her with no expression. "Okay, maybe not. I thought it'd be funny."

We made our way to the main street with all the bars, sticking to the alleys. I scanned every dark corner in case a vampire lurked in its endless depths. Many times I would get ahead of Zac, and he would snare me around the waist to lead me back into the safety of his reach; his discomfort was almost palpable whenever I was too far away. We walked around the back of a bar and froze when we heard some whimpering noises. Zac signaled for everyone to halt, snaring my waist again when I kept going.

In the shadows of the building were a man and a woman. Her back was against the wall, and he was pressing against her. She held her head to the side, her mouth opened in a dazed fashion, exposing her neck where the man appeared to be kissing. He also looked like he was shoving her, perhaps holding her down, because his body was moving, making hers jerk in response. My jaw went slack when I realized my first assumption had been wrong, and it dawned on me what I was witnessing.

The man *was* kissing her neck and not biting it. The shoving he appeared to be doing was him thrusting himself inside of her. And she was loving it. They had come out here for a little lover's rendezvous. I couldn't stop from flushing when I thought about how it would feel to be in her position with Zac kissing my neck like that. Thank God it was too dark to see me blush. When I looked at Sarah, she was snickering behind her hand

and I motioned for us to continue on.

We prowled the back alleys of every building and still had no success. A faint growl sounded from around the corner. I was there in a silent second, stopping to peer around a chain link fence. There were three guys loitering around in the dark, but a fourth one was holding a young woman in his arms; she was limp with a thin trail of blood sliding down her throat, her life was slowly leaving her.

"Hurry up, Avery. I'm bored. Cymbal told us we needed to kill at least three a night. I don't want to be on the end of the shit stick if we don't do what he says," the biggest one said to the other three in an Irish accent.

"You wouldn't be so pissy if you hadn't decided to keep one of them and change her, Aaron," Avery replied, condescension filling his tone. At his name, my blood began to boil. "And look what happened: she loathes you, and has taken off. It would have just been easier to end her, like you were supposed to."

That bastard was going to die. An idea came to mind and I acted on it. I motioned for the others to creep around them while I distracted the vampires. Then I stepped into view before Zac could stop me. "So who is this Cymbal guy?"

Their eyes shot to me and I could tell they were surprised that I had caught them unawares. The guy holding the woman dropped her on the ground, and the four of them faced me. They showed their fangs but I didn't move. Why should their fangs scare me? I had a pair of my own. The biggest one circled around me, eyeing me like a piece of meat, and taking in the ancient runes on my vest while failing to spot the sword strapped to my back.

"Well, well, well. It looks like we have a kitten in need of a new home. Maybe we'll fill our quota tonight after all."

The thought made me want to rip his throat out. "You wouldn't like the way I taste."

He came to a halt in front of me, tilting his head in curiosity.

"Oh, I think I'd like the way you taste." His fangs shot down and his claws grew longer, darkening in color.

His pupils dilated as he attempted to enthrall me. He frowned when he realized he had no control over me. I reached behind my head and between my shoulders to grasp the handle of my sword. I drew it from its sheath and brandished it.

"Either way, I don't think you'll get the chance," I said.

His smile vanished and I attacked; he had no time to react before I chopped off his head in one smooth motion. It was weird that I felt no hesitation to take his life. Zac leapt out of the shadows and removed the female victim to safety. Sarah and Caleb attacked two others with their swords at the ready, but when I searched for the last vampire, he was nowhere to be found. After Caleb and Sarah dispatched the other two, they came to stand with me. Zac came back as I searched for the last vampire.

"Is everyone all right?" Zac asked.

"We're fine. What did you do with the girl?" Sarah asked, wiping the blood off her sword.

"I set her on a doorstep and rang the doorbell. Someone should be calling an ambulance right about now."

"Did anyone see where the last guy went?" I asked. There were only three bodies.

"We killed them all. There's no one else," Sarah said.

"There are only three bodies. Where's the fourth?"

"There were four?" Caleb said.

Sarah jolted forward; her mouth opened and blood trickled out. "Sarah!" I screamed, and Caleb caught her when she fell forward.

The last vampire had stabbed Sarah with a knife which he was licking the edge of. The tip was missing and I figured we would find it in Sarah's wound. Zac appeared behind him, dug his claws into the vampire's throat, and separated his head from the rest of his body. When he let go of the vampire, his body dropped to the ground with a loud thump. Zac stepped around him and helped Caleb lift Sarah into his arms, despite the blood covering his hands.

They started to leave, but I stopped and moved the four bodies into a large pile, then set them on fire. Zac came back to get me. We looked at the burning mass for a second and then departed.

We ran as fast as we could without Caleb jostling Sarah too much, and made it into the woods before Sarah started screaming. Caleb almost dropped her in surprise. When he set her down, she rolled onto her side and I saw the stab wound was even worse than before; the skin was black and oozing blood.

"What's wrong, Sarah?" Caleb asked.

"The knife. It's in the knife." She clutched at the wound.

"What's in the knife?"

"Silver."

The three of us exchanged horrified glances, and then Caleb slapped his sister's hand away and stuck his finger in the wound, trying to pull the silver out. Each time he touched it, he would yank his hand away in pain, the smell of burnt flesh accompanying it. After the third time, Zac pushed him out of the way and tried to pull the silver out. He was no more successful than Caleb. It had to be me. I was the only one not allergic to silver.

"Dammit! How are we going to get it out of her?" Zac asked. Caleb cringed in agony, tears welling.

"Move," I said, and he moved out of habit, even though he knew that, as a werewolf, I wouldn't be able to accomplish it.

"We need to get back to our house or she'll die," Caleb said.

"I can do it." When I reached for Sarah's wound, she flipped over onto her back so I couldn't get to it. "What the hell are you doing?"

"I can't let you." She was pale with dark circles under her eyes. If I didn't get the silver out soon, her system wouldn't be able to recover.

"But you'll die."

Zac and Caleb looked between the two of us, baffled as to what we were talking about.

"I made a promise and I won't let you reveal it because of me." She wiggled away when I tried to get near her again.

"No one else is dying because of me. The consequences be damned." I looked to Caleb. "Hold her down."

Caleb nodded and did as I commanded. Sarah struggled, but I reached into her wound as far as I could and felt around for the tip of the knife.

"Got it." I pulled the silver out of her body and she stopped trembling.

The silver of the knife glittered as I held it up to the light of the moon, and saw that the outside of the knife was steel but it was merely a coating over pure silver; my immortal eyesight could easily discern the fine difference between the two metals. I threw the piece of knife away, wiped Sarah's blood off on my pants, and stood. Caleb carried Sarah in his arms again, and we ran back to their house so we could flush the wound.

It took us ten grueling minutes before we were back in the safety of the house with Sarah lying on the couch. I texted Aunt Lenore to tell her we had gotten back, and Caleb washed and bandaged Sarah's wound. Zac was sitting on the arm of the couch, staring at me from across the room with a strange look on his face, and his arms were crossed over his massive chest. His mind had to be going a mile a minute. When Sarah was able, she sat up and looked from Zac to me with an upset expression.

"How were you able to hold the silver?" Zac asked.

I sighed and my hands shook. "Because I'm not allergic to silver."

"So you aren't a werewolf."

"I am a werewolf." I glared at him. This was the reaction I had been waiting for. What surprised me was the amount of anger I felt towards him.

"Then how do you know so many things about vampires?"

"Because I have to know how to defend myself if they were to find out what I am."

"And what is that?" Zac stood. He was very angry.

His anger set me off, and I stood as well, though I didn't dignify his outburst with an answer. He had no right to be mad at me. Sarah said he believed in the same things she did, and I wished he would prove me wrong.

"You've been keeping secrets from everyone."

I strode over to him, and got in his face. "They're my secrets to keep. I don't have to tell you anything."

"Tell us the truth."

"I'm a hybrid!" He took a step back. "My father was a werewolf and my mother was a vampire. That's why they were murdered. Do you feel better knowing you've been kissing someone who's half vampire?"

He hit me so hard I was catapulted across the room, colliding with the wall and smashing it. My face stung and I could feel a line of blood trickling down my cheek, the flesh swelling in seconds. By the time I stood up, Zac had pinned me against the wall by my throat so that my feet weren't touching the ground. My throat burned and my vision started going dark. All I could do was look into his eyes, which were solid black, and I knew I was going to die.

CHAPTER 12
REALITY

"Stop it," Sarah screamed, and I saw shock ripple through Zac before he dropped me, the black clearing from his eyes.

My legs crumpled beneath me, and I coughed as I tried to get air back into my burning lungs. My eyes watered, not from the pain, but because I knew this would happen. Zac backed away, gazing down at his hands, like they had betrayed him. My heart hammered in my chest, my legs trembling as I got to my feet.

"You looked an awful lot like your father when you were choking me," I said, my voice rough since my larynx had almost been crushed. My gaze passed over Sarah before I spun on my heel and left; the last image I had was the puzzled look on Zac's face.

I burst out the front door and broke into a sprint. Going home was out of the question and so I ran. As I ran, I realized I was living one of my dreams. My injuries were the same, but I never thought it would be Zac who was behind it.

It didn't escape me that the rest of my dream involved me getting hit by a car, but that didn't matter. No pain could compare to what I was feeling right now. The pain was one massive hole where my heart used to be. Where Zac was supposed to be. A fence appeared and I slowed, recognizing it as the perimeter fence around Stone Mountain. In the haze of riotous emotion, I hadn't realized I had run so far. I jumped the fence and continued.

The night lit up and I dodged the car too late. It grazed me on the right side and propelled me across the street, like David Beckham shooting for the goal. I laid on the ground, shocked that I had been hit, and tried to get my body to obey my mind. The effort was monumental but I began to crawl toward the curb. The car didn't stop and I assumed the driver didn't have a license or something like that.

The going was slow. Every time I moved my right side, there was a sharp stabbing pain and I had to wait for it to subside before I could continue. Inch by inch, I gained ground. It took a long time before I made it into the darkness and shelter of the woods, and then leaned against a rock and rested.

The tears came back in a rush, and nothing I did could stop them. Zac's hatred and disgust for what I was overshadowed all the pain. Somewhere deep inside me, I had hoped he would be as accepting as Sarah had been, and I guessed I was hoping for that more than I knew, because his reaction hurt more than any pain I had ever endured. It was like my heart had been broken, ripped out of my chest, stomped on, buried, dug back up, and stomped on again.

My whole right side felt sticky. I touched a hand to my abdomen where there was a tear that had gone through both my vest and shirt, and it felt wet. Great. Now I was bleeding. The night air had gone from chilly to freezing. The loss of so much blood meant I didn't have enough to circulate through my veins to keep me warm. Everything became sluggish. My heart beat slower and more time elapsed between breaths. My limbs shook at how cold I had gotten just sitting there, but after a while the trembling stopped when my core temperature matched the air around me. It wasn't good when you lost so much blood your body couldn't even shiver as a sign it was trying to keep you warm.

A twig snapped nearby, but I couldn't move myself to hide. At this point, I didn't care if a whole coven of vampires or pack of werewolves found me and killed me. At least it would end my suffering. A flash of gold caught my attention, and I moved as far to the side as I could to see what it was. Sarah skidded to a halt, a shocked look on her face. Her dark blue eyes hid nothing of the fear she felt for me.

"Skye!" she said, and Zac came running into view, followed by Caleb. His face was pale and his heart beat faster the moment he set eyes on me.

The heat coming off Sarah and him wafted towards me; I could hear the blood rushing through their veins. My mouth watered and my fangs elongated, my lips parting in case they got close enough for me to bite. Instinct was taking over, doing what it was supposed to for me to survive. If they got any closer, I would attack them. Never had I taken blood from a source, besides that of my parents, because you would share their memories and feelings. It was hard enough dealing with my own thoughts in my head. Zac took a step towards me, more frightened than I had ever seen him.

"Stay away," I croaked.

Sarah grabbed his arm. "Her aunt said to stay away until she got here." He clenched his jaw tight, but stayed where he was. His eyes pleaded with me, wanting me to understand, but the pain flared and I looked away.

Not a word was spoken as we waited. Aunt Lenore arrived soon after and knelt next to me, her stormy gray eyes dark with worry, and her pale blonde brows furrowed with concentration. She pulled a bag of blood from a bag at her side. She held it to my lips but my fangs receded back into my gums.

"Schuyler, drink it," she said, pressing it against my mouth.

"No." I turned my face away.

I couldn't drink the blood in front of Zac. He thought I was some disgusting creature, and I didn't want him to see me at my weakest. My chest was on fire and I felt like I was going to be sick. My eyes watered against my will. Crying was not an acceptable option.

"You'll die," she insisted.

"I don't care."

Aunt Lenore looked to the others. "What the hell happened? Why is she acting like this?"

"Everything would be better if I just died." When those words left my lips, I could have sworn I heard Zac's heart skip a beat.

When I glanced at Sarah, I saw a decision cross her features.

"Zac leave," Sarah said.

Zac's head whipped to the side. "What? Why?"

"Because I said so."

He stood adamantly and then growled. "Fine!"

Sarah marched over, grabbed the bag from my aunt, and shoved it in my face. Her attitude was if I refused she would force it down my throat. My hunger flared and I gave into it, sinking my teeth into the bag and drinking. My wounds began to heal after a few seconds. There was a grimace when my ribs popped back into place, and the bones healed, but the emotional pain remained.

"Are you feeling better?" I asked my aunt.

"Yeah," I said.

"You ready to go back?" Sarah asked.

"Not with Zac."

"I can make him leave the area, but I can't make him leave entirely. He's really upset about what he did, and he wants to tell you how sorry he is."

"He already had his chance."

"It doesn't make sense. It goes against the instinct inside of us to harm our mates in any way," Sarah said. Aunt Lenore glanced at Sarah, and then in the direction Zac had left, but said nothing.

It didn't take long for the blood to heal the wounds, but when

Aunt Lenore tried to give me another bag of blood, I refused it. Zac's reaction made the act of drinking blood distasteful.

Aunt Lenore left first, then Caleb after he looked at Zac, while Sarah stayed. She was the buffer between Zac and me. He had made me hate what I was for the first time in fifty decades. Sarah walked alongside me for a good part of the trip and Zac on the other side of her. Zac and Sarah communicated in hushed voices, like they were trying to decide something.

Sarah slid to the side so Zac could get closer to me. "I'll be back," she said, and glared at Zac. Maybe he had blackmailed her for five minutes alone with me.

He didn't say anything for a while. What could he say? I'm sorry for trying to choke you to death?

"Are you okay?" he asked.

"Why is that any of your concern?"

"Because I care about you."

"You sure showed how much you cared about me when you were crushing my throat." Out of the corner of my eye, he flinched and, for some reason, I felt bad for my harsh words.

But why should I feel bad about it? He was the one that flipped out and hurt me. Zac sidled closer.

"Why won't you believe I'm really sorry about what happened?"

If I looked into his eyes, I would get lost in them, and then he would think he could get away with doing whatever he wanted. Zac reached for my hand, but I jerked away from him. I didn't want to remember his touch as a bad thing.

He had messed everything up. He had found a way to get inside of my barriers and convince me letting him in was okay. How stupid I was to believe that.

Zac stood in front of me and grabbed my shoulders. "Skye, will you say something?"

My traitorous eyes watered again at his pleading tone. "Don't touch me."

Part of me wanted him to let go of me, but at the same time I wanted him to pull me close and kiss me like he had never kissed me before. I wanted him to tell me that he didn't care I was a hybrid and he wanted me no matter what.

Zac let go of me and then Sarah was beside me once more. With her there, I wouldn't be tempted to run into his arms. But the powerful, almost unbearable, urge surged through me nonetheless. I broke into a run, with Sarah close on my heels, and tried to escape the pain I was in. Zac watched as we ran out of sight. He knew he had hurt me. And he realized there was nothing he could do to change my mind.

Holding my emotions in once I got home, I gave Aunt Lenore a nod, and went upstairs to my bathroom. I turned on the hot water and stepped in. My arms were wrapped around my torso as I watched the water turn red and swirl down the drain. Too bad I couldn't wash away my memories of Zac, the ones that hurt too much to remember.

When the water ran clear, I got out of the shower and toweled off before pulling on some pajamas and crawling into bed. Exhaustion drained me of every drop of energy. I closed my eyes and tried to erase my memory. In the black depths of my mind, an image of Zac's face, strained in agony over what he had done to me, floated to the surface.

CHAPTER 13
AMULET

Darkness surrounded me, a level of pitch no light could penetrate. There was no sound, and it was cold. I knew my breath would be a cloudy fog, if I could see it. I didn't know where I was, but I knew I was lost. The beacon that had been my guiding light was forever extinguished.

My lips trembled as tears spilled down my cheeks, stinging as they froze against my skin. There was a tearing in my chest and I was bombarded with never ceasing pain; it was my constant companion.

The world was dark and depressing. Then I saw it. A light in the darkness, a warmth beating back the cold, fighting it for the right to be there. I ran headlong, tripping over my numb feet, falling a few times and scraping the skin of my palms, toward the light in the distance. But I ran the way dreamers did in dreams, like your feet were made of lead. The closer I felt I was getting to the light, the further away it seemed to be.

When I got closer, I reached for the light with an outstretched arm, but it evaded my grasp. Pain shot through my body and I collapsed to the ground in agony. My whole body felt like I had been dipped into acid, like my bones were trying to grow through my skin, like I was trying to become something I wasn't.

There was a tapping noise coming from somewhere, but it was still too dark to see. I was in pain yet I couldn't help but get annoyed with the incessant sound. It was distracting and I couldn't let anything distract me. I needed to get to the light before the cold could freeze me.

There was an annoying tapping, like the one in my dream, but coming from my window. My heavy eyes cracked open and I threw the covers off of me, slinging my feet to the ground. There was a chill in my room and I wanted to crawl back into my warm bed, but I wasn't about to let the irritating sound persist. Pushing aside the curtain, I saw Zac hanging there, using the gutter on the eave as a hand hold. After opening the window, I moved out of the way so he could climb in. Not letting him in would be more of an effort than listening to what he had to say. He could be stubborn when he wanted to be.

I trudged back to my bed and got back under the covers, where it was warm, and laid my head down. With narrowed eyes, I scrutinized him as he climbed in and closed the window.

"Are you all right?" he asked, and sat on the end of my bed.

I tucked my knees to my chest. "I'm fine. Couldn't be better. Why do you ask?"

"Because you've been asleep for three days."

My head spun when I sat up and reached for my cell phone. I checked the date and, sure enough, I had been asleep for three days. In the uncomfortable silence, I looked at Zac and saw purple bags under his eyes. His skin was pale and, I wasn't sure, but he looked sick. Immortals never got sick. Not in the way humans did. It appeared he hadn't gotten any sleep in the past three days.

I set my phone down, averting my eyes, and took a deep breath. "How are *you*?"

He looked at me. I could feel his eyes on me, even though I wasn't looking at him. "I haven't slept or eaten in three days." He paused and I glanced at him to see him shaking his head. He seemed lost. "I feel sick to my stomach about what I did. Every time I think about it, it causes me pain."

So, he felt pain when he thought about it, too. Zac did look tortured, and I went soft for him, again.

"Why did you react like that?" I asked.

"I've been asking myself that question over and over again. I have no idea why I acted the way I did. It was like I wasn't in control of my own body. I saw that I was hurting you but I couldn't stop myself. It was like I was in a trance." He stared at the bed sheet as he spoke; his mind was in the past, reliving my nightmare come true. "When Sarah yelled, it broke the trance I was in and I couldn't believe what I'd done. If you could just see into my mind, you would know what was going on inside my head, and you would know I would never willingly do that to you. I can't sleep because whenever I close my eyes, an image of you lying dead at my feet, by my own hands, haunts me like a ghost."

I edged forward and placed a hand over his mouth to stop him from talking. Nothing more needed to be said. He was suffering more than I understood. "Well, there's only one way for me to see what was going on in your mind, but I can't do it."

His eyes shot to my face. "What way is that?"

"I drink your blood. When a vampire does that, they gain the person's memories and form a powerful connection that causes extreme pain when it's broken."

"What can break a connection like that?"

"Death. And it feels like death for the one still living."

"You sound like you've felt it."

"I did. When my parents died. I'd fed on their blood when I was younger, because I didn't want to drink from those bags. When they were murdered, I felt a pain I've never felt before in my life."

"I'm sorry, Skye." Zac took a deep breath. "So you'd have to drink my blood, and then you'd be able to read my mind."

"Yes."

"How much blood would it take?"

"For something so recent, it would only take a drop. If I wanted to know something from long ago, I'd need to take a lot more. Blood memories are like dropping a sponge in water; the older ones have soaked up the years, like water, and have sunk to the bottom, while the newer ones are still floating around on the top."

"Please take my blood. I want you to know what happened from my point of view."

"I won't take your blood, Zac. I won't do it." I sat away from him.

"Why not?" He scooted closer. His proximity unnerved me.

"It almost killed me when my parents died. If I take your blood, then I put myself in danger of that again."

"But I won't be killed."

"You know about me, and eventually someone will learn of that connection and use you against me. They'll kill you for helping me. The same goes for Sarah, Caleb, and my aunt." My chest tightened. "Especially my aunt. They'll likely torture her. It'll only make things more painful when they killed either of us."

"I'd never let them hurt you." He held my face and forced me to look into his eyes. I wanted to believe him, wanted it with everything inside of me.

I missed his touch so much, and just the feel of his warm palms against my cheeks made me ache for the tender kisses we used to share. My mind was saying no, but my heart was screaming to let him in, to take the comfort he was offering. As he was looking into my eyes, his thumb began to stroke my cheek.

"I feel like I'll die if I don't kiss you," he said.

My heart needed him, and I was going to take the comfort I needed.

"Then kiss me." I reached for him as he brought my face to his. Time itself slowed the closer we got to one another, and I wished I could make it last forever.

My hands clutched the sides of his neck, and slid up until my fingers wound through his hair as I pulled his mouth to mine. The moment our lips touched, I felt the same electricity that was always there when we kissed, and I wanted more. I rose back up onto my knees, forcing his head back. Even with my body crushed against his, I couldn't get close enough. Zac wrapped both arms around my waist, squeezing me to him, before pressing me back onto the bed with his body slanted across mine. His hips were wedged between my legs, my feet wound around his waist, sliding over his thighs.

He opened his mouth so I could slip my tongue in, and there was an explosion of taste and my senses heightened. I jerked my mouth away from his and saw that his lip was bleeding. I flicked my tongue against my fang. Strange. I hadn't felt them descend.

One drop of Zac's blood was like fire on my tongue. Warmth spread through me and I sensed every single nerve on my skin firing where it touched his, like we were linked. The urge to bite him intensified, as I felt the need for more of his delicious blood. Zac reached a finger to his lip, and drew it back to look at it.

"I'm sorry," I apologized, covering my mouth with my hand, trying to hide my reaction to his taste. I expected him to jump off me with disgust.

"It's fine, Skye. Are you okay with taking my blood even though it was an accident?"

"I guess my body didn't have a problem with taking your blood though my brain knew I shouldn't have." I looked at him and saw his eyes were bright in the darkness. "Did I hurt you?"

Instead of answering, he just chuckled and averted his gaze. I gave him a questioning look and then gasped when he grasped my hips and pressed himself against me. "I wouldn't say you hurt me." He grinned, making me melt for him, and then kissed me.

Embarrassment had always stopped me when things got too hot and heavy with Zac, but now I had his blood on my tongue, and I could care less about what he had done, as long as he didn't stop. Gripping the bottom of his shirt, I pulled it upwards, wanting to see and feel his chest. Zac understood and, without a word, removed his shirt and tossed it onto the floor before lying back in my arms.

My hands ran along his sculpted back. His hand slid down my arm, my side, and then behind my knee, and he hitched one of my legs around his hip, locking it in place. His lips trailed down my neck, my fingers curling through his black hair. My door opened and light spilled in from the hallway. In a blur, Zac was standing next to the bed.

"Aunt Lenore," I said, and sat up in surprise.

"Forgive me for interrupting." She smiled, and turned to yell down the staircase. "He's in here!" She turned back to us. "So sorry."

Aunt Lenore closed the door, plunging us back into darkness. Zac and I looked at each other before bursting out laughing.

"I guess Caleb and Sarah have been looking for me," Zac said, and reached down to grab his shirt.

"Why would they be looking for you?"

"Because I've been avoiding them."

"Why?" I got off the bed and stopped him from putting his shirt on to look at me.

"I figured they'd be ashamed of me after what I did." His eyes were unfocused and in them I could see the shadow of pain.

I rose up on my toes and pressed a kiss to his lips. He closed his eyes, like the feeling caused him pain, and I knew I would never be able to withhold a kiss from him again. When I sifted through the recent memories in his blood, I saw that he had no control over himself, and so I wondered what made him do it. His memories showed he never thought anything bad about me, and he was truly shocked when he couldn't stop himself from choking me. What fascinated me even more was how strong his feelings were for me. They were so strong that sometimes he had thoughts of finding me wherever I was, and taking me until I couldn't remember my own name. The pain in my chest faded and I could breathe easier. It wasn't his fault, and I needed to make sure he didn't punish himself any longer.

"They're your friends and they'll understand," I said. "You weren't in control. Your memories prove that. I'm not mad at you and I forgive you for what you did."

Zac dropped his shirt again and pulled me against him, kissing me like I meant everything to him. When I broke away, I was breathing hard, as was he, but I let go of him and headed towards the door. Zac didn't follow so I turned around.

"What's wrong?" I asked.

He reached back down to get his shirt, and looked up at me with a lopsided grin. "I need a minute to compose myself." When he saw I didn't understand, he pointed down at his pants.

"Oh! I'll see you downstairs then." I grabbed some clothes and changed in the bathroom.

Sarah and Caleb were sitting in the living room while Aunt Lenore was cooking in the kitchen. It must have been somewhere around dinner because she had a lot of food sitting on the counter waiting to be cooked. Aunt Lenore glanced at me as I entered the kitchen. I nodded at her before walking into the living room and sitting down.

"How's Zac?" Caleb stood when I came into the room. He and Sarah looked like they hadn't gotten any sleep either.

"Was I the only one that got any sleep in the past three days?" I asked.

Sarah smiled. "Probably. Are you okay?"

"He's fine now. Everything's fine."

Caleb sighed, like he was releasing a lot of pent up stress, and relaxed. "Your aunt seems to be cooking for an army."

"That's because we're staying for dinner, you idiot," Sarah said, tossing a pillow at him.

Zac came into the room then, sat down on the couch next to me, and wrapped an arm around my shoulders. I leaned into the curve of his side and snuggled into his warmth.

"Food's ready," Aunt Lenore called, and Zac went in to help her divvy out dinner. When he came back in, he handed me a bag of blood, which I hesitated to open.

"What's wrong?" he asked.

"Nothing. It's just no one has ever seen me drink before. I feel kinda awkward."

"It doesn't bother me," he whispered, and kissed my cheek before he started eating.

Now that I had tasted Zac's exquisite blood, the bag of blood was positively bland. It was like drinking room temperature water after having tasted the sweetest, coldest water from the spring of eternal youth. It had magical qualities to it that were gone when they made contact with the air. All of them were talking to each other across the room, but I had zoned in on the news being displayed across the screen.

The breaking news said a woman had escaped her death by some hero who had left her on a porch to be found. She didn't remember what had happened and that everything was fuzzy. Thank God she couldn't remember our faces seeing as immortals had to keep a low profile. The reporter continued, saying police had later found a burned area, but all that was left was a pile of ashes. I smiled to myself. No more innocent people would die.

The news faded as I was enveloped in darkness. Somehow I was in a dark room, in an unfamiliar bed. A door opened and Zac's father walked in. My body moved on its own, and I realized I was seeing things through Zac' eyes. Whatever was happening wasn't happening to me, and it wasn't happening presently. Craven approached with arrogant strides. A stone dropped in front of Zac's eyes, dangling on a thick chain. The stone looked like solid hematite, but it had an aura around it that reeked of power, a power I had never felt before.

Zac's eyes were glued to the stone, but since I was witnessing it second hand, I had no problem looking away. The stone swayed from side to side, and Zac's eyes followed.

"You will obey Cymbal. Cymbal is your master. You must do everything for Cymbal," Craven said.

"I will obey Cymbal," Zac chanted in a monotone, his English accent crisp and clear.

Oh, hell no. Zac's father was hypnotizing him.

"If you see the hybrid, you will kill her. If she reveals herself to you, you will kill her. If any of our kind interferes with your mission, you will kill them."

"I will obey Cymbal." Craven snapped his fingers, and everything went black.

With a sudden jerk, I was back in my living room, not knowing when I had gotten to my feet, my body swaying with dizziness, before I collapsed. Zac caught the bag of blood before it spilled everywhere, and then handed it to Aunt Lenore before he helped me onto the couch. My hands clutched at his shirt as I tried to make sense of what I had seen. It would seem that Craven was the one sending Zac out after innocent vampires. That was why he was losing time. I looked at Zac. He never had a chance. He had been hypnotized to kill me, and from what I could tell, the hypnotic element was strong.

"Skye, are you okay?" Zac asked when I stayed silent.

"It's your father. He's Cymbal."

"How do you know that?" Caleb asked, scooting forward in his seat.

"A blood memory." Aunt Lenore sucked in a breath. "It was from Zac's point of view. Craven came into your room and dangled a stone in front of your face. Then he hypnotized you. He said you must obey Cymbal and that if you found me you were to kill me and anyone of your kind that stood in your way."

Zac paused for a minute, frowning in concentration. "I remember part of that. He came into my room and then I woke up hours later. That was one of the reasons I left home. I couldn't remember things, and I was losing huge chunks of time." He shook his head in frustration and looked at the others, and then back at me. "Is that why I choked you?"

"You had no control because your body was obeying the spell he had placed on you. You broke the trance, but I don't know how. How were you able to break the trance? Surely Sarah yelling wasn't what did it?"

"It definitely wasn't me," Sarah said. "You're Zac's mate. He could never kill you because the instinct would take over and override any command that was forced on him."

Zac tensed next to me, and my hands tightened around his shirt even more. He pressed his forehead against mine.

"I can't believe my father's Cymbal. I knew he was biased, but I never thought he'd take away my free will. I never thought he'd stoop that low."

"I'm sorry," I said.

He looked down at me, his brows pushed together over his

beautiful eyes. "It's not your fault. He's the one that betrayed me, not you. If my father would stoop to the level of trying to get me to kill my mate, then he's dead to me."

"How did you know he was Cymbal, Skye?" Sarah asked.

"He was speaking in third person, saying things like, 'You must obey Cymbal'."

"Maybe he wasn't talking about himself in third person. Maybe he was telling Zac he needed to obey Cymbal, but that Zac had never met him before. Your father may just be a pawn."

"Either way. He'll die for what he's tried to do," Zac said, fury pulsing through him.

"Let's go for a walk, Zac," I suggested.

Zac nodded and followed me out the garage door and into the night. He wrapped an arm around me until I was tight against his side. I hooked my own arm around his waist, and we walked in silence for a bit.

"Are you gonna be all right?" I asked, and he slowed our pace.

"I don't know. I knew my father hated vampires, but I never thought he'd go this far. He tried to make me kill you, Skye. And we don't know what triggered it. What if it happens again?"

"You won't hurt me. I know you won't let that happen again."

He stepped in front of me. "I don't want to hurt you. God knows I'd rather die. But what if I can't stop it the next time?" He cupped my face and kissed me before I could even think to answer.

"You know, if you want an answer to your questions, you can't keep kissing me like that, because it makes me lose my train of thought."

Zac gazed into my eyes and brushed my hair behind my ear.

"I love you," he said. I froze, and readied to pull away from him. Zac grabbed my hands to keep me from leaving. "I didn't mean to make you uncomfortable. I just wanted you to know how I felt. I don't expect anything in return."

"But you'll want that eventually. And when you don't get it, you'll leave."

He put a hand to the small of my back and tugged me closer. The skin of his palm was rough, and my breathing hitched when his skin slid along mine.

"I'll take you any way I can get you." He kissed me again.

I may not be in love with Zac, but that didn't mean I wasn't attracted and attached to him. It would be harder being alone after having a relationship with Zac because then I would know exactly what I was missing.

Zac and I strolled around for a while and when we came back inside, Sarah and Caleb had left to go home. Zac kissed me good night and left. As soon as I entered the living room, Aunt Lenore motioned for me to sit. I knew she was going to want to talk about me taking Zac's blood.

"Are you going to tell me why you've been having blood memories?" she asked.

"It was an accident. We were kissing and I bit his lip. I didn't realize I'd done it until it was too late."

She was quiet for a moment. "There's something I've been meaning to tell you since I met Sarah the day you got shot."

"What?"

"Zac, Sarah, and Caleb…they're from the same pack as Andrew and me."

Bile rose in my throat. "The same pack that had mom and dad killed?"

"The very same."

CHAPTER 14
SILVER

Back in my room, I had trouble falling asleep. After everything I had learned and having fresh blood from an immortal werewolf, my body was alive with hypersensitivity and my brain wouldn't stop processing the information. Quiet sounds were amplified, and I could feel every single fiber in my sheets. Never before had anything felt so detailed. I thought about Zac, and his thoughts toward me; the way his skin felt against mine and how warm he was. After everything Sarah, Caleb, and Zac had done, I knew they weren't a danger to me. But Craven was actively looking for him.

Those thoughts gave me a headache, so I went back to the few intimate minutes with Zac. It was easy to recall the way his chest and abdomen moved when he held himself above me. Even now I could see him lying on his bed, asleep, wearing only a pair of boxers. The sheets were at his feet, like he had kicked them off. He bent his leg and placed one of his arms behind his head then settled back down.

"Skye," Zac said in his sleep.

Okay, I wasn't dreaming this. It was the connection we had formed when I took his blood. That meant I was spying on him as he was sleeping at this very moment, at his most vulnerable. And he was dreaming about me. His naked chest rose and fell as he breathed, one of his strong hands splayed across his chiseled abdomen. What else could I do with this connection? I imagined my fingers stroking down the side of his abdomen, and smiled when he moved, like it tickled.

Next, I imagined being in his room with him, crawling onto the bed, and straddling his waist. My mouth opened at the real sensation, and I took it further by imagining I was leaning over him, my face hovering just over his, with my hands on each side of his head. I lowered my head until our lips were touching and ran my lips across his. He shuddered beneath me.

"Zac," I whispered.

His head twitched back and forth at the sound of my voice. Once more, I imagined kissing Zac, and his body moved in response. He moaned, and my eyes widened as his hand moved down his stomach toward the edge of his boxers, where he had grown hard.

<*Zac,*> I said in my mind, and when he opened his eyes I did the same, back in my room.

I shot straight up, breathing hard, and as sensitive as ever. Zac was about to touch himself because he was thinking about me. I jumped when my phone beeped, and snatched it off the nightstand, seeing a text from Zac.

< *I heard your voice in my head. What just happened?*>

<*It's the connection.*>

He texted me back in a second.

<*The connection we made because you tasted my blood?*>

<*Yeah. Are you okay with that?*>

There was a pause that worried me. My hands started to shake.

<*It's fine with me. I thought you'd have a problem with it since you didn't want to do it in the first place. Is it always like that?*>

<*Well, I only had a taste of your blood, so it wouldn't be that powerful.*>

<*What would it be like if you had more? If you drank from me?*>

<*It would feel like we were actually in the room together, and we can speak to each other in our heads. We can use it to find one another.*>

Our connection was strong when I had been thinking about him, so I wondered how much stronger it would feel if I had had more than a taste.

< *I could feel you there with me, and you're saying that's only from a drop? It'd be really interesting to know what it'd feel like if you'd taken more.*>

<*I told you having a connection was interesting.*>

There was a long pause, and I figured the conversation was over when the phone beeped again.

<*What did it feel like when your parents died, and the connection was broken?*>

My eyes watered and a lump formed in my throat. I took a deep breath and texted the answer, pausing twice to wipe my eyes.

<*It feels like you're being ripped in two. It feels like everything in your world falls down around you. The pain is so intense you wanna die. You feel like the pain will kill you yet death never comes. It never grants you the peace you so desperately need.*>

I sent the message and wiped away a tear that fell down my cheek. The phone beeped again, and I opened the message.

<*Please, don't cry, Skye.*>

<I forgot you'd be able to feel that.>

<Do you need me to come over? I can if you want.>

<I'm okay.>

There was a shattering of glass, and then a sharp pain in my shoulder. The force of the projectile that hit me flipped me backwards off my bed, and I landed on the floor with a thud, smacking my head against the wall, creating a hole.

<Skye!> I heard Zac in my head right before my phone started ringing.

My thumb mashed down the answer button. "Someone's shooting at my house!"

"We're on our way."

More glass broke and another projectile whizzed through the air, went clean through my mattress, and embedded itself into the wall next to my head. Time to move. After the next shot, I scrambled across my room to the wall where the window was. My door was thrown open, and Aunt Lenore's hand and the side of her head peered out as she crouched in the office. She zeroed in on the blood coming from my right shoulder, covering the tank top I was wearing and I saw a flicker of darkness—the beast inside—cover her face before going back to normal.

The gun continued to fire into the room. Blood dripped down my shoulder as I clambered to my feet, using the wall as a crutch, and after the next shot, I bolted through the door. A bullet grazed my left arm before I could get out of the way. Aunt Lenore hauled me into the office and slammed my door shut so they couldn't see when we went past. She switched off all of the lights as we thundered down the stairs, and made it into the kitchen. She snagged some blood out of the refrigerator and tossed it to me.

Another window smashed when a bullet flew through the kitchen, tore through the bag of blood, spilling its contents. Aunt Lenore reached to grab another one, but I signaled for her to stop. The nearest towel on the oven handle sacrificed itself to clean my hands, and then we crawled under the windows of the kitchen, out of sight, and grabbed my shoes from the living room.

"We need to get out of here," Aunt Lenore whispered.

"Zac and the others are on their way." I put pressure on the wound at my shoulder but I was still losing blood. After feeling around the back of my arm, I discovered another hole; the bullet had been a through-and-through.

Aunt Lenore curled her fingers and her claws grew black and razor sharp, digging into the floor. Our living room floor was made of hardwood slats, but she shredded through them like they were cardboard. Once she was under the house, she reached up and dragged me through the hole, and then we crawled to the side of the house where we could get out of the door leading to the crawl space. She ripped off the lock and we escaped into the night. All I was wearing were shorts and a tank top with my sneakers, so I was feeling the dry, frigid air blowing against my exposed skin.

Aunt Lenore led the way as we wound through the woods, getting as far away from the house as we could. Our breaths were loud in the silence. Not too much later, I heard the muted sound of bullets piercing the earth. Aunt Lenore heard them too, and sped up the pace. More bullets struck the ground, and then a bullet lodged itself into my thigh, making me cringe when it dug into the bone.

A painful cry left my lips, and I was forced to stop. Someone crashed through the trees behind me and I spun around to face them. My thigh screamed in protest at the weight I was putting on it, but I paid it no heed and strode forward to meet the shadow closing in.

"I'm sick of getting shot," I said. "Show your face, coward."

His eyes glinted in the darkness, and his shadow proved he was enormous as he approached. His face was hidden in shadow, but I saw the moonlight reflecting off the gun he raised at me.

In the blink of an eye, he pulled the trigger multiple times. I cringed for the foreseeable impact but it never came. Zac appeared in front of me and when I tried to pull him out of the way, he gripped me tighter, holding me in place.

"No," I said, but I couldn't budge him. He grunted as each bullet pierced his body.

There was a loud snarl and then a fight started. I peeked around Zac's shoulder and saw Caleb squaring off with the stranger. Zac pulled me away from the man. There was no way he was going to get to me.

"Let me at him," my aunt said. She had grown bigger and her eyes had turned black. For once, she looked like the predator she was.

"Let's go," Zac said, and I could hear the pain in his voice.

He led me to a car where Sarah was sitting in the driver's seat, bouncing up and down, like she was going to jump out of the car at any second. A few minutes later, Caleb and Aunt Lenore hopped in. Sarah sped away from the house as fast as she could when Zac started fidgeting in his seat. The third time he twitched I realized something.

"Stop the car," I said.

"What?" Sarah looked at me through the rearview mirror.

"Stop the damn car." Sarah pulled over into a neighborhood. I looked to Caleb. "Get out." Caleb obeyed without question.

Zac was even more baffled when I took him by his shoulders and flung him across the backseat to lie on his stomach.

"What are you doing, Skye?" he asked, and tried to flip over onto his back.

I sat on his legs and forced him back onto his stomach. “Lie still. This is going to hurt.”

My claw tore his shirt down the middle so I could get to his wounds, and saw nine holes in his back. I scrunched my hand up a few times and then my nails grew, knowing I wanted to protect what was mine. My claws reached into the first wound and plucked the bullet out. When I got each bullet out, I chucked them over my shoulder. But the last one kept slipping out of my fingers.

“Skye, I don’t want to worry you, but I might pass out,” Zac said, his fingers clutching the sides of the seat, his extended claws piercing the gray leather.

“I can’t get it,” I said.

Zac growled low in his throat, and then I got a hold of the bullet and pulled it out.

“Yes.”

With a smile, I gazed at Sarah, but looked back down when I felt something wet dripping down my fingers, moving faster than blood. Trust me; I knew what dripping blood felt like. The bullet appeared to be melting down my fingers.

“Shit! Liquid silver.” I tossed the bullet over my shoulder and wiped my hand off on my shorts so I wouldn’t smear silver all over Zac’s bare skin. Zac began to cough and his back arched at a painful angle.

“How are we gonna get it out?” Sarah asked.

Silver was one of the ways to kill a werewolf, unless they could shed the silver. But there was no way Zac could shed something liquid, something that could enter his blood stream. What could I do? The pain from the connection being severed would be like torture.

The night on the rooftop forty-four years ago resurfaced. Something had happened then and also when I had been with Zac at the clearing. Maybe I could do it again. I placed my palm over the last wound and drew my hand away, my fingers closed together like I would around a loose hair. As I drew my hand away, the silver came out. It looked like someone was pouring it into the wound, only we were watching it in reverse. Once it was out, Zac’s body relaxed, and he gasped for air. I opened my palm and the silver hung suspended in midair before curling into a perfect ball and solidifying. It dropped into my flattened palm, and I threw it out the window. Zac caught his breath and rolled over to look at me. He and the others stared.

“What?” I asked.

“What did you just do?” Sarah narrowed her eyes.

I looked at each of them. “I have no idea.”

“Let’s get back to the house so we can figure out what to do,”

Caleb said.

Sarah pulled into the driveway as I was ushered into the house by Zac. Aunt Lenore scanned the neighborhood before following. Caleb went around the house, closing all the blinds while Sarah got some hot water and fresh towels.

Zac checked the wound at my shoulder and went about cleaning and bandaging it up. While he worked, I examined his stoic face, looking for any sign he was freaked out about what I had done. When he was done fixing my shoulder, he looked at me.

"I felt it," he said, averting his eyes, only to look at me a second later. "I felt it when he shot you."

"That's the connection."

"It hurt."

He was probably regretting me taking his blood now that he knew he would even feel my pain. "I know. I'm really sorry you have to go through that. I wish I could take it away."

"No, Skye, you mistook my meaning. It hurt because I thought I was going to lose you. I wasn't there to protect you when I should've been."

"It was bound to happen. It's just the way my life is."

Zac nodded and touched his forehead to mine. As he was peering down, his brows came together in a frown. He let go of my face and touched a hand to the dark upholstered couch. It came away red.

His gaze traveled from his hand to my face. "Why didn't you tell me you were bleeding?"

"Don't," I said, when he tried to reach into the wound. "There's silver in it."

Zac seemed at a loss. "What am I supposed to do then?"

No one could do anything; I would have to fish it out on my own. I reached around to where the bullet was lodged in my leg, and started digging. It hurt like a bitch, but I kept on, since no one else could get it out. After ten grueling minutes, I was met with success.

Zac cleaned the wound on my thigh as I seethed with anger. Zac glanced at me a couple of times while he was working, so I knew he could sense how I was feeling through the connection.

"What are you thinking about?" he asked.

"The bullets were laced with liquid silver. Someone knew werewolves were helping me."

"Well, maybe they thought you'd be allergic to silver," Sarah said.

"They already know I'm not allergic to silver after they shot me the first time. That means the silver was meant for you."

Aunt Lenore came forward then. "I need to go back to the house."

"Take a roundabout route and be careful," Caleb said.

"Son, I've been doing this a lot longer than you have."

"Be careful Aunt Lenore," I repeated to get her to acknowledge it.

"I will, sweetheart. Zac, you keep her safe while I'm gone."

"With my life," he said, looking her straight in the eye.

Aunt Lenore left out the back door. When it closed, I touched a hand to Zac's cheek. It was hard to believe he had taken nine bullets for me. His promise to Aunt Lenore sounded like he would be ready to do it again. Thirty minutes went by before Aunt Lenore came back, out of breath, with smudges of soot on her skin and clothes.

"What happened? Are you all right?" I was on my feet in an instant, only to be reminded at the last second I was still injured. Zac caught me when I stumbled.

"They burned the house down," she said, as she caught her breath.

"Shit."

"What is it? What does that mean?" Zac asked and held me closer, as if my words meant danger was nearby.

"That's all the blood we had," Aunt Lenore said.

"How long can you go without?" Sarah asked.

"I need it every day to stay at my strongest, otherwise I get really hungry. We've never had to go without before, but the longer I go without it, the harder it gets to resist biting someone." I sat and Zac sat next to me, his arm around me. He was on high alert for more danger, but I was thinking about other things.

"What are we going to do?" I asked.

"Tomorrow, when the bank opens, I'm going to get some money and we're going to find another place to stay where we can set up our new lives," Aunt Lenore said.

"We can help you." Caleb got to his feet.

"Thanks."

"Is it safe to stay here tonight?" I asked.

"I think we should stay at a hotel just in case there are more of them," Sarah said.

Aunt Lenore got to her feet. "I think that's a good idea."

"Let's get some things and get out of here." Zac helped me to my feet.

Sarah gave me a pair of her pants that tied around the waist and a jacket for the trip to the small hotel near us. The receptionist was a woman with an ugly brown bob and a dark tan pantsuit. It clashed with her yellow skin and the overall effect was reminiscent of a camel. She wasn't in a good mood when we entered. But she didn't have the excuse that immortals were after her, had just shot her three times, burned her house down, and shot her boyfriend nine times in the back—all for the purpose of trying to kill her.

We rented three rooms right next to each other, two of them connected by a door. Zac and Caleb were sharing a room, Sarah and I had another, and Aunt Lenore took the room on the other side of Sarah's and mine. Aunt Lenore made sure everyone got settled in before she went to her room. Sarah curled up in her bed and turned the light out, but I was still standing with Zac in the doorway connecting to his and Caleb's room. He cradled my face in his hands and kissed me with an aching tenderness that struck my heart. This kiss felt different. It was like he was trying to tell me everything in one kiss, in case he wouldn't get the chance later.

"I'll see you tomorrow," he whispered, and we both closed our doors.

My thigh screamed at me as I climbed into my bed and closed my eyes. I hoped sleep would come to me easier this time, but all I could think about was the haunting intensity of the kiss he had given me, the way his lips crushed against mine, like his biggest fear had almost come true.

Once I fell asleep, an image rose up of a werewolf with flaming orange hair, raking his claws down Zac's chest. Deep furrows were opened and blood gushed. Zac was losing the fight for his life and there was no one to help him.

CHAPTER 15
SWEET SCENTS

The dream kept me from getting back to sleep. I couldn't stop thinking about the brief pain I had experienced when I thought I was going to lose Zac. There was a sensation pulling me toward the door separating my room from Zac's. The pain in my leg protested as I limped over to the door, and placed both of my palms on the cool wood. After my nightmare, I needed to see Zac, put my hands on him to convince myself he was all right. I opened the door between us to find him waiting on the other side, like I knew he would be. No words were spoken as I took his hand, led him back to my bed, and got under the covers. He tucked my body against his, wrapping his arms around me. His strong heart lulled me to sleep in seconds.

When the sun peeked through the curtain, I sat up in the bed, Zac's arm sliding off my waist. My limbs were still stiff and painful and that irritated me. In the bathroom, I washed my hair and scrubbed any excess dried blood from my body, then brushed my teeth. When I came out of the bathroom, Sarah was dressed and had pulled her shiny golden hair back into a sleek ponytail. A bad tangle was garnering all of my attention when Zac came into the room from his.

"Your aunt has already left for the bank, and while she's doing that, we're going to buy you some clothes. Your aunt will meet us wherever we are when she's done," Zac said.

Aunt Lenore had left money for me to buy clothes for at least a week. Zac and I sat in the back of the car; Sarah sat in the front with Caleb driving. Sarah chatted but I zoned out. My attention was out the window, watching the scenery as it passed by. My dream had frightened me, and I was afraid to mention it to the others.

My thoughts were so heavy, I didn't even realize we had made it to the mall until we pulled into a parking space and Caleb shut off the engine. Zac nudged me and I tugged the handle to open the door. Zac had his hand at my waist as we walked through the parking lot and, right when we got to the entrance, a couple of dyed blondes walked out the sliding doors. Both of them were wearing low cut shirts and skin tight jeans that showed off their perfect butts. When they saw Zac, they swayed their hips in an exaggerated manner, checking him out. They didn't notice me so I narrowed my eyes at them and growled deep in my throat.

"You wouldn't be able to handle him," I said as they passed, and they both frowned.

They walked off in a huff, and Zac's arm tightened around me. "Why did you do that?"

"I have no idea."

"I kinda liked it."

Zac growled in my ear, giving me goose bumps. Sarah laughed and I knew she had heard the entire exchange. We passed store after store, but I didn't care for the styles. We walked all over the mall, and after a while I found a store that looked like its clothing would be more durable.

The others perused the clothing as I grabbed five pairs of jeans and some long sleeve shirts, all of which were dark colors. After I paid for the clothes, I was walking back to where Zac and the others were standing, when the store around me dissolved and I was dropped into a car driving along a rain drenched road. The fat rain drops splattered against the windshield, and the wipers attempted to keep up.

It was Zac's point of view again. He was sitting in a car talking to a man with dark red hair and green eyes—the one from my dream the night before—who took up almost half of the back seat. Maybe this had something to do with my dream.

"The way to find someone trying to hide in a crowd is to search for the smell that makes them immortal. The smell is quite different from humans, and you can find anyone, even if you don't know what they look like. Human scents are the most powerful around their groins and immortals have that, too, but the place where immortals smell different is around the neck." The man had a Scottish accent, and he must have been giving Zac tracking lessons before they went hunting. Was Zac doing this off his own free will?

"What does Cymbal wish?" Zac asked.

Nope. His father had hypnotized him and was forcing him to kill vampires while he was under his control. How many had he killed under his father's influence?

The red haired man leaned in, his scent like pine needles. But I didn't understand why I was seeing all of this. When the image faded, Zac was standing before me.

"Skye?" he asked.

"I'm here."

"What happened?"

"Another blood memory."

"Will I remember this one?" There was worry in his eyes, but I didn't want to lie to him.

"Probably not. Do you know a red haired man with green eyes?"

"No. What did he have to do with me?"

About to explain, I took a deep breath and got an overpowering whiff of pine trees. That was why I had the vision. The red haired man was in the mall at this very moment and the vision had shown me how to evade him. We had to split up, but first we would need to find a way to cover up our immortal scent.

All of those thoughts passed in a nanosecond before I took Zac's hand and rushed out of the store. Without a word, I tugged him along behind me, like he was a resistant toddler pitching a fit. Sarah and Caleb saw what a hurry I was in, and rushed to catch up. Zac stayed silent as I moved, knowing it had something to do with his memory. There was a Victoria's Secret store, and I pulled Zac in with Sarah and Caleb close on our heels.

"What's going on, Skye?" Sarah whispered.

"You have to trust me and do exactly what I say. I'll explain everything later."

The perfume tester was on the shelf, and I sprayed Sarah three times on her neck before doing the same to me. Then I got some cologne and repeated the process with Caleb and Zac.

"That's really strong, Skye. Why do we have to wear this?" Zac asked.

"Didn't I just tell you to trust me?" I snapped.

"Sorry." He held his hands up in surrender, his nose wrinkling in silent dissatisfaction at the powerful scent.

"Now I need all of you guys to leave this store in different directions and wait for my signal. At the signal, I want you to head for the car and take different routes."

"What signal?" Caleb asked.

"You'll know it." I had no idea what I was going to do to signal them to leave.

Zac's anxiety level peaked. "Skye, don't ask me to do this."

"I'm not asking, I'm telling. If we stick together, it'll be more noticeable. We'll only be apart for five minutes at the most." I pushed at him until he obeyed me and left. Hopefully the cologne would keep him safe.

After the three of them were gone, I went left out of the store. I ducked into another store when I smelled pine needles and hid behind one of the racks. Above me, I spotted the sprinkler system and concentrated as hard as I could on it. The sprinkler system turned on and water sprayed across the entire mall, screams of surprise erupted all around me. There was the signal.

I draped my hair around my face, and rushed out of the mall. The red haired man would have a hard time finding us in the wet and chaotic mass of people. Humans squeezed past me as I went down a hall, and out a separate door before heading towards the car. Weaving through the cars, I ran as fast as I could—within human range. When I made it to the car, Sarah and Caleb were already there, so I turned around to look for Zac. There was a painful spike in my heart. Where was he?

There was a loud crash and the screech of crushing metal. Our heads whipped to the left, and my jaw dropped when I saw a car flip through the air, setting off car alarms in a ten foot radius. Then I saw my nightmare come true. The red haired man was fighting with Zac. The bag slipped from my slack fingers and I ran, careless of who saw me going faster than any human could. My heart almost stopped when I saw Zac's wounds, his shirt shredded. He was so wounded he couldn't even react to each blow he received. He was defenseless, vulnerable, easy prey for the warrior at his back, dealing brutal blows.

Zac went down and I stood before him, shielding him, when Caleb tackled the monstrous werewolf. The man threw Caleb off, and flung him into a nearby car, collapsing the side of it. He dropped to the ground in a heap, knocked out cold. The red haired man wasn't even out of breath. A good number of humans were creeping toward the fight. If they got any braver, they would see something they would never forget.

When the man saw me, he stopped in surprise and sneered. "Well, well, well. You should have kept running. You might've had a chance at escaping if you had left when you could. Now I'll bring you to Cymbal. I might even have a little fun with you before we get there. Or maybe your blonde friend there. I do so prefer my own kind," he said.

Anger boiled within me. "If you try anything, you'll lose a paw. Or something else."

He barked with laughter. "The little bitch knows how to gamble. How quaint. But I have no time for this. I'm on a tight schedule."

My legs started shaking, but I felt powerful at the same time. He marched toward me and I threw my hands at him. An invisible pulse hurled him through the air, and as he arched back down, he took out seven cars, mangling them beyond recognition.

"Schuyler, get in," someone shouted.

Aunt Lenore had arrived in the nick of time in her car, and Caleb was helping Sarah place Zac in the backseat. Worry suffused me when I saw that Zac was still unconscious and bleeding heavily. My eyes watered as I climbed in the front seat with Sarah, and whirled around to see what Caleb was doing. Caleb tore open Zac's shirt to inspect his injuries. Each cut was at least six inches long and an inch and a half deep. My aunt had taught me how to assess injuries without emotion, but when it was someone you cared about it was extremely difficult. Most of the claw marks were on his abdomen and arms, but one swipe clawed down the side of his neck, all the way across his heart. The blood drained from my face, and my stomach dropped to my feet.

Zac's breathing was shallow, and I held my breath whenever he stopped breathing. Tears clouded my vision and I was scared to death he was going to die. Caleb used Zac's shirt to wipe away the blood as it welled to the surface, but it kept coming back in a rush. Caleb cursed and jerked his own shirt off, and used that to stem some of the more serious bleeding.

"We need to get to Zac's house. Sarah, tell Lenore where to go," Caleb said. "We're low on supplies, but there should be plenty at his house."

Time crawled by as I watched Zac's chest rise and fall, praying he kept breathing. My eyes darted to his face, but there was no change the entire ride to his house. The car came to a screeching halt in his driveway, and I leapt out of the front seat. Sarah ran inside to get everything ready, and I helped Aunt Lenore and Caleb carry Zac into the house. Sarah tossed me some gauze from the kitchen, while she carried over a bowl filled to the brim with hot water. My hands shook as I dabbed some gauze in the hot water, and started to wipe the blood away from Zac's ravaged chest. He was losing blood at an alarming rate.

It had been at least one day since I had had any blood to drink, and his blood smelled tantalizing. My wounds screamed at me, and they needed blood if they were going to heal as fast as my body demanded of them. My hands shook harder. Zac's blood was covering them like warm, wet gloves and I knew my eyes had taken on a feverish glow. If I didn't leave now, there was a good chance I was going to take the rest of the blood he needed, and if I did that, I would never forgive myself. My fangs lengthened and sharpened. My instincts were taking over and I couldn't stop it.

"I can't do this," I said, and ran to the kitchen.

I snatched the soap off the sink and started scrubbing my hands like I had OCD. The scent of his blood on me was still strong, and it didn't help that it was wafting through the door to the living room. My hands were raw and red by the time I dried them off. I snatched an orange on the way out and went to the upstairs bathroom, peeling it on the way, and sat in the tub with it under my nose. The scent of the orange was so sharp and strong that it overpowered the need for Zac's blood. What kind of girlfriend was I if I couldn't stop from biting him when he needed me the most?

Thirty minutes went by before I heard footsteps on the stairs, and then a soft knock on the door. Sarah came in, wiping her hands off with a sterile cloth, and pulling off her bloody jacket. She tossed her jacket back down the stairs. There was a sad look on her face, and I wasn't sure how to take it. My breath caught and tears welled; Sarah got on her knees when she saw I was about to lose it.

"He's fine," she said. "The bleeding has stopped, and we even saw healing before we put the bandages on. He's sleeping. Caleb and your aunt are carrying him to his room right now."

Relief flooded through me, I dropped the orange, and watched uncaring as it rolled to the other side of the tub. My limbs felt weak after tensing them for so long, and I slouched down in the tub, laying my head on the cold porcelain siding.

"Thank God," I said.

"Why the orange?"

"It's the only thing strong enough to overcome the smell of blood. Any citrus will work." I looked at her, still on the verge of crying. "Tell me he's going to be okay."

"He's going to be fine. He's strong, always has been. He'll pull through this in no time. Do you want me to come and check on you later?"

"I'm okay. I just need to be alone for a while."

Sarah left the bathroom and closed the door behind her. My eyes slid shut as I focused on the clean and sharp smell of the bathtub I was in. I told myself over and over no matter how good Zac's blood smelled to me, I refused to take it. It would be counter-productive for his healing if I kept taking his blood when I was thirsty.

It took two hours, but now I was in control. After discarding the ruined orange, I washed all of the juice out of the tub, removed my jacket and took off my shoes. They remained in the bathroom as I headed to Zac's room. The door was ajar and I stole into the room, closing it behind me. A few calming breaths were needed before I could look at him lying prone on his bed, covered in bandages. Before I knew it, I was standing next to the bed, looking down at him. There were traces of pain on his face, and I wished I could take it from him. I knelt on the bed and sat next to him, far enough away that I didn't move him with the shifting of weight.

I reached out and touched his face. He made a sound and stirred at my touch, his face angling towards me, and his lips parted. My fingers caressed his face until he opened his eyes. And I was never happier to see them. They were so blue it made me want to cry, and I didn't know if the blood loss had caused it or not, but even the lavender flecks were lighter than usual.

"Hey," I whispered.

"Hey."

"How are you feeling?"

"Like shit." He chuckled and then grimaced. "But I'm better now that you're here."

"Zac, what happened when we split up?"

"He spotted me and I couldn't shake him. When we got outside, he attacked. The last hit he gave me knocked me out, so I don't know what happened after that. Obviously we won considering I'm lying here and you're still alive. Please tell me you didn't do anything stupid."

"I stood in front of you and then Caleb tackled him. He tossed Caleb off like he was nothing and knocked him out for a bit. He said something about taking me and using me for his…pleasures." Zac growled when I said that. "Then he said he'd rather have Sarah. I threw my hands up and he was launched across the parking lot. Then my aunt showed up and we hauled ass."

"I wish I could've seen that." He chuckled and winced again.

"He was definitely surprised."

"How did you know to do the perfume thing?"

"I had another blood memory where you'd been hypnotized. The red haired man was sitting in the back seat with you, telling you the best way to track immortals. Our immortal scent comes from our neck and I hoped if we disguised our scent, then we'd get out okay. But I was wrong." I touched his face again. "Once he saw you, nothing could stop him."

His hand came up and covered mine. "We had no idea he was going to find me out of the four of us. I'm just glad you made me leave without you. I'd never forgive myself if you'd been with me and gotten hurt." He turned his head and kissed my palm. "But enough about me. How are you?"

"What do you mean?"

"Sarah told me you were helping to clean my wounds then you ran out of the room."

"My hands were covered in your blood, and you know I find your scent irresistible. Suddenly it was too much. My mouth started watering and all I wanted to do was bite you. It took everything in me to leave."

"So you still haven't had any blood?"

"Not a bit. But why are you worrying about me? You're the one that's hurt."

"Skye, I care more about what happens to you. You can take my blood if you need it," he said, and I shook my head. "Why not?" He seemed put out that I was saying no.

"Zac, I just spent two and a half hours in the bathroom telling myself I wouldn't drink your blood, and it will undermine everything I did if

I took it anyway." I prepared to stand. "You need to get some rest."

"No." Zac sat up and reaped the reward by falling back in pain. "I'm not tired. I'm actually hungry." His stomach growled. "See?"

"Fine. I'll cook you something."

"I'm coming, too." He leaned forward, with less pain this time.

"You most certainly are not." I pushed him back down onto the bed, avoiding his bandages.

"Either you help me get down there, or I hurt myself trying to do it alone."

"Fine." I helped him to a sitting position before ducking under his arm, lifting him to his feet.

He was heavy, but once he could stand on his own two legs, he could hold most of his weight. It took us a couple of minutes to get down the stairs, but we made it. We looked around but there was no sign of Caleb, Sarah, or my aunt.

"Where is everyone?" Zac asked.

"I don't know." I shrugged out from under his shoulder as he balanced himself using a wall, and walked through the house.

"Skye," Zac called.

"What is it? Are you okay?" I asked, rushing over to him.

"I'm fine. They left a note saying they're patrolling around the house. They aren't taking any chances of what happened at your house to happen here. Apparently, I'm too injured to move in a hurry."

He crumpled the piece of paper in his hand. He didn't like being a hindrance, wounded, so helpless he wouldn't be able to protect me. "Let's get you something to eat," I said.

He leaned against the counter as I rifled through the cabinets and refrigerator, finding a fresh steak.

"Can you even cook?" he asked. I paused and turned to give him a vacant look. "I mean, you don't eat so there's never been a reason for you to cook, and I wasn't sure if you could." He received the same unblinking expression. "Okay, I'm sorry. Please continue what you were doing?"

"Thank you." I went about pulling out pots and pans.

Since he was wounded, I knew he would need meat as a main part of his diet. It helped werewolves heal faster and get their strength back. I thawed the steak in the microwave before putting it in the skillet. If he was going to get the most out of his steak, then I didn't need to cook it much. All werewolves loved their steaks rare and bloody, because it was the closest thing to feeding on a live animal without hunting. And werewolves thought drinking blood was disgusting.

Zac's eyes were trained on me while I was cooking. After just a few minutes, I took the steak off the burner, cut it into strips, and brought the plate over to where he was standing. I dangled a slice in front of his face, and his tongue darted out and snatched it. He swallowed and snared me with his arm and pulled me close, wincing when I pressed into his bandages.

"How'd you know that's how I like my steak cooked?" he asked with a smirk.

"I do live with a werewolf."

The plate scraped along the marble counter as he pushed it away from him. It didn't seem like he could do it injured, so I was surprised when he lifted me onto the counter. My hands clasped his face with worry when his face went white, but he recovered. He brushed the hair out of my face, leaned in close like he was going to kiss me, and then sniffed me. I didn't move a muscle.

"Why do you smell like oranges?" he asked.

A laugh escaped. "I took one in the bathroom with me."

One brow rose up. "Did you eat it?"

"No, I don't eat food."

"Then why did you take it?"

"I could smell you no matter where I went in the house, so I did something I did when I was a kid, when I had to deal with blood being spilt. I peeled the orange and held it under my nose. It's the only thing that overpowers the smell of blood to me. I carried an orange in my pocket every year of elementary school. I used it so much I started smelling like oranges." I paused and took a deep breath. "I really thought I could've killed you for a second there."

Zac brushed away the tear that escaped and kissed me. "I know you wouldn't have done it. You have the strength to do anything you want to."

His lips brushed against mine again. My heart stuttered and skipped a beat. His kisses were intoxicating, like he was baring his soul for me to see. I wanted to join in on the kiss more, but I was afraid if I touched him I would injure him further. He was covered in bandages and it was complicated finding an injury free spot. Zac maneuvered his hips between my legs and pulled me flush against him.

"Well, it's a good thing we're keeping an eye out," Caleb said as he walked in. "A tornado could come through here and the two of you would never notice."

Zac stepped away from me, knowing I would be embarrassed that Caleb had walked in on us, and grabbed some of the steak. Caleb sniffed the air, turned around, and took a step forward. My hand went up to signal him to stop, and he slid back a few feet, like an invisible force was pushing against him.

"Never mind. I'll make my own." He went to grab one out of the freezer, acting like nothing happened.

When Zac finished eating, I helped him limp back upstairs and got him settled in bed. When he was lying down, I sat down and peeled off the tape to his bandages, making sure his wounds were healing. They were, but the one along his neck, extending all the way down his chest and over his heart, worried me. The ointment was on the nightstand so I put more on his cuts, and then replaced the bandages. My fingers ran through his soft black hair, and caressed the uninjured skin around his wounds to relax him. When I started to stand, his hand snaked around my wrist and pulled me down.

"My instinct to protect you would be greatly eased if you stayed here tonight," he said, his voice thick with sleep and his eyes still closed.

"What if I get thirsty?"

"You won't bite me if you don't want to."

He pulled me against his chest and rolled onto his right side so he could tuck my body against his. It was comfortable, being in his arms, and I liked being held so close. His warm breaths fanned across my neck, his arm wrapped around me, holding me so tight, even though he was no longer conscious. It was like he was afraid I was going to leave, like he was going to lose me.

Lying there, my mind was free to wander, and it centered on Zac being hypnotized. How was his father controlling what he did when he was so far away? That train of thought brought up another question. Could Zac's father find him because of the hypnotism?

CHAPTER 16
LOVE LOST

Zac's weight shifted and then his warmth was gone. I shivered at the chill. My eyes cracked open to see Zac staggering away from the bed, hunched over in pain.

"Are you okay? Where are you going?" I asked.

He turned so I could see his face. "Since you don't eat, I can understand why you'd ask. I have to go to the bathroom."

"Oh, right." My cheeks flushed bright red, and I set my head back down to hide my embarrassment. My living radiator was gone, so I tucked my knees to my chest and reached for the comforter at my feet. Once it was within my grasp, I yanked it up to my neck. What was I doing? Someone was after us. The time for sleeping in was over.

Zac was back out in a minute, but I was up and walking about his room. Aunt Lenore had left some more bandages and tape on the dresser and I motioned for him to lie down.

"Can we do this downstairs?" he asked.

"Okay."

Zac needed little assistance getting down the stairs, and then he sat on the couch and studied me as I applied new bandages. Most of the cuts had healed completely, while others were closed but the skin was still raised and pink. While I worked, he kept sliding away from me until I had to straddle his hips to reach his neck. When I finished, he wouldn't let me get back up. I narrowed my eyes at him.

"What are you trying to do?" I asked.

"Me? Nothing." He tried to look innocent. And he almost succeeded.

With a shake of my head, I stood to gather the old bandages to throw them away. There was a click from the front door, and I figured it was either Sarah, Caleb, or my aunt, coming back from patrol. After throwing away the bandages, I headed for the door. When I saw who it was, I slid to a stop, falling backwards onto my butt as I scrambled away. The man from my dream stepped into the house. His long, sable black hair reached his shoulders and his towering frame barely fit through the door.

"Zac!" I shouted, and he came running from the living room.

He saw me and took position in front of me, between me and his father. Then, bafflingly enough, Zac relaxed and smiled at his father.

"It took me a while to find you," his father said to Zac, and then they hugged like they hadn't seen each other in a long time. Any air in my lungs left in a rush. My face blanched and pain erupted in my chest to the point I clutched at my heart. "Um, is she okay?"

"Shit! Skye." Zac knelt down beside me. He grabbed my face when I refused to look away from the man staring down at me, and forced me to look at him. "Skye, look at me."

"It's him," I whispered.

"No, it's not him."

"I think I'd remember him, Zac. He was in my dream. I described him to you and you showed me a picture of him." Did he forget he had told me his own father was in my dream? Was this a part of the hypnotism?

"Yes, my father was in your dream. But that's not my father."

He appeared to be lucid. "What are you talking about?"

"He's my uncle. My father's twin." Zac helped me to my feet and pulled me close.

Frightened, I dragged my feet, but Zac pulled me nonetheless. His uncle didn't move, which made things a little easier, since Zac insisted on getting closer.

"Look at his eyes." Zac watched me, and I gazed back at him. His eyes were unique and I was glad he had those lavender flecks making them so soft. Not like his father's eyes at all.

After a minute, I found the courage to look at Zac's uncle's eyes and they were different from my dream. They were a warm lavender color. When I relaxed, Zac pulled me against him.

"Skye, this is my Uncle Jared. Uncle Jared, this is Schuyler," Zac said, and I reached out a shaky hand and took his.

"It's nice to meet you, Schuyler," he said.

"It's nice to meet you, too. Now that I know you aren't here to kill me."

"I don't understand. Why would I want to kill you?" He looked from me to Zac with a quizzical expression.

"She had a dream about dad choking her to death. And obviously you look just like him," Zac said.

"That doesn't explain why I would want to kill her."

"She's half vampire, half werewolf."

"So that's what that scent is. I was curious about that." He walked past me, making me shrink against Zac. "Don't worry child, I won't hurt you."

Just then Jared took a good look at Zac and the fact he was shirtless and bandaged up. "What the hell happened to you? You get in a fight with your girlfriend?"

My face paled at the thought of doing something so horrible to Zac. "No, it was a red haired man with green eyes," Zac said, and that wiped the smile off Jared's face.

"Damn." He got to his feet.

"Do you know him?" Zac asked, and settled me down on the now vacant couch.

"His name is Liam. He's very old." He looked at me. "Did you know him?"

"No," I said.

"What about you?" This was directed at Zac.

"No, but he knows me," Zac said.

"Tell me everything from the beginning."

Zac told him everything, starting with when I started hanging out with them. He even mentioned the part where he choked me, his uncle made a look of surprise at that, but he continued on. Zac mentioned me being shot and Jared made a guilty face.

"That's my fault. My men sensed you weren't human so I told them to figure out what you were," Jared said.

"You told them to shoot her?" Zac asked shocked.

"No. That they decided on their own," Jared said. Is there anything else that happened?"

Zac continued his story. When he was done, his uncle nodded and held up his hand.

"How did Schuyler know to leave the mall?" he asked.

The answer died in my throat, because even though Jared was cool with me being half and half, and that Zac was with me, I wasn't sure how he would take the fact I had drank his nephew's blood.

"She saw it in a blood memory," Zac said for me. At least he was confident his uncle wouldn't care.

His uncle gave me a look I couldn't describe, nodded, and that was the end of it. Good. I wasn't in the mood to hear anything about it.

"I should probably warn the others that you're here. Her aunt might try and kill you unless we warn her first." Zac got up to call Caleb's cell.

"Who's your aunt?" he asked.

"You'll meet her soon enough," I said. I may not have been much of a threat, but it irked me that he wasn't even concerned someone stronger was on their way here.

"You're smart to not to trust everyone immediately. Your aunt taught you how to survive well."

"She's the only one that looked after me when my parents were killed. I mean, it wasn't like she could go back to her pack. They'd have killed her on sight." I relaxed in Jared's presence. Just being around him, I could sense he was different.

Zac came back into the room. "Your aunt is on her way. She wants to meet you." The first part he said to me, and the second to Jared. Zac seemed sure it would go well, and I prayed it would go better than I was imagining.

Aunt Lenore stalked in a few minutes later with her golden hair tied back into a ponytail, and her stormy gray eyes wide with worry. She pulled me into her arms and thoroughly checked me over. She paused when she sniffed the air, her eyes widening, and whirled around.

"Jared," she said.

"Lenny?" A second passed before they embraced and kissed.

Zac's brow went up. "You two know each other?"

"Yes." My aunt was the first to speak. "Jared's my mate." My aunt had never mentioned she had a mate. Disappointment and anger sank in.

"Sixty years ago, you disappeared without a word. News came later that your brother had been killed. What happened to you? I thought you were dead," Jared said and pulled her close to him again. It didn't escape my notice when pain flashed in her eyes. Jared looked like he was seeing a ghost.

"Schuyler needed me. I made a promise to my brother." She turned to face me. Her voice caught when her emotions threatened to overwhelm her. "I'd shut everything out about my old life so I could protect you. I didn't expect this to happen."

"And when were you going to tell me that you'd left your mate behind?"

"It didn't matter." She didn't look at Jared so she didn't see his expression.

"Obviously it did." I walked out the front door.

The sun was setting as I ambled down the street and away from the house. My aunt had lied to me. It was obvious she had missed him. And he was so in love with her. There was more to her old life than I had been led to believe. I would fall to pieces if Zac ever left me. Where did she find the courage, the strength, to let him go?

Before I knew it, I made it all the way to the clearing Zac and I had been to just as the sun sank below the tree line. I sat on a rock, and watched the sun go down the last few inches. Zac's presence could be felt at the edge of the clearing before he sat next to me.

He wrapped an arm around me and kissed my cheek. "Sorry I'm late. Your aunt thought it wouldn't be a good idea for me to leave the house without a shirt. I actually had to put on clothes before she let me leave. It made me feel like I was sixteen all over again."

"Well, we know how good her ideas work out," I said.

"I'm sorry she didn't tell you."

"Around the time when I first met you, I asked her if she regretted leaving everything. I asked her if she regretted never getting the chance to find someone she could love and have her own family with. A family that would be accepted by the pack. She told me she'd never thought she could be happier than when I was born. She lied." Tears fell as his thumb stroked my cheek.

"How do you know she lied?"

"Did you see her face? Obviously she loves him. And she left him without a word because of me. Not to mention the face he made when she said it didn't matter."

Zac pulled me closer, heedless of the fact that I would be pressing against his cuts, and held me. Everything was so confusing, and I wasn't sure what to think anymore. If Aunt Lenore had loved Jared, then it was time I learned how to take care of myself, so I didn't take any more of her life away from her. She deserved it after all she had done for me.

"I know what you're thinking, and I want you to stop thinking it," Zac said.

"Why shouldn't I leave? I only make everything worse."

"Do you really feel that way?"

"Yes."

"Your aunt may have left things behind, but she did it because she loves you. She wasn't lying when she said she'd do it again. You're the only thing she has left of her brother and the woman he loved. Have you ever thought about it that way?" Zac asked. No, I had never thought of it that way. "Besides, Jared will help us and they can be together again."

"Yeah, they can."

"Here." He tugged at something in his pocket. "Your aunt brought this for you, but you left in a hurry."

Zac handed me a bag of blood, and I pierced the bag with one of my fangs. The blood tasted good after two days without. While I was drinking, Zac moved my shirt to the side, exposing the back of my shoulder, to make sure the bullet wound healed completely. Any soreness in my body melted away, like I just received an amazing massage. He kissed my shoulder, sending shivers through me, before he put my shirt back in its place.

"We should get back. We aren't safe out here at night," Zac said, and pushed me up so I could stand, then got to his feet behind me.

My muscles and every other part of my body were more energized, but I craved a hot shower.

"I feel disgusting," I said.

"You can get a shower when we get back."

Back at the house, in the bathroom, Zac followed me in. He closed the door behind him and pushed me against the wall and took my mouth with an urgency I had never seen in him. His kisses were rough, and soon, I could think of nothing but the way his lips crushed upon mine, the way his touch made me dizzy, and the way his kisses made me quiver with anticipation. His hands were at my waist, pulling me against him, while my arms wound around his neck and my fingers twined through his hair. He lifted me onto the bathroom counter and stepped between my legs. There was a rush of excitement and I kissed him even harder. When he pulled away, I looked at him like he was crazy, but he just shook his head.

"I don't want to do anything you aren't ready for," he said. "I don't want you to regret it. I want you to enjoy it." He kissed me once more, and then left me alone in the bathroom.

I wasn't expecting that. And I wasn't ready for him to leave, not when I was so hyped up because of him. My entire body was shaking with feeling as I got off the counter, and turned on the shower.

I stripped out of Sarah's clothes and stepped under the warm water. It relaxed me even further, and I felt a lot better once my hair was washed clean, the dirt scrubbed away. When I got out of the shower and wrapped a towel around my torso, I went into Zac's room and saw a spaghetti strap top and a pair of shorts on the bed. Nothing looked better right now than clothes that fit. The shorts I slipped on under the towel, and then let it drop to the floor before I slipped the top on.

Someone cleared their throat and I whirled around to see Zac sitting in a chair next to the window. How long had he been there? How much had he seen? The angle he was at led me to believe he didn't see anything but bared skin but, for some reason, I couldn't muster the anger I should have felt that he hadn't declared his presence sooner. He stood and approached me. My heart stuttered at the intimacy of being alone with him in the dark.

"You haven't said anything about me being in here while you changed." His voice was like velvet sliding along my body. Goose bumps rose on my damp skin.

"I guess I haven't said anything because I don't care." I closed the rest of the distance between us. My palms laid flat on his chest, avoiding the area where his shirt was raised from the bandages. I rose up on my toes and touched my lips to his. The kiss was gentle, but serious.

"Are you feeling the same thing I've been feeling every time I kiss you?" he asked.

"What have you been feeling?"

"There's this energy inside me that reaches every nerve when I kiss you." He brushed my hair out of my face, giving me that aching kiss again. "It takes everything in me to go slow."

"I wish I didn't always get so embarrassed."

"You don't ever have to be embarrassed with me."

I yawned in his face and he laughed. "Sorry. I'm tired."

"You've had a long day. We're going to split up patrols during the night, so why don't you get some sleep?" He led me to his bed and I got under the covers.

"Wake me when it's my turn?"

"Sure." Knowing Zac, I had a feeling he wouldn't wake me up, but I was too tired to dwell on it for too long.

My eyes closed when my head hit the pillow. Zac settled next to me and covered me with his arm, pulling me against him in a possessive way. The bed was so warm and soft I fell asleep in no time.

****

I was in a dark room somewhere—nothing natural could be that claustrophobically dark—and it was cold. There was no sound at first, but then I could hear moaning. A door to my left flew open and four men barged in. To my right, I saw a man lying prone on the floor, his hands bound behind his back. He wore no shirt and his filthy pants were torn in myriads of places. His flesh was mottled with dark bruises and large cuts. The four men dragged him up by the arms, even though his wrists were secured behind his back. He groaned as he staggered to his feet, his head fell back and lolled around on his neck.

Not knowing what else to do, I followed as they lugged the man out of the room and down a concrete corridor. The corridor was lit by fluorescent bulbs, giving it a sterile and depressing feel. After a few steps, the man couldn't walk any further, but they kept marching while his bare feet dragged along the ground behind them. They took him to another windowless room, but at least this one was lit. The injured man had greasy hair and the light cast clarity over his injuries, making them appear more gruesome.

The prisoner had his back to me, slumped over onto his knees, in a chair they had thrown him into. One of the four men closed the door behind me, while another pulled the half dead man into a sitting position. The biggest one, with dull brown hair and dark brown eyes, took his place in front of him, and hit him with one of his meaty fists. A bone snapped as it broke and the man was flung to the side. He made a small sound of pain before the guy pulled him back up. He punched him again and again, and I flinched each time. With each hit a bone would break. They were merciless, never giving him a moments rest.

"Tell us what we want to know and we'll stop," one of the men said between

punches, studying his nails.

The man they were beating said nothing. He didn't even shake his head, or acknowledge that he had heard them. What did they want to know? And why wouldn't he give it to them? The interrogator waited a few blows and then posed his question again. There was still no answer, but this time he spat his blood at the one punching him. I wanted to scream at them, hit them, but I knew this was only a dream and it wouldn't do a thing.

"Enough," the interrogator said. "Use the paddles."

The huge man wiped his hands off on a towel, like he had just finished changing the oil in his car. I wanted to kick him where the sun didn't shine.

My eyes followed the fourth man as he exited the room, leaving the door open. He came back in, pulling a machine on wheels. It was a defibrillator, but this one had been modified to torture a life rather than save it. They charged the paddles, and then stuck them against the prisoner. He tensed and every muscle clenched as thousands of volts of electricity surged through his body. He groaned as his muscles rippled painfully, and I wanted to smack those paddles away from him.

"Tell us what we want to know," the interrogator said again, and held up his hand so the other man waited. He was giving the prisoner a chance to talk.

"Go to hell." The injured man spat blood, again, this time at the interrogator.

No. No, no, no, no. Please, God no. Please tell me I didn't recognize that voice. I circled around the chair and gasped when I saw through the bruises, cuts, and swollen face to see Zac. Now their questions made sense. He wasn't answering because he didn't want to tell them where I was. Zac was being tortured for my location and he wasn't even contemplating telling them. My hands clutched at my hair, threatening to pull it out. My thoughts went wild and the pain in my chest increased tenfold.

They shocked him twenty more times, and I screamed along with him. I tried to hit the men torturing him, even knowing it was pointless. I wanted to escape my nightmare, but it was like pushing against solid steel.

"Has he talked?" Liam asked when he entered the room. A snarl ripped through my chest at his voice.

"No, he hasn't," one man said. "We've beaten him, drowned him, buried him, and electrocuted him. But he won't talk."

They had drowned and buried him? He was using past tense which meant Zac had died each time, only to have his immortality bring him back to life.

"I had something made especially for you, Zac. No one has ever resisted saying anything for this long. This," he held up a knife, "is a knife forged completely of silver. It's a little tricky to handle, but it holds a lot of promise. I want to test it and see how well it works."

Liam dragged a chair over from the side of the room, and placed it in front of Zac so he could see him. He held the knife aloft and waved it in front of his face. The knife shimmered, while the handle was plain steel so the werewolf wielding it was safe. He shoved the tip of the blade into Zac's shoulder, and drew it down his chest. Zac opened his mouth and screamed at the top of his lungs. Blood rose to the surface and trailed down his chest. He tried to move away from Liam but others held him still. His screams echoed in my head, haunting me, as the knife made of silver ravaged his chest. Zac threw his head back, breaking the nose of the man behind him. Then he kicked Liam in the chest, slamming him into the concrete wall. Zac gripped the handle of the knife and yanked it from his body. Before he could stand, another man came up behind him and snapped his neck. Zac dropped.

"NO!" I screamed and sat up, my arm extended, reaching for the Zac in my dream.

CHAPTER 17
TRANCE

Zac burst into the room and was on the bed in a second. "Skye, what is it?" He grasped my face to calm me down. "You're freezing."

My skin felt clammy and cold to the touch. My limbs were trembling after what I had seen in my dream, and I couldn't shake the sight of Zac's neck being broken. Even though he was fine before me, I couldn't stop seeing him beaten almost to death and tortured by Liam with a silver knife. My heart beat out an erratic rhythm, and I gasped for air as I clutched Zac to me and refused to let go.

"Skye, are you all right?" Zac asked.

When I didn't answer him, he threw the covers off and lifted me out of the bed. Without the warm comforter, I shook even more and felt like all the heat was leaving my body. It was just a dream. It hadn't happened. I wasn't going to let it happen. Zac rushed me into the bathroom. He set me on the toilet and started the hot water in the bathtub, once he could pry my hands off him. Aunt Lenore came running in, followed by Jared.

"I heard Schuyler. What's wrong?" she asked, and knelt in front of me.

"I don't know. She hasn't said anything," Zac said.

When I looked at Zac, images of him lying broken from my dreams entered my reality, only to switch back to normal in the next second. Sarah and Caleb appeared near the door.

"Why are you starting a bath?" Jared came further into the bathroom.

"She's freezing. I don't know what's wrong with her, but I need to get her warm."

When I tried to imagine the heat of the water, I only shivered more. My eyes wanted to close, but the nightmare was behind the lids, waiting to pounce.

"Did she say anything when she woke up?" Aunt Lenore asked.

"All she said was 'no', I don't know what she was dreaming about, but it had to be bad." When the tub had a little water in it, Zac moved me off the toilet and lowered me into the tub. Stinging stabs of heat pierced me. The hot water was almost painful against my frigid skin. Zac cupped his hands together and poured water over me. "C'mon, baby, snap out of it."

Even as I stared into his eyes, I had trouble breathing, and I did everything to ignore the pain radiating from my chest. Part of me wanted to tell him what I had dreamed about, but I couldn't form words when my mouth felt frozen. In fact, I started shaking even more, making Zac growl in frustration. He stood, removed his shirt, and stepped into the tub with me, gathering me into his arms to warm me with his body along with the hot water.

I clung to his chest like it was my life support, and tried to make myself stop shaking. Zac didn't have a bandage on his chest anymore, and the worst cuts had healed across his neck and down over his heart. My mind flashed back to the image of his beaten body, and then I was clutching the ruined chest from my dream.

"How long has she been having these dreams?" Jared asked.

"At least a month. But none of them has ever been this bad. I've never seen her react like this," Zac said.

"I've seen this once before," Jared said, "when someone had a terrifying prophetic dream. They gave no warning to what they saw and there was no way to stop it."

"What happened?" my aunt asked.

Jared looked at me before he replied. "Her family was massacred. She never recovered and committed suicide seven years later."

The moment those words passed my ears the shaking intensified. I didn't want my dream to come true about Zac. They couldn't hurt him because I needed him. There was a spike of pain in my chest and I placed a hand over my heart, clutching at it, trying to hold the pieces of myself together.

Zac's hand covered mine. "So what you're saying is Skye had a dream so bad she may not be able to talk about it?"

"Yes." Jared got on his knees next to the tub, and looked at me. "Can you at least tell us who it's about?"

My eyes stared into Jared's lavender ones, and then I raised my gaze to Zac's face. Jared followed my gaze, frowning when he understood.

"You need to tell us what happened so we can avoid it," Jared said.

"Don't push her," Zac said.

"We need to know what happened."

"If we push her, she could retreat inside herself."

"We need to know," Sarah said. "Can I help you, Skye?"

I nodded. Sarah got down on her haunches and held my face in her hands so I was peering into her dark blue eyes. As she stared, everything became lighter, and the shock melted away and left behind a numb feeling. The flashing back and forth from dream to reality stopped. My mouth opened and I started to describe my dream, like a zombie, repeating what I saw with no emotion.

Sarah released my face. "Just so you know the effect of what I did won't last long. She'll revert to the way she was before."

Zac's arms tightened around me, and just like she said, the despair came back in a rush. My dream was going to happen unless I stopped it, and I was going to do just that. Forcing the emotions into a box, I pushed away from Zac until he let me sit up.

"We need to leave this place," I said. "In my dream, they torture Zac for my location. We need to leave here. They can't find us if we're unpredictable. We need to lose ourselves to the point that even we don't know where we are."

No one said anything. Jared cleared his throat. "I think that's a good idea."

"How are we going to do that?" Sarah asked.

"We buy some tents and camping gear and we go on a trip," I said.

"Damn, just when I was loving clean hair," Sarah said, and stood.

"So we leave tonight?" Caleb asked.

"We leave tonight," Zac said.

Caleb stood and left, followed by my aunt. Jared mentioned something about getting the tents and other camping gear ready, and then he was gone, too. As I stood, all of the water splashed back into the tub before I stepped out. There was more splashing when Zac stood and got out of the tub. He grabbed a towel and wrapped it around me before leaving the room.

"I'll get you some clothes," he said.

With expert maneuvering, I took off my sopping wet clothes, keeping the towel around me. When Zac walked in, he paused to look at me, in nothing but a towel, before handing me my clothes and leaving. I slipped on the dark pair of jeans and a black, long sleeved shirt. The design on the bottom of the shirt looked familiar, like the one I had picked out at the mall. When I studied the jeans closer, they looked like the ones I had picked out as well. But I had dropped them in the parking lot.

"Where did my clothes come from?" I asked as I came back into his room.

"Your aunt picked them up while you were sleeping," Zac said. I gasped when I looked up at him, in only his underwear. I spun around and put my back to him. "What?"

"You're in your underwear."

"So?"

"So? You could have warned me."

"I could care less if you see me in my underwear." I heard his feet, light as a feather, on the carpet as he walked towards me.

"But I care." I turned around and smacked into his solid chest. An explosion of his scent wrapped itself around me. My lips pursed and I refused to look down.

"I put pants on. I didn't mean to make you uncomfortable."

"Thank you." I didn't move away from him. My chest still ached, and being close to him helped ease the discomfort. A minute passed.

"I'll be all right."

"How do you know?"

"I just know. I'll be fine, as long as I have you." He gave me a tender kiss on the lips, making my legs go weak. "I love you."

My breath hitched. We stared at each other and I knew he was waiting for something. "What do you want me to say?"

"I want you to say you love me."

"Zac…I don't believe in love. How many times do we have to go through this?" I asked.

He put a hand under my chin, lifted my face, and kissed me before I could protest. "Until you admit it."

****

The backpack I had on would have been heavy to a girl my size, but I found it easy to carry. Zac had a similar pack but it was much bigger. Jared had found four tents and had come back to the house within an hour with all of the things we needed. We were packed and ready to go in less than twenty minutes.

Jared led the way, followed by my aunt, me, Zac, Sarah, and then Caleb bringing up the rear. Jared had decided the order and I wasn't going to argue. He was the best man to put in front, because he was the oldest and most experienced at situations like these. We walked out the back door and into the forest behind Zac's house.

The woods were silent except for the chirping crickets and night time predators. The rays of moonlight that could pierce the trees felt like a touch, soothing me like a lullaby. Zac walked behind me, giving me plenty of time to think about what he had said. I knew he loved me and I knew he would want more eventually; I just didn't think it would be so soon.

Since I was so absorbed in my thoughts, I tripped over a large root I hadn't seen. Zac's hands were around me, steadying me when I lost my balance. After a couple of hours, Jared stopped our journey, and decided we should make camp. Zac, Caleb, and Jared set up the four tents, while Sarah, Aunt Lenore, and I started a fire to eat dinner.

A rock became my chair, and I stared into the flames as everyone passed around food. Prior to leaving, I drank a bag of blood. I was still uncomfortable drinking in front of a bunch of werewolves. They didn't care that I was half vampire and needed blood to survive, but it was still hard for me to let people see my weakness. A weakness none of them shared.

There was a chill so I crossed my arms to brace myself against the cold. While I was observing everyone, I saw Jared watching Aunt Lenore, and my heart ached for her. My anger at her for lying to me had long since dissipated, but I was sad that she had had someone she loved and had missed. Jared glanced up and saw me staring at him, so I jerked my head in the direction of the woods behind me and got up. He set down his food and followed.

"Did you need to talk to me about something?" he asked when I stopped walking, far enough away from the camp that the others wouldn't overhear us.

"Do you ever get gut feelings that something bad is going to happen?"

"Yeah, I had a really bad one when…right before Lenny went missing. Everyone thought she was dead, but in my heart I knew she was alive."

"Well, I'm getting a feeling like that. And what it's telling me is something big is going to happen. Something I won't be able to stop. When the time comes, I need you to do something for me without question."

"What do you want me to do?"

"When whatever is going to happen happens, I want you to get Aunt Lenore out. I will not let her die for me. You're the only one I trust to take care of her because you love her and she loves you. She wasted sixty years of her life on me. Don't let her waste the rest of it." I turned on my heel without waiting for him to promise because I knew he would do it. Just like I knew he wouldn't tell Aunt Lenore we had had this conversation.

When I sat back down on my rock, Zac gave me a questioning look, but I just shook my head. What could I tell him? That I had a bad feeling we were going to be caught no matter what we did?

After dinner, Zac and I crawled into our tent, and I nestled in his arms.

"Are you okay?" Zac asked.

"I'm afraid my dream will come true."

"I don't want you to worry about it. It won't happen."

I wanted to ask how he could be so sure, but he silenced me with a kiss. As I settled down to sleep, Zac hummed my lullaby, and I drifted off to the sound of his voice.

****

My eyelids felt heavy when I opened them. The sun was shining on the other side of the camouflage tent, a small circle the only indication of the sun's position in the sky. Zac was still asleep beside me. He looked so young when his face relaxed. I knew I looked young for my age, seeing as I was sixty years old, but I also looked young for a human eighteen year old. My aunt said it had to do with when we froze into our immortality, which was when we were at our strongest. Since I was a hybrid, and had the strength of both, I froze at sixteen. I crawled from the tent into the sunlight. The warmth felt good on my skin as I stretched my cramped and aching limbs.

The area was crowded with trees. For a moment, I stood and listened to the sounds of the forest around me. Animals could be heard burrowing in the ground. Nearby, a bird was flapping its wings as it settled into its nest. The light caressing the earth split into rainbow shards as it covered the world.

When I listened closer, I could hear the quiet and swift trickling of water nearby. I headed toward the sound and found a thin, deep stream of clear water. The ground sloped down to the water's edge, and I carefully made my way to the edge.

The stream was beautiful, with its clarity and sharp, fresh scent. My fingers swirled through the water and I watched as the rainbows of light danced around my hand. A low growl sounded from across the tiny stream, and I froze before raising my eye line. On the opposite bank was a large black wolf in a defensive stance, his amber eyes trained on me.

The wolf's eyes angled upwards to something above me, and growled even fiercer, planting his feet further apart and lowering into a crouch.

"Don't move, Skye." Zac's voice reached my ears, soft and calm, but I didn't turn around to check.

My gaze stayed on the wolf as he tried to keep an eye on the two of us. Fear mingled amidst courage in his amber eyes as he debated on who to attack first. It was understandable. His senses were driving him crazy because he could smell two predators, but they looked like humans.

"Look him in the eye," Zac said. "I want you to back up toward me slowly without turning around. Don't break eye contact. Stare right back at him."

Zac knew more about wolves than me, and I did as he said, taking small steps backwards until I felt his warm hand along the small of my back. When I got closer, he pulled me beside him in one swift motion. Only then did I take my eyes off the wolf. Zac stared the wolf down while he moved me behind him with an arm holding me along his back. I peeked around him and watched as the wolf prepared to jump, then stopped itself mid-thought, sliding forward as its claws dug into the muddy bank. His jowls came back revealing his long fangs, there was growling low in his throat. Zac stood as still as a statue. After what felt like forever, the wolf stopped growling, lowered his gaze, and scampered off with a whimper. Zac rose and turned to face me.

"Are you all right?" he asked, cupping my face, tilting my head up until I was looking at him.

"I'm fine. What did you do?"

"Every werewolf learns that they have a special talent outside the norm. Sarah demonstrated hers after you had that dream. She has the ability to control emotions, but she has to be touching you. It took Sarah a long time to figure out her talent, but mine showed early. I have the ability to communicate with animals. Wolves are the easiest."

"So you can speak to them?"

"Not necessarily in words. I give them impressions." He moved some hair from my face.

"I'm not sure what you mean."

"For instance, with the wolf just now, I gave him the impression if he attacked you, he'd see a human become a predator stronger and smarter than him. He made the right choice."

"Has Caleb figured out his talent yet?"

"Not yet."

"How do you find out what your talent is? I mean, what do you do to find out?"

"You just find out. Someday something happens you can't explain so you test it out. That's how I found out."

"How did you test it?" We started walking back to the campsite.

"My first encounter was with a wolf, so I went and found a wolf. When that worked, I tried with other larger animals."

"Larger animals? Like what?"

"A bear."

"A bear?" I slapped his shoulder. "What were you thinking?"

He laughed, pulling me into his arms, and fogged up my mind with a kiss. "Skye, I'm fine. Calm down."

"If I'm only half werewolf, would I have a talent?"

"You might." We resumed walking back toward camp. "I'm not sure if vampires have talents like werewolves do."

I thought back to when I threw that vampire across the roof. "I wonder what it could be."

"Maybe you already know what it is. Maybe that's how you pulled the silver out of me and threw Liam across the parking lot. Maybe you have telekinesis or something."

Everyone else was up and about when we got back. Looking at all of them, I wondered if my aunt or Jared had talents.

"Aunt Lenore, have you figured out what your talent is?" I asked when we started breakfast.

"I think it has something to do with people believing what I say to be the absolute truth. But it doesn't work unless I want it to," she said.

"What about you, Jared?" I asked.

"I'm always stronger than the opponent I'm fighting. I figured that out very early in my life. Out of all my friends, I was the strongest. But my parents just thought I was strong for my age. Then a werewolf from another pack came to our town. He started attacking people. He grabbed a young girl and was strangling her when I tackled him. I was still very young, so there should've been no way I was stronger than an adult werewolf with so many years on me. I killed him and the girl survived."

"Why do you ask, honey?" Aunt Lenore asked.

"Zac just explained his talent to me, and it got me thinking about whether or not the rest of you had figured out your talents."

"I was thinking maybe her talent was telekinesis," Zac said.

"I had a feeling that was why you could do that," Sarah said.

Jared got to his feet. "Everyone finish up. We're leaving in ten."

The guys dismantled the tents and placed them back into their carrying cases. Jared meandered through the trees and underbrush, and we followed. Caleb camouflaged our trail as we went. As we walked, I mulled over Jared's story of the werewolf.

"There's a clearing ahead. We'll take a break there," Jared said.

It took a good thirty minutes to get to the clearing. When we broke through the trees, I set down my bag and sat under the shade of a tree to cool off. My eyes were glued to Zac as he pulled out his water bottle and took a long swallow. I hadn't felt lonely in a long time, and I knew Zac was the reason for that. The aching wasn't there when he was around.

Since I had been watching Zac, I noticed when he paused with the water bottle halfway from his lips. He lowered the bottle but his hand was shaking so hard the water sloshed out of the opening. Something was wrong. Before I knew it, I was standing and making my way towards him. Zac saw me coming and clenched his jaw.

"Stop. Don't come near me, Skye," he commanded.

The others noticed him just then. Every part of him was shaking, like he was fighting an internal battle. Then I realized what was happening.

"Something's triggered the hypnotism. We need to do something," I said.

"I know what to do," Sarah said.

She grabbed my arm and started pulling me away from Zac. "What are you doing?"

"Taking away his target."

"No. Zac!"

"Go with her Skye. It's too dangerous for you to be around me. Go with her before I can't control myself anymore," Zac said, and shook even more. His claws sank into the water bottle, crushing it, and he began to turn into his werewolf form.

It was hard, but I let Sarah pull me away from Zac. Nothing could tear my eyes from him. He charged suddenly, but Jared was ready for that. He hooked his arms through Zac's from behind him and clasped his hands together behind his head. Zac couldn't move because his uncle was too strong. Sarah and Caleb grabbed their bags and mine.

"We'll find a way to contact you. Keep Zac from coming after her," Caleb said.

"Be careful." Jared held onto a struggling Zac.

Caleb nodded in response and yanked at me to get moving.

"Zac," I said as I was dragged away by my friends. If we left, then I couldn't keep him from getting captured.

"I love you, Skye. Now get out of here," Zac said, his voice showing the strain of the hypnotism.

It was odd hearing him say one thing, and watching his body do another. Once we were out of sight, there was a roar from Zac that got cut off. Using the connection, I saw through Zac's eyes as Jared punched him. I would have run back but Zac's thoughts told me he wanted Jared to do it. If he was unconscious, he couldn't come after me.

CHAPTER 18
TAKEN

"Are you sure you're okay, Skye?" Sarah asked when she sat next to me, and handed me a bag of blood.

"Did you see his face?" I bit the bag and started drinking. My chest was hurting and I couldn't stop the images from my dream from popping into my head.

"All he cares about is you, Skye," Caleb said. "He'll be fine. He'll only be worried about you."

"Caleb's right. Zac only cares about whether or not you're safe," Sarah said.

They were right and I knew they were. Zac couldn't control the fact that his father had hypnotized him to kill me. How did his father manage to do that anyway? Immortals were different from humans and hypnotism didn't work because our subconscious wasn't open to suggestions. How was Zac's father able to hypnotize him? Maybe the amulet had something to do with it. But a crucial piece was still missing.

"What's Craven's talent?" I asked.

Sarah and Caleb looked at each other and then back at me. Caleb was the first to speak. "I'm not sure."

"Did he ever do anything strange?"

"Not that I know of."

"There was this one time. I was walking by Zac's house and when I looked into the window…" Sarah said, and shook her head. "Everything gets fuzzy after that. It's like I had this cloudy film over my eyes."

Something occurred to me. How could Sarah's memory have been tampered with? Was it possible Craven had the talent of suggestion, that whatever he wanted to be true became the truth? Or whatever he said wouldn't just be believed, they would be forced to obey. It would explain why he was able to hypnotize Zac and get him to do what he wanted, even from a distance, and how Sarah couldn't remember something she had seen.

"I think he has the talent of persuasion," I said.

"What do you mean?" Sarah asked.

"Well, think about it. Say Sarah saw something in Zac's house and Craven found out. If he had the talent of persuasion, then all he'd have to say is she didn't see anything and then all of a sudden she no longer has the memory. It would explain why her vision gets cloudy when she tries to remember what happened that day."

"What about Zac?" Caleb asked.

"Zac said he was missing chunks of time. Then I had the blood memory about Zac being hypnotized by his father using a stone. If he had the talent of persuasion, then he could command Zac to kill me and then wipe the memory from his mind so he wouldn't know he'd been commanded to do that. It seems like something almost powerful enough to overcome our instincts."

"That sounds plausible, but there's one thing wrong with that," Caleb said. "I don't know why I forgot about this until now, but I remember it as clear as day. Zac came to me one night, covered in blood and freaking out. I asked him what happened and he said he couldn't remember a thing four hours before. He just remembered looking down and seeing blood. I took him to his house and his dad was home. We both got him cleaned up and his father looked worried." He paused before going on with a confused expression. "But when Zac was clean, his father looked at me and told me nothing happened and I wouldn't remember any of it. Then he turned to Zac and said the same thing. It was weird because I watched Zac's face go blank, and then he saw me and said he hadn't realized I was there. It was like everything that had just happened, that I'd seen, never occurred. But I remembered everything. What would explain that?"

The flames of fire danced and the wood crackled as I thought. Craven's talent couldn't only work on family members because he had altered Sarah's memory, so there was something about Caleb that was different.

"Maybe there's a reason you weren't affected," I said.

"What do you mean?" he asked.

"What if your talent is that you can resist Craven's talent?"

He was silent for a moment, contemplating my theory. "That's possible. I don't know how to test it considering I'd rather not go looking for Craven."

"I think it might be something like that," Sarah said. Her golden hair was shining a fiery red as well and her sapphire eyes reflected the flames. "When we were younger, I tried my talent on him but it didn't work. I thought I was wrong about what my talent was. Now I look back and see I wasn't wrong. It just didn't affect him."

"Yeah, I remember. You seemed really upset when you couldn't help me. I'm sorry, I guess," he said, and chuckled. "Well, as much as I want to continue this interesting conversation, we need to get some sleep. We're leaving at dawn. I'll take the first watch."

A few minutes later, Sarah doused the fire and we went to bed. I thought about Zac and whether or not he was okay. Was Jared going to have to knock him out repeatedly to keep him from coming after me? I didn't want him to hurt himself because his body was trying to follow my scent, and his mind couldn't overcome it. The pain was so intense I curled into a ball, my knees drawn to my chest, and wrapped my arms around my legs.

I had been away from him before, and it didn't unnerve me as much as right now. Maybe it was because there was a chance he could be taken, and I wasn't there to stop it from happening. Or was it something more? My whole body ached with how much I needed him. Sarah and Caleb could protect me, but I just didn't feel as safe as when he was near. I closed my eyes and cleared my thoughts, praying for the oblivion of sleep.

****

The forest was dark and the trees loomed like giants in the shadows. Ahead of me, I saw two shapes that stood out against the rest of the forest background. I headed for those two shapes, and when I got closer, they materialized into a pair of tents. Zac emerged from his tent, stumbling around in the dark, like he couldn't see where he was going. He made his way to Jared and Aunt Lenore's tent and opened it. They came out confused, but alert and ready for a fight.

"What's going on?" Jared asked, scanning their surroundings.

"They're coming," Zac said, and I noticed the trembling had returned.

"How much time do we have?" Aunt Lenore asked.

"Ten minutes. You need to get out of here."

Jared rushed to pack the tent away, after throwing Aunt Lenore's bag at her. "What do you mean? You're coming, too."

"They're tracking you through me. That's how I know they're coming. You need to leave me here."

"What am I supposed to tell Schuyler when she asks where you are?"

"I have a feeling she's watching this right now." My hand reached out until I was almost touching his shoulder, and he glanced in my direction. "Now get out of here."

Jared was done packing and was jerking Aunt Lenore away from Zac. I watched with him as they ran away and out of sight in seconds. Zac was shaking even more when he turned around and waited for whomever it was to show. Footsteps could be heard coming closer in the pitch of the woods, but when I looked to my right, Zac was gone.

Some men came out of the darkness and searched the abandoned campsite. There was a growl and Zac dropped from the trees, attacking the man closest to him. The man had no time to react, and when Zac stood back up, he wasn't moving. Zac took down two more before a deep voice spoke out over the din, soft, commanding, and impossible to refuse.

"Stop fighting, Zac."

Zac fell to the ground, shaking even harder as he tried not to obey his father's command. Two of the men kicked him while he was down, and he cried out in pain. I ran to him, though I knew I couldn't help him. Then the two men grabbed his arms and held him in place as another guy beat him until his father commanded them to cease.

"Where's the girl?" he asked, and Zac looked at him.

The shaking stopped since he wasn't resisting the command—he didn't need to—because he didn't know where I was. "I'm not telling you anything."

His father looked surprised. "Tell me where the girl is."

"No." His father struck him in the face.

"Zac," I cried, and his eyes darted to where my spectral body was.

"Take him to the base," his father said, and they began to drag him away.

I couldn't let them take him, but when I tried to follow I couldn't go any further, like there was an invisible force holding me back. I was a mime trapped in my own creation. Zac turned his head around to look at me once more, and then I heard his voice in my head. <Don't come after me.> A tear slipped down my cheek because I knew he understood exactly what was going to happen to him.

****

"No," I screamed, waking Sarah.

Caleb rushed over and unzipped our tent. "What's wrong?"

"They have Zac. He felt them coming. Aunt Lenore and Jared got out, but he stayed behind because they were using him to track us."

"He bought us time. We need to leave." Caleb left the tent.

"We need to pack up, Skye," Sarah said, and yanked her shoes on.

We shoved everything in our bags and were ready to go in a matter of minutes. We took off, Caleb leading the way, and Sarah behind me bringing up the rear. They were doing their best to keep me safe, but all I could think about was Zac's fate. We ran until the sun had risen above the horizon and then stopped. We took a few minutes to rest and catch our breath before we were off again. Our pace became harder to maintain as Zac's beatings leaked through the connection until I felt like a punching bag.

Days went by and we slept and ate when we could, because we

could never stay in one place for more than a few hours. When the food and blood ran out, I would take down an animal, drink its blood, and then Caleb would cook the meat for Sarah and him. Once we were forced to stop when I gasped for breath and collapsed. A look through our connection revealed Zac surrounded by water. The same thing happened when they buried him. The pain never ended.

It had been a week since Zac had been captured. When I had had that dream about him, I had no idea how long he had been there. How long would it take for him to get in that condition? Sarah and Caleb kept an eye on me because they knew I was thinking about a way to get him out of there. And, of course, that was *exactly* what I had been thinking about.

They would kill him when they realized he didn't know anything. Every day they increased the torture, and I prayed he would survive it. Zac had become my whole world and I didn't know what I would do if I lost him. My heart felt like it was being ripped in two if I even contemplated him dying. I needed him. My heart needed him.

We were running when I collapsed in agony. Sarah stopped and Caleb made his way back. There was a sharp pain spiking through my heart. I had felt it before when Zac had drowned and when he was buried. The pain meant he was dead.

CHAPTER 19
JUMP

"Skye, what's going on? No matter how much blood you take, you keep getting paler and then you collapse and scream like you're being burned alive." Sarah said after the pain subsided.

"I can feel everything they do to him. The pain I felt meant he was killed," I said.

"What?" Caleb went pale.

"It wasn't a true death. They didn't cut off his head." His immortality would keep bringing him back. He would only truly die if he was decapitated. "We have to get him out of there."

"We can't. If you go there, then his sacrifice will mean nothing," Sarah said.

"I can't let them hurt him anymore." I felt like I was going to have a complete mental breakdown.

Sarah gave me a look. "We told Zac we'd protect you and that's what we're going to do. We aren't going to let you go and find the enemy. That would be counterproductive."

I understood they had made a promise, but they also didn't understand how painful it was to have a blood connection severed. My system wouldn't survive another loss like that. Especially if it was the death of my mate.

Every time we made camp or stopped to eat, I had been practicing what I thought was my talent. Since we had stopped, I created a bubble like structure in my mind and pushed it outwards. It acted as an alarm of sorts because it would alert me when something crossed its path. The bubble gave us protective shield at least two miles out, enough time to have a head start.

I breathed out and the air fogged up around me. It had gotten a lot colder in the past few days and we were going even further north. The trees were sparse and any leaves still attached were all brown. The protective shield rippled as an indecipherable number of immortals crossed the barrier.

I leapt to my feet. "They're coming. I don't know how many." We scrambled to grab everything, and then started running for our lives again.

No matter how fast or how far we ran, it was only a matter of time before they found us. They had good trackers and sooner or later they were going to catch us off guard. Numerous men came crashing through the woods behind us, barreling toward their prize. The wind shifted and they had our scent in their nostrils.

"I hear water," Sarah said, and sprinted towards it.

Caleb pushed me after her. When we broke into the open, we skidded to a stop before we catapulted over the edge of a cliff, a raging river below us. Caleb clutched the neck of my shirt and yanked me back so I didn't fall over, and I nodded in thanks over my shoulder. But that didn't solve our predicament.

"They have to be tracking my scent," I said.

"Then let's confuse the trackers." There was a sudden pressure between my shoulder blades when Sarah pushed me over the cliff.

The air cut off my scream, and I vaguely heard as Sarah and Caleb jumped behind me. There was a loud pop in my side when I slammed into the frigid water, like hitting a wall of concrete. I kicked towards the surface, but my legs were numb and losing feeling, the rest of my body was just dead weight. And it didn't help I was still wearing my pack. My ribs screamed and my lungs burned from the lack of oxygen and I felt like I could spew fire. White light shimmered near the surface, but my clothes were weighing me down and I hadn't been drinking enough blood. Drowning was not a pleasant option, and I hoped Zac wouldn't feel it the way I did with him. He didn't need more pain.

The water rushed around me, blocking out any other sound, so I was surprised when my pack was torn free, and an arm looped around my waist. My head broke the surface, and I sucked in freezing air to my burning lungs. Water sloshed around me, making me cough when it went into my mouth. Caleb swam with strong strokes, his blonde hair falling into his eyes, and breathing hard as he fought the current to pull us to the riverbank.

Every time I kicked, my ribs would burn, and it hurt to move or even breathe. We were edging to the right where Sarah was reaching out for us, with a tree to keep her from being pushed further downstream. Caleb reached out and snagged her hand, and she pulled the two of us to the bank. We climbed out of the river with Sarah's help, and then the three of us collapsed on the ground. My breaths were coming in short rasps, my ribs crying out in protest with each one. Caleb got up after a second and pulled off the over shirt he was wearing, and ripped it into three long strips.

He threaded the strips under my back, then pulled them tight and tied them at the side. I looked at him, wondering how he knew.

"I felt your rib was broken when I pulled you from the bottom," he said before he collapsed back onto the ground, his chest heaving as he tried to catch his breath.

"We need to get out of here." Sarah panted. "They'll find us if we don't move soon. And we need to find warm and dry clothes."

I shivered when the cold wind hit my wet clothes, skin, and hair and I was sure Caleb and Sarah were freezing as well. Caleb and Sarah stood, and Caleb hefting me to my feet. Our packs had been taken by the river, robbing us of our only dry clothes. We ran as fast as we could, though our pace was slowed because of my ribs. We ran until the sun went down, then Caleb left the two of us in a nook against a cliff while he went to pilfer some dry clothes. Sarah and I sat huddled together, trying to keep warm until Caleb got back.

He came back after what felt like hours with a change of clothes, and a large blanket. "Change quickly. I passed a television in the house. It's supposed to get colder." He tossed me and Sarah the new clothes. Sarah held up the blanket while I changed, and I did the same for her. When Caleb came back, he grabbed the blanket from us and sat on the ground.

"Sarah, lie closest to the rock and Skye lie next to her. I'm the warmest so I'll take the open side," Caleb said.

Sarah curled up by the rock and I settled next to her. Caleb was next to me, and covered us with the blanket, which was thinner than it looked. Caleb wrapped his arm around me and pulled me flush against him, which was a little awkward at first, but once I started warming up, I didn't care. Sarah snuggled closer to me as well and soon our body heat mingled together. We got some sleep, but the temperature continued to drop.

At some point, I must have fallen asleep because I woke up, conscious of a burning sensation over my chest. In seconds it increased in intensity. It grew until it felt like my skin was being burned with acid. Caleb woke abruptly when I twitched.

"Skye, what's wrong?" he asked.

"My chest feels like it's on fire." I gasped between words.

Sarah stirred and sat up when she saw we were awake. She opened her mouth to say something, but was cut off when I screamed at the top of my lungs as my skin split.

CHAPTER 20
NOT A DREAM

The pain was so intense across my chest it was like someone was holding a live flame to my skin, branding me with red, hot metal. Caleb pinned me down so I wouldn't exacerbate the wound that had been created. In the haze of pain, I swore I heard Zac screaming in the back of my mind.

When I peered down, my skin looked like it was being sliced by an invisible knife, continuing down, devastating my chest, until it reached my waist and mercifully stopped. There was a sharp pain at the back of my neck, followed by the pain from Zac's neck being snapped. Sarah and Caleb looked at each other in shock and bewilderment.

"What the hell just happened?" Caleb asked.

"They cut Zac with the knife," I said. Now I knew just how much silver hurt a werewolf. "I knew I'd feel it, but I didn't know this could happen."

Caleb put pressure on my chest and abdomen to stop the bleeding. "So this has never happened before?"

"Never," I said. "I didn't even know it was possible."

"Zac's your mate and you're a hybrid. You already have a strong connection based on one drop of blood. Not to mention Zac's so tuned to you he can't think of anything but you. It wouldn't surprise me that you're connected in more ways than one." Sarah and I were both surprised with Caleb's theory.

It hurt when Caleb pushed down on the cut, but it stopped bleeding. He ripped up part of the blanket, used it as a pad to cover the long cut down my chest, and then we moved out. We had no idea where we were going, and we were out of sorts ever since we had fallen into the river. Caleb walked with his arm under me for support, but we still weren't moving very fast.

"We need to get a move on," Sarah said.

"Then just leave me," I said.

"If you keep saying that, I'm going to think you don't like us."

Caleb stopped and whipped his head around to sniff the air. "They've caught our scent. We need to do something. We can't outrun them." Caleb passed me over to Sarah and ran ahead of us.

Sarah pulled me along and I ignored the pain I was feeling, forcing myself to go faster. Sarah and I erupted out of the woods near a two lane road and stopped, at a loss for which direction to go. Screeching tires caught our attention. A car skidded to a halt next to us. Caleb rolled the window down and shouted for us to get in.

Sarah and I got in the back of the car and Caleb took off. The heat was on full blast, and I stopped shaking as my body temperature returned to normal. We sped around corners, trying to get as far away from the men chasing us as we could. A couple of minutes passed, and I figured we had lost them when tires squealed behind us, and a black SUV turned a corner and sped up.

"Hang on," Caleb said, and floored it. The engine revved loudly.

Sarah and I buckled up, and I glanced over my shoulder at the car following us, praying Caleb could elude them. The car was catching up to us, and it was only a matter of minutes before they were parallel to us.

"Go faster, Caleb," Sarah said.

"The car won't go any faster. I didn't know they'd have a car to follow us," he shouted, and hit the steering wheel.

The SUV maneuvered closer and Caleb rammed the side of it, forcing it off the road. The crunch of metal against metal was loud, and it kept on until the SUV swerved to the side, barreling past a telephone pole. A horn blared and another car came out of nowhere, hitting the side of our car, and pinning us to a tree. There was a woman in the car that hit us, and she looked as shocked as we were.

My head was ringing as I looked at Sarah. She was awake and shaking her head. Caleb was slumped along the front seat, the side of his head bleeding profusely.

"Caleb?" I said, and reached over the seat to see if he was okay, but Sarah grabbed my hand and pulled me out of the car. "What about Caleb?"

"He'll be fine. We need to get out of here," Sarah said, and her blonde hair was coated in red.

"Sarah, this is my dream." She pulled me further away from the wreckage. I glanced over my shoulder, praying Caleb would get to his feet.

"I know."

"But you die."

"I know!" She turned to face me. "I've come to terms with that.

Even knowing I'd die, I knew I'd make the same decision when the time came. I'll die if I can protect you."

She started pulling me away from the car again; I followed because I was too weak to resist. "You know how I feel about people dying for me."

We heard the black SUV screech to a halt at the wreckage, and then Sarah shoved me ahead of her. "I'll buy you time. Don't come back to save me." I stared at her for a second, angering her. "Run, Skye. Run."

Against my instincts, I turned on my heel and sprinted in the other direction. I hid behind a tree to watch. Sarah growled and attacked the men when they got close. They pummeled her to the point that she was swaying on her feet and dropped to her knees, fighting the urge to cross into unconsciousness. The man closest to her pulled his sword from its sheath and readied to cut off her head.

"Stop!" I screamed, and leapt out from behind the tree.

The men turned, ready to take off after me, but I held up my hands and headed towards them. They fanned out around me the closer I got, and then closed in a circle when I came up to Sarah.

"I thought I told you to run," she murmured, struggling to keep her eyes open.

I got on my knees. "You know I never listen."

"We've been looking for you," the man with the sword said, before a black hood was thrown over my head. There was a sharp pain at my temple, and then I hit the ground and lost consciousness.

CHAPTER 21
THE CELL

The black hood was ripped off. A single light above me swayed to and fro. My head was pounding and I couldn't focus. There were men around me wearing black clothing so they blended in with the dark background. They kept moving, never staying in one place, creating havoc with my sense of balance. They just watched me, and whenever I looked at any of their faces, I would get punished.

I memorized their features for when I sought revenge. And I recognized three of them as the ones who tortured Zac in my dream. They would pay for what they did to him, too.

My lip was bleeding after being hit so many times, but I could do nothing but let it drip onto my stolen jeans. My hands were tied behind my back, chafing my wrists, and they forced me to keep my head down, causing more discomfort. When I peered up at the guy in front of me, he frowned because I had the audacity to look at his face. He brought his hand back to strike me, but I pushed a bubble of energy around me and thrust it outward, slamming him into the wall.

He hit the wall hard, throwing dust to fill the air, and then crumpled into a heap on the floor. The others stood stunned for a moment, and then they all attacked at once. When they stopped, I was lying on the floor, on top of my tied hands, panting as I tried to breathe around my bruised ribs and battered lungs. My muscles were cramped because of the position I was forced to stay in.

Later, two of them dragged me out of the room and down the hall into another windowless room with no lights, and tossed me in. My head skidded on the stone floor and my vision swam, making the room spin. Thinking it would feel better, I rolled onto my side, but it hurt just as much.

A groan escaped my lips and I tried not to think about all of the things they would do to me. They couldn't torture me for information since I was the only one of my kind. I didn't understand why they didn't just kill me. I thought that had been their goal since my parents were murdered.

I wondered if Sarah was alive and if they had taken Caleb from the car. But mostly I needed to know how Zac was doing. I thought about him, concentrating on the way he made me feel. After a moment, I could sense his presence in my mind.

<Skye?> His voice was so raspy. <Why can't I see you?>

<Because they're keeping me in the dark.>

<They caught you? What happened?>

<We've been on the run. They caught up with us. It happened like my dream.>

<Sarah's dead?> I could feel the dizziness pass through him when he sat up, and just as quickly lied back down.

<No. I came back before they could kill her. But we've been separated ever since. I don't know what happened to them.>

We were both silent for a moment, and then Zac spoke again, his voice deep and scratchy. <What have they done to you?>

<Nothing a little blood wouldn't fix, but I doubt they're going to give me any of that.>

<How long have they had you?>

<They caught us this morning.>

<Skye…> Zac murmured my name, and then there was silence.

<Zac? Zac?> Either they had taken him for more torture, or he had passed out.

The lock clicked before the door flew open, and a man walked in. He had a lantern in his hand, which he set on a ledge, and closed the door behind him. When he started unbuttoning his shirt, I clambered to my feet, trying not to sway, and moved away from him. His toned and muscular body could wreak havoc upon mine.

He came toward me and I back-stepped until I touched the wall. The guy smiled and I shivered with fear. His features were familiar and I recalled that he was the one who had thrashed Zac in my dream. He boxed me in with his arms, and when I aimed a kick at his crotch, he caught my foot before it made contact, squeezing painfully.

"I don't think so, pet. We'll be needing that," he said, grasped my chin, and forced his tongue into my mouth.

When I tried to bite his tongue, he shoved me away with a sneer, spinning me until I faced the wall. He shoved me against the stone, hard enough to rattle my teeth. The rough stone abraded my cheek. He pressed his chest against me, and I could feel the bulge in his pants against my back.

"Get off me," I said with a growl.

"I will when I'm done."

My survival instincts flared and I struggled against him, but it was no use. He reached around to my front and undid my pants, shoving them to the floor, then did the same with his own. He was too strong to fend off so I retreated within myself, thinking instead of what I would do when I got out. And I *would* get out. My nightmare continued as more men had their way with me, though I struggled and fought each until I lost count. Some came back for seconds and thirds. The first few were violent with me, breaking my will and my body. Then they would come when I was weak and tired and unable to protect myself.

****

The door opened again and I whimpered, thinking one of the men had come for his turn, but he snatched me up, directing me to a room with a pool full of hot water. The man unbound my hands and shoved me further into the room, closing the door behind me. Rubbing at my chafed and bloody wrists, I looked around the room. There were towels and soap on a stool, so I assumed I was supposed to clean myself. The door opened again, and I turned in time to see Sarah shoved into the room.

"Sarah?" I said.

"Skye. You're alive." She rushed over to me and we hugged. Her tight grip caused a severe amount of pain, but I made no sound. "What are we supposed to do?" Her hair still had blood in it, there was a gash across her forehead, and her skin was covered in cuts and bruises, but she didn't seem too worse for the wear.

"I assume we're supposed to get clean." I took my shirt off, and then my pants and was about to step into the water.

Sarah gasped and I whirled around to find her staring at me, her mouth gaping. "What the hell? What have they done to you?" She stared at the bruises shaped like hands covering my thighs and stomach. Not to mention all of the bite marks on my shoulders left by the men as proof that they had had me. I covered myself with a towel.

The fact Sarah would see the evidence of their treatment of me had never crossed my mind. Then I had a chilling thought. "Did they touch you?"

"No. Who did it?" She paused, her mouth opened soundlessly when she couldn't form the words. "How many times?"

"More than one and more times than I can count."

"Have you seen Zac?"

"He's beaten all to hell, but he's alive. He'll kill them when he finds out."

I frowned. "He doesn't already know?" From Sarah's expression, I could tell that she didn't have an explanation. "Maybe he doesn't know because I don't want him to know."

"Are you going to tell him?" Sarah asked.

"He's not going to." I turned away from her.

"What do you mean? You aren't going to tell him?"

"No. And you aren't either. Promise me you won't tell him." She opened her mouth but didn't say anything. "Promise me."

"I promise."

We got into the water without a word said between us. It hurt to clean the area where those men had clutched me so hard to keep me in place. Sarah would look at me, but never said anything. Part of me wanted to cry, but if I broke down now, I wouldn't survive any more of my time here. Once we were clean and dressed, they came back for the two of us, putting our hands in iron manacles this time. The manacles were tight and had jagged edges that cut into our wrists.

I watched over my shoulder as they took her down the hall the opposite way I was going. Once back in my cell, I laid there in the dark, waiting for more to come and they didn't disappoint. Without food or blood, I was growing weaker each day, and fighting off the men was becoming harder and harder. Even when I didn't fight, they still left bruises. It was like they enjoyed seeing my pain, or maybe it just turned them on when they could see the result of their last encounter. Insignificant bastards. They would pay. They would *all* pay.

****

Days went by, though I wasn't sure how many. Most of the time I wasn't conscious, but I stayed sore, so I knew they would do what they wanted, even if I wasn't awake. My body was so weak I couldn't lift my head, and when the door opened and light spilled in from the hallway, I couldn't stop from crying. The man chuckled at me, grabbed my manacled hands, and lugged me out of the room.

There was no resisting the man as he dragged me down the hall, almost wrenching my shoulders from their sockets. He was nice enough to pick me up when he went down the stairs, but dropped me back on the ground when we were at the bottom.

Another loud creak signaled a door being opened, but I didn't have the strength to look. Once inside the darkness, he threw me across the room. I heard the rattling of chains as he tugged them over to me, and hooked them to my manacles, attaching me to the wall. They had never chained me to the wall before.

He closed and locked the door behind him, leaving me in the dark to ponder on their motives. A haze settled over my mind and I knew I was close to passing out, but the lock clicked and jarred me awake. What now? The door hinges screeched and I struggled to lift my head to see what they were doing. Three of them entered, weighted down by a fourth.

The men chained the unconscious body to the opposite wall, and left the room, the lock sliding in place once more. We were immersed in darkness. Across the way was the body, lying in the dark. The severe aching in my chest returned. It was Zac. It was hard to see him when they brought him in, but he was the only one they would put in the cell with me. He had lost a lot of weight. My heart clenched and I had to remind myself to breathe.

"Zac?" My voice was hoarse from screaming and then disuse when I refused to scream.

He stirred and moaned before settling down. My vision went blurry when tears welled in my eyes.

"Zac!"

He jolted, and I watched as he looked around before his eyes found me.

"Skye?" His voice was hoarse, too.

"I'm here."

The chains rattled as he moved, and then a curse when he reached the end of his tether. "I can't reach you."

A light bulb clicked on. "I think that's why they chained us. They'll let us see each other, but they won't let us touch."

"Are you all right? Have they hurt you?"

I wasn't going to tell him what they did to me. Even the idea of them hitting me would torture him. "A lot less than what they've done to you."

"Did you…" his words caught in his throat, "did you feel it when they tortured me?"

"Yes. But there was something else."

"What?"

It would be difficult to explain, so I pulled my shirt aside, showing him the tip of the long cut identical to the one on his chest. He had put it together when he touched his fingers to the infected cut on his chest.

"I don't know how it happened. It didn't do it with anything else they did."

"Oh God, Skye. I'm sorry. I thought I was making things better by leaving." He tried to come closer again. "Dammit!"

"You had no way of knowing. It's not your fault." He kept pulling on the chains and the scent of fresh blood filled the air, as the manacles tore into his wrists. "Stop doing that. You're just hurting yourself."

He stopped, breathing hard, collapsed onto the ground, and we laid there staring at each other. It had been so long since I had touched him and

I needed it, but I was afraid if he could touch me he would figure out what they had done. I couldn't let him get killed because he was consumed by rage.

"I don't wanna live in this world, Zac," I said.

"What are you talking about?"

"This world is full of nothing but death and darkness. My parents were murdered just because they loved each other and I've spent all my life running away from people I don't even know. What's the point?"

Zac gazed at me through the darkness. "I can't imagine what life has been like for you. We are the children of darkness but even in the darkest places there are cracks where light can find its way through. Even the midnight sky is illuminated with specks of starlight. You just need to find your light. I already found mine. It's you, Skye. You're my star in the darkness."

His words brought tears to my eyes. After a while, I passed out from exhaustion.

****

The pain always woke me up, but this time it was something I had never felt before. Nothing had ever hurt like this. It was like fire was searing my flesh away. My eyes cracked open and I saw Zac's face a few feet away from me, his eyes closed, breathing in shallow pants. The room was flooded with light, covering my body like a spotlight. There had to be a shaft or something because there was no other way the sun could get in.

The sun! But the sun never burned me. When I rolled onto my back and the sunlight washed over my face, the pain intensified. I had to get out of the sunlight before it killed me.

"Ow. Ow. Ow." The pain grew. "Zac. Zac!" I screamed. I heard his chains move when he woke up. "Zac, it hurts."

"What hurts?" He blinked and squinted through the bright light.

"The sun."

Zac growled as he strained against his bonds. The chains groaned in protest but weren't breaking. Each breath came in harsh rattles, as my lungs turned to liquid.

"Zac…" My voice was faint. I wished I could touch him one last time before I died.

CHAPTER 22
UNEXPECTED

"SCHUYLER!" Zac roared, and then there was the loud sound of metal breaking and stone crumbling, skittering across the ground in a jumble of pieces.

The chain clattered along the floor, and then I felt him trying to yank my chain out of the wall to no avail; he had used all his strength on his. He cursed and settled next to me, blocking the sunlight. He pulled me against him, and held me so I wouldn't fall back into the sunlight.

My breathing was still labored, but it started to get better. My face snuggled against Zac's chest as close as I could with the manacles. His arm was shaking, and I wanted to cry because of how much they had hurt him.

Zac didn't budge an inch while the sun was shining, though I thought his body would have given out long ago. Hours later, the sun was down far enough that the room was dark. When he felt it was safe enough, Zac collapsed onto his back, breathing hard. I reached a hand up to touch my face and feel my burned skin. Zac turned his head to look at me, his finger grazing my skin.

"It's okay. It just looks like a bad sunburn," he said. He looked to the ceiling, and licked his dry lips before turning back to me. "I can smell their scent on you, Skye. What are you not telling me?"

"They've dragged me everywhere and hit me when I didn't do what they wanted. Their scent is probably all over me. I can't do anything about that." I glanced at him. "I'm more worried about what they've done to you."

"Nothing I couldn't handle."

So, he was doing the same as me. He was going to evade my questions since I wasn't going to answer his. Well, if he wasn't going to tell me, I was going to see for myself. With great effort, I rolled onto my side and reached out to touch his ribs. His skin was purple along his ribcage, and when I touched it, he hissed in pain.

"Sorry," I said, and used all my strength to sit up.

My fingers probed around his ribs, finding two of them broken, and then felt his chest, which was also covered in bruises. Every single injury added to the seething rage brewing within me. It amazed me he had been able to pull his chain from the wall.

His breaths were coming in harsh rasps. One of his broken ribs must have punctured his lung. I settled both palms on his chest, above the long, deep cut, and thought about the skin knitting back together and pushing out the poison of the infection.

My palms began to glow, and Zac arched his back and gritted his teeth against the pain. Once that was healed, I moved from the cut to his broken ribs, hearing two cracks as they snapped back into place. His muscles relaxed and he fell back to the floor, while I choked for air. Black spots dotted my vision, and everything went fuzzy before I fell toward the floor. Zac caught me before I hit the ground and then I passed out.

CHAPTER 23
INCENTIVE

"Skye." Zac was shaking me. "Skye, please, baby, wake up."

My head hurt so much it felt like it had split in two. My eyes slid open to see Zac staring down at me. He had my head balanced on his arm and was holding me close. When he looked at me like he was so in love with me, his eyes shone like the stars. I wanted to always wake up with him next to me looking at me the way he was right now.

No words portrayed the emotions I felt for Zac. My heart hurt when he was hurt, and not just because of the blood connection we shared. Zac pushed my hair back, caressing my cheek before giving me a gentle kiss on the lips. Everything besides us disappeared in that moment. He reared back to look at me again, and my heart swelled with feeling.

"Zac, I think…" I paused to gather the strength to say the words out loud. "I think I'm in love with you."

Zac smiled and it was the best thing I had ever seen. "I love you, too." He pulled me closer with one of his hands holding me behind my neck and kissed me.

There was so much emotion in that kiss that it filled my heart. Even if they killed us tonight, I would die knowing we loved each other. When I looked back on every moment we spent together, I wondered why I didn't recognize it before. Now there was no way he could learn what those men did to me. It would kill him. I would live with that secret for the rest of my life. And the rest of my life could very well mean the next few days.

Zac stayed on my side of the cell since I was still chained to the wall, and he didn't have the strength to break the chains. It appeared I had merely healed the major breaks in his body, but I couldn't fix everything when I was so weak.

"Why did the sun burn you?" he asked.

"I don't know. I haven't had blood in a long time so that may be why. I've never tested it before, but it's possible that I could be allergic to sunlight if I don't have enough blood."

"When was the last time you had any?"

"The day before we were taken. How long have we been here?"

"It's been three weeks." My vision swam again. "Skye?" Zac nudged me.

"Hmmm?" I grunted, my eyes flashing open.

"Skye, you need blood. Take some from me." I shook my head, but he insisted. "Skye, you need it."

"I can't. I can't hurt you."

"Please, baby, just take a little. You're as pale as a ghost."

"I just can't."

I was too exhausted to resist when Zac lifted my top lip to look at my fangs. They had receded back into my gums, and wouldn't lengthen again. Zac bit his finger and forced his thumb into my mouth, but even the taste of his exquisite blood didn't get a reaction. My body just wouldn't accept his blood, which scared the hell out of me.

The door squealed and swung open to admit five men. They frowned at the destroyed wall until they saw Zac on the other side of the cell with me. He was stronger than they expected. They never thought about what he would be able to do if they put my life in danger. Nothing would stop him short of death. The men came at us; three of them held Zac down as they tore me out of his arms. He thrashed and yelled, but they were too strong for him when he was so weak. They unhooked the chain holding me to the wall and proceeded to drag me from the room.

"Skye," Zac called, but they were bringing him, too.

At least they were keeping us together.

They took us to the room where I had seen them torture Zac in my dream, and chained him to the chair bolted to the floor in the middle of the room. His arms were secured behind him at an awkward angle, and he watched while I was chained to the wall in front of him. My hands were secured above my head so I couldn't sit down. Once I was secure, I looked at Zac and saw that I had only healed a few of Zac's injuries. And he had wanted me to take his blood.

Since I could see, it meant Zac could see my tattered clothes. He looked me over, his gaze stopping on the claw marks in my pants; there was no way I could lie and say they weren't from someone's hands. One of the men noticed our silent transaction. It was the same man that had come to me the first night I had been captured. My hands jerked as my muscles tried to obey the urge to end his miserable life.

The man leered at me, and when he walked closer, grabbed me by the hair and wrenched my head back. Zac growled and strained against the chains. The man stopped and looked at him.

"So you think she belongs to you," the man said. "Well, then I dare say you'd mind if I did this…" He bent down and kissed me.

"Don't touch her!" Zac shouted.

I spit on the floor when he let go of my head. "You'll regret that."

"Will I now? We'll see," he said.

My eyes stayed on him, but my attention was drawn away when Liam stalked in. He saw me and smiled. Liam closed the door behind him, and pulled up a chair next to where I was forced to stand.

"We meet again. It took us a while to find you, but now here you are," he said as if I was a guest who took a long time to arrive.

"What do you want, Liam?" I asked.

He frowned, like I had surprised him. "How do you know my name?"

"Lucky guess."

"Then I'll get right down to business. I want to know what you can do."

"What do you mean? Be specific now." I was tired of being jerked around, and I was ready for them to get it over with.

"What's your talent?"

"I don't know." Liam looked from me to Kresham and nodded. Kresham moved and, in a flash, stabbed Zac in the side. "What did you do that for?" Crimson blood wept from his side, soaking into his pants.

"Because I know you're lying," Liam said.

"Well, then hurt me, not him. He doesn't know anything." I waited for Zac to look at me.

<Don't tell them anything,> Zac said through the connection. His light blue eyes never showed any fear. He had complete confidence in me, even though he knew I couldn't answer his questions. Love was a hard thing to understand. It completely went against self-preservation.

"What's your talent?" Liam asked.

"How should I know?"

Kresham stabbed Zac in the chest close to his heart. Zac cried out and my legs buckled so I was hanging there like a limp rag doll. My shoulders protested as my weight tugged me down, my head sagging until my chin touched my chest.

"What the hell?" Liam leapt from his seat when blood seeped through my shirt above my left breast. Liam looked from me to Zac, and then held a hand out to him. "Stop, Kresham. Apparently this won't work."

I started laughing.

"What do you think you're laughing at?" Kresham asked.

"Now I know your name," I said.

Kresham rammed the knife into my stomach. My air was cut off when pain assaulted my brain, and it was all I could do to stay conscious.

"Schuyler," Zac yelled as Liam punched Kresham and yanked the knife from my body.

"What did I just say? Now you'll answer to him. I'll not take the fall for your stupidity." He shoved him towards the door. "Get out."

Zac leaned forward as far as the chains would let him. When I could breathe again, I looked from Zac to Kresham, who was still standing in the doorway, and imagined a knife slicing through his skin. His hands flew to his throat, blood gushing through his fingers. Liam hit me in the temple with the knife's hilt. Someone must have unhooked the chain holding me up because I fell to the floor, hitting my head, and then everything went black.

CHAPTER 24
INJECTION

There was a light swinging above me, making the darkness behind my eyelids flash from bright to dark. When my eyes opened, Sarah was standing over me. I surged to a sitting position and almost lost consciousness again.

"Slow down Skye. You have a nasty bump on your head," Sarah said.

"Why am I in here?"

"They brought both of you in here a couple of hours ago. We've been waiting for you guys to wake up."

"Zac and Caleb are here?" I surveyed the room and found Caleb squatting next to Zac's body on the floor. "What happened to him?" He looked worse than before.

"We were hoping you could tell us. They brought the two of you in here and both of you were out," Sarah said, and I got off the ledge I was on.

My legs shook and I wobbled on my feet, catching myself when my legs couldn't support me any longer. Zac had fresh wounds on his body, and there was so much blood I wasn't sure how he was breathing. I touched his face and he leaned into my hand, so that was a good sign. He must have put up a fight when I was knocked out. My thumb caressed his cheek as I fought the tears.

"What happened? We haven't heard anything since Sarah said she got cleaned up with you. It's been longer since I've seen Zac," Caleb said.

"I was kept alone before I got cleaned up with Sarah, and then they took me back there. At some point, they took me out of my room and dragged me downstairs to an empty cell and chained me to the wall. Hours later, they dragged Zac in." I summed up the rest, telling them about the sun burning my skin, what they asked me, and what they did to Zac when I didn't answer.

"What happened to the long cut on his chest?" Caleb asked.

"I somehow healed it and two ribs, but then I passed out." I leaned my forehead against the cool concrete wall in exhaustion.

"Skye?" Caleb put a hand against my cheek and then flipped his hand over and touched my forehead with the back of his hand. "You're freezing. They haven't given you any blood?"

"None." I slumped against the wall before he could catch me.

"Take some from me. Or Sarah."

"I can't. Zac already tried."

Everything was going hazy again. My eyelids were so heavy it felt like they were metal shutters. I passed out and fell into a deep sleep, and of course, I dreamed of things happening far away.

****

It was a random hotel room I had never been in. There was a single queen sized bed with a dresser, and a desk with a chair and two lamps. Voices could be heard in the hall and then a click at the door before Aunt Lenore and Jared entered the room. They were arguing, but I couldn't make out what they were saying.

There had to be a way to contact Aunt Lenore. They didn't know we had all been taken. But how was I going to get in touch with her? I could communicate with Zac because of the blood connection, but I had no such connection with my aunt.

In the past four weeks, I had been demonstrating supernatural talents. There didn't seem to be anything that I couldn't do, so maybe I could communicate with her mind, like I did with Zac's.

Concentrating, I imagined her feeling my presence. She was arguing with Jared when she suddenly went silent and turned toward the window. Jared stopped talking when she turned around and his expression went from annoyance to concern.

"What is it, Lenny?" he asked, and brought her face to look at him.

"I don't know. I just sense someone's here with us."

I needed to try talking or something before I lost the connection. <Aunt Lenore?>

Her eyes widened. "Schuyler?" She looked around.

<You can't see me because I'm not there. I'm in your mind.>

"How's that possible?"

"What's going on?" Jared asked. "How are you talking to Schuyler?"

<Shut him up for a moment. I don't know how long this will work.> Aunt Lenore hushed him with a finger and he waited.

"How is this happening?" she asked.

<I don't know, and I don't have time to explain right now. Zac was taken by

his father when he made the two of you leave. About a week after Sarah, Caleb, and I were captured, and have been held somewhere ever since.>

"They have you? Where are you? How do we find you?"

<We were blindfolded and knocked out, so I don't know where. The four of us are in the same room in some sort of abandoned building. Zac's in bad shape and I don't know how much longer he'll last. If they take me into the sun, then I'm not going to last either. If I'm deprived of blood, I can be killed with sunlight. You need to find us. You're our only hope.>

I couldn't hold onto the connection and the image of Aunt Lenore and Jared faded and broke down. Her lips began to move, but I couldn't hear her. I hoped she would be able to follow my directions. If they didn't get here soon, then we were going to die. After everything I had gained, I didn't want to give it up.

****

It was strange how heavy and bent out of shape your body could feel when your eyes were closed and your muscles ached. There were voices, but they were deep, sluggish, and difficult to comprehend. As I lay there, the voices became clearer and their words distinguishable.

"She can't raise her own body temperature. She told us she couldn't take blood and that you had already tried." Caleb was the one talking.

"I wonder why they're keeping us alive," Sarah said.

"I think they're waiting for someone. They keep talking about a 'him'. Maybe they're waiting for their boss to get here."

"I think you might be right," Zac said. "Liam freaked out when Kresham stabbed Skye. He even told Kresham he wouldn't take the fall for his stupidity. They need her alive until whoever they're waiting for gets here." I felt his hand along my brow and neck, feeling how cold I had become. "We need to get out of here. Skye can't take much more of this."

"She's cold as ice. We need to do something. For all we know, she could be dying if she doesn't get blood," Sarah said.

"Her wounds have stopped bleeding so that's a good sign," Caleb said.

Zac came close enough that I could feel the heat radiating from his body. Never had I been so tired that I didn't even have the energy to open my eyes. I felt Zac's hands on me; one slipped underneath my waist and the other cupped the back of my neck. His arms shook with effort as he lifted me and hugged me against his bare chest. He kissed my forehead before resting my cheek against his shoulder, my nose pressing into his neck.

I started shivering again, since my body was trying to warm itself, and Zac held me closer. "I made contact with Aunt Lenore," I whispered.

He jumped. "What do you mean, Skye?"

"I talked to her."

"I'm confused," Sarah said.

"I don't know how I did it. They're going to try and find us. Don't put too much hope into it."

When I was done speaking, I went limp in his arms. There was nothing left to go on. I was a train that had run out of steam, a car that had run out of gas. It wouldn't surprise me if even adrenaline wouldn't help me survive the next time they tortured me. Maybe it was better this way. If they killed me now, I wouldn't feel anything before I died.

Hope surged through Zac at my words, and I wished I could feel the same way. Zac had already been killed multiple times, and there couldn't be much time left before whomever they were waiting for showed up. My mind wanted me to cry, to release the stress, but that took energy. I just wanted Zac to hold me like he was doing so if we died, we would die together.

Zac tucked me against his chest again and I breathed his scent, managing to open my eyes. Sarah's matted blonde hair and wide blue eyes could be seen in her sunken and pale face. She and Caleb looked terrible. They looked like they had been beaten and starved, and I thanked God the men hadn't done to Sarah what they had done to me.

The door opened but none of us moved. Two men yanked my limp body out of Zac's arms with little effort, which enraged him. Zac leapt to his feet and charged the man that had snatched me, but two others held him back so another could kick him in the stomach. Zac coughed and made a retching sound before spitting up blood. A single tear rolled down my cheek and dropped, mixing into the dirt on the floor.

"Don't," I whispered. "Just let me go."

"I can't."

The man holding me laughed, and then took me from the room. They carried me to a room where there was a hard metal table with two manacles attached to each end. The man set me down, and hooked the manacles to my wrists and ankles.

I tried to do what I had done to Kresham, but nothing happened. Maybe I needed blood to be strong enough to use so much of my talent. Or maybe it was because of the rage I felt when they had hurt Zac.

They stuck a needle into my arm and hung up a bag filled with clear liquid; I watched as it slid down the tube toward my arm. It would be stupid to think they were going to make me feel better, so I wondered what it was. When the clear liquid hit my blood stream, I felt a burning sensation begin and increase in intensity. Pain beyond belief. Searing like fire. Unbearable agony. That was why they had strapped me down. I couldn't help but thrash against my bonds, screaming at the top of my lungs. Somewhere, down a long tunnel, at the other end of the connection, Zac screamed with me.

A very long time later, the man unhooked me and carried me back to the cell. No one attacked the man when he brought me back in, and when I heard the sound of chains, I realized why. The man set me down on the ground, and when the door slammed shut, Caleb picked me up and handed me over to Zac.

His hand was trembling when he touched my face. "What did they do to you?"

"They stuck a needle in my arm and hung a bag of clear liquid. I don't know what it was but it hurt like nothing I've felt before."

"We need to get out of here," Sarah said. "We need to get out now."

We all knew what we needed to do, but doing it was something different all together. A lot of noise came from outside our door, like the men were arguing about something, but I couldn't understand what was being said. The door slammed open and Craven entered. Sarah and Caleb scrambled away from him, and Zac set me behind him and stood between me and his father.

"Well, now I see why you weren't able to complete the mission I gave you," he said to Zac, a sneer marring his face.

"Gave to me? You forced it on me. I never wanted it."

I thought he would strike Zac down, but he didn't even flinch, like he expected his defiance. Craven chuckled and snapped his fingers, and the guards rushed forward to grab me. Zac broke through the chains and fought them.

"Stop, Zac," Craven said, and Zac dropped to his knees, a snarl ripping through his chest. "Take the girl." He turned to leave, and then stopped, turning back to his men. "Bring all of them."

Sarah and Caleb fought against the guards, but Zac was still under his father's spell and could do nothing but obey. The man carried me behind the others as they took us down the corridor and up a staircase. We emerged into a room bigger than all the others, with a chair against the far wall, which Craven sat in.

They couldn't have been waiting for his father to get here. There had to be someone else running things. They were keeping me alive for some reason, but I couldn't fathom why. Something needed to be done. It was up to me to find a way to get them out of here. I owed them that much for bringing doom upon them.

<Help is coming,> an unknown voice said in my mind. <Be ready.>

CHAPTER 25
BLOOD

There was no time to wonder who had spoken to me when Craven said, "Bring her forward."

The man holding me set me on my feet before Zac's father. My legs shook and then I collapsed, catching myself so I didn't hit my head on the floor. It wouldn't do for me to lose any more blood.

"Skye." Zac's voice was weak and reedy as he cried out for me, and I knew he was resisting Craven's talent as hard as he could.

"Stand," his father said, but I remained. "I said stand." He stood, like that would make the command more effective.

"Sir, she hasn't been allowed blood as ordered. She's been weak ever since," one of the men said.

"Fine." He took a deep breath. "It seems my men have been unsuccessful in figuring out your talent. I've been sent to retrieve that information."

"If they weren't so stupid, then it would've been obvious to them what my talent is," I said. "But *you* aren't stupid, are you?"

"Did my son tell you that?"

"No, he tries not to think about you. But I'd feel the same way if my father forced me to kill innocent people for him."

"He was born to hunt. He betrayed everything he is by being with you and helping you."

"No, he's better because of it. You're just too much of a coward to realize there's no reason for vampires and werewolves to be fighting. Even your name describes what kind of man you are." He was next to me in a flash, and struck me across the face.

"Don't touch her!" Zac struggled to his feet and stood before me again.

"You don't command me," Craven said with a sneer. "You will not move from that spot."

It was obvious when Craven's command took effect because Zac didn't even sway with exhaustion. He was frozen in place and there was nothing he could do. Craven beat Zac until even the power of his talent couldn't hold him up anymore.

"Stop it! He can't fight back," I cried, and covered him with my body so I would receive the blow. Zac didn't even have the energy to push me off him so I wouldn't get hurt.

"You can move freely," Craven said, and went back to his mock throne. I growled low in my throat.

As Craven walked away, I looked at Zac; there was blood falling from a cut above his eye, which was swelling shut. The light blue of his other eye was red from a burst blood vessel, and his breathing was labored. My eyes watered for what his own father was willing to do to him. Zac's lips parted and he said something I couldn't hear.

There was a crashing sound that drew everyone's attention to the door. Metal clashed against metal and the angry snarls of werewolves battling reached us. The door was thrown off its hinges, landing across the room and breaking into splinters. When the dust cleared, I saw Aunt Lenore and Jared standing amidst all of the dead bodies strewn about the floor of the hall, their swords bathed in red.

Aunt Lenore rushed in with Jared behind her. She skidded to a halt once she saw the four of us. Her stormy gray eyes widened with rage and her lips pulled away from her teeth, which were elongating, as her instinct to protect began to consume her. Craven got up from his seat with a smile on his face.

"Well, I never thought I'd see you again, Lenore. I thought you'd been killed," Craven said. "I should've known someone was taking care of her. There was no way she could have survived without help. And I guess I shouldn't be surprised to see you as well, Jared. You always did have a soft spot for leeches."

"You'll pay for what you did to my brother," Aunt Lenore said.

Craven had gone after my father and mother when they fled for their lives? Rage I had never felt before surged through my body, reaching every nerve. Now he was going to die. And I was going to be the one to do it. But I was too weak to do anything more than shield Zac from further attack with my body.

Zac's hand brushed against my cheek and my attention returned to him. His mouth opened to say something, but I couldn't hear him. When I leaned my ear next to his mouth, his words were clear.

"Take my blood," he said.

"But you need it."

"Take what you need."

Here was my chance to get the strength I needed to kill Craven. Zac turned his head to the side, exposing his neck to me. It had been fifty-six years since I had taken blood from a source. My fangs sank into the soft skin of his neck and tapped into the vein.

His blood flowed into my mouth like rich, hot cocoa to a person traveling through a blizzard. Instinct kicked in, and I clutched his body to me as I drank. Zac's hands tightened around my waist, holding me against him. My body became hypersensitive as the blood reached every nerve ending. My strength returned as well as the very strong desire to be intimate with Zac. His hands dropped to the floor. Removing my fangs, I jerked away and saw his eyes were closed, and he was barely breathing. Anger fueled me as I stood to face Craven.

"You will pay for what you did to my parents," I said.

"Stay where you are," he commanded and everyone froze.

But for some reason I could still move, and so could Caleb. We were the only ones who were immune to Craven's talent. Liam came running into the room and looked around at all of his slain soldiers. He roared and charged for Jared, who was still frozen.

"Look out," Caleb said to Jared, who whipped his head around to stop Liam when he charged. The others were somehow freed as well. Caleb had managed to break the spell Craven had over the rest of them.

They had everyone covered, so I turned my attention back to Craven, and he looked scared. Raising my hands, I sent Craven flying through the air until he collided with the wall, smashing through it and landing in the rubble. The sun shone through the gaps in the wall, but I knew it wouldn't hurt me now that I was full of Zac's blood.

Growling and snarling erupted behind me, but my gaze never strayed from my foe. He was going to die for killing my parents, for what he had done to Zac, and for what he had allowed his men to do to me and my friends. Craven stumbled to his feet and held his hands out in front of him, like he was trying to pacify me.

"Think about what you're going to do. It takes a lot to kill someone and I don't think one as innocent as you has the rage it takes to end a life."

"You gave me all the incentive I needed when you killed my parents."

A calm, killer demeanor came over him, and he ran at me. Craven went for the easy kill, but before he could grab my throat, I slashed my claws across his face. He stumbled, blinded for a second, and then kicked out at me, sending me across the room. His blows were powerful but he didn't have my speed. Staying within arm's reach, I evaded most of his punches, and pummeled him with rapid hits. His claws raked across my side, making my back spasm. I pretended I was badly hurt and, as he lunged for the killing blow, my claws sunk into his throat. Craven gurgled and with one great lurch, I wrenched his head from his body; a dull thud sounded when his body hit the floor.

I stood there, peering down at Craven's body, when a hand touched my shoulder. I whirled around, ready for a fight. "Skye, it's just me," Caleb said, grabbing my hands when I tried to attack him. "Are you all right?"

The cuts along my abdomen burned, but I didn't care. "I'm fine." I glanced over Caleb's shoulder and saw Zac lying where I had left him. "Zac." I ran back to his side with Caleb close behind me.

He wasn't breathing. Dropping to my knees next to him, I turned his head to straighten his esophagus, while Caleb kneeled on the other side of him. He placed one hand over the other and started doing chest compressions. I tilted Zac's head back, plugged his nose closed, and breathed air into his mouth. I lowered my ear to his mouth while watching his chest fall as the air left his lungs. Sarah, Jared, and Aunt Lenore stood by as we tried to revive Zac. But no matter how many compressions we did, his heart wouldn't beat.

"It's not working, Schuyler," Jared said, and Caleb stopped doing compressions.

"No, it has to work," I said with my hand lingering over his heart. It wasn't beating. "Dammit, Zac, don't leave me!" I slammed my fist down on his chest, above his heart.

"Ow!" Zac coughed and opened his eyes, blinking a couple of times. I flung my arms around his neck and hugged him. His hand patted my back. "You're really strong after you drink blood."

"Sorry." I sat back on my haunches and settled my hands in my lap.

"Are you all right? How long have I been out?" Jared stopped him from sitting up, gave him a stern look, and Zac stayed down.

"I'm fine and you've only been out for a couple of minutes." I glanced at Jared and then looked back at Zac. "You stopped breathing. I thought I'd killed you."

"I'll go and get the car," Jared said.

Aunt Lenore searched through the backpack she had dropped and was tending to Sarah's wounds with Caleb. The swelling around Zac's eyes was starting to go down, and his handsome countenance was once again visible. His hands edged toward me and I cradled his face and kissed him. Zac's hands skimmed along my waist, making me chuckle and lean back up.

"What?" he asked.

"You're still feeling the effects from me taking your blood, aren't you?"

"Yeah, I guess so. I didn't know the feeling was going to be that strong."

"Now you know why I have to be careful when we kiss. You have no idea how hard it is for me to not give in to that feeling."

Zac attempted to sit up again. "I never said I didn't have as much trouble. It's really hard to stop when I know you feel the same way, but I know I need to go slow with you."

I smiled. "I love you."

"I don't think I'll ever tire of hearing that." He pulled me down to kiss him again. "And I love you."

Since taking Zac's blood, every sight, sound, and smell became more acute. So I heard when police sirens were approaching.

"Shit. Cops," I said to the others.

If we were still here when the humans arrived, our secret would be exposed. And that could be the beginning of a mortal versus immortal war.

CHAPTER 26
SECRET

Jared came back with the car, and he helped Aunt Lenore and Caleb get Zac in while Sarah and I set the building on fire. By the time the cops got there, the building was completely consumed and we were long gone.

We were all scrunched together in the back seat with me next to Zac. He leaned his head against my shoulder and fell asleep. He was heavy but I didn't care. He needed the rest. He had refused to sleep when I was there because he was afraid they would take me while he slept.

Jared drove us to Zac's house, now it was safe to go back there. Jared carried Zac into the house and put him on his bed, as if he weighed no more than a child. I got a bowl from the kitchen and filled it with hot water and draped some clean towels over my arm. When I got to Zac's room, I set the bowl on the nightstand and dipped the edge of one of the towels in the water, then dabbed at the cuts on his chest.

Zac's head moved as he unconsciously reacted to the pain. I hated hurting him, but I didn't want any of the cuts to fester. And there were so many of them. When I was done with his chest, I tugged the sheet up to his waist. It took some finagling but I got his pants off and disinfected the rest of the cuts.

I stole into the bathroom, leaving the door cracked, and started the shower. The water heated up and I removed my destroyed clothes and stepped in the shower. It felt good scrubbing the grime from my hair, and I watched as the dirt and dried blood swirled down the drain.

Once out of the shower, I wrapped my torso in a soft towel and brushed my wet hair out, then took a good look at my clothes. Zac had seen the claw marks in my pants and I knew he was wondering who had made them. I ripped up my jeans so no one else would see the claw marks, and went over to Zac's dresser and rummaged through his clothes.

"If you wanted something to wear you could've just asked," Zac said through a gaping yawn.

Turning around, I leaned against the dresser to look at him. He was still lying down but his head was angled toward me. Too late I remembered I was only wearing a towel and adjusted the way I was standing, which only drew his gaze to my legs. The bruises stood out against my pale skin and the bite marks on my shoulders still lingered.

I moved so he couldn't see the inside of my thighs, but I heard him sit up, like he was getting ready to interrogate me either way.

"What the…? Why am I naked?" he asked, and I laughed. When I looked back at him over my shoulder, I saw he had the sheets bunched around his waist. "Did you do this?"

"Don't worry, I didn't see anything." I rifled through his dresser.

"I wouldn't care if you did," Zac said.

Snaring a pair of boxer briefs from the drawer, I tossed them to him. I found a long sleeved shirt that was long in the waist, and pulled it on before letting the towel drop to the floor.

Zac came up behind me, his hand touching my neck, and when he moved my hair to the side, I prayed he wouldn't inspect the bite marks. The feathery light touch of his lips caressing my neck sent shivers throughout my body that was growing stronger with each touch. Good. His mind was going in a different direction. He spun me around to face him, and I gazed into his eyes. His hand cupped my face before going behind my neck to pull me forward, so he could give me a tender kiss.

"You're keeping me out. What is it you're trying to hide from me?" he asked.

"Nothing. I'm just tired. And you need sleep, too."

Many of the cuts on his chest were healing now that he had been given the chance to recuperate. All he needed was a good meal and he would be on the mend.

"I'll bet you're hungry. Come with me, I'll cook you something." I grabbed his hand to lead him from the room.

He jerked me back after a few steps. "You're not going downstairs wearing only that." He grabbed another pair of boxer briefs for me to wear.

It was endearing that he didn't want anyone else seeing me half naked; I smiled as I slipped them on while he slung on a pair of jeans. I led him downstairs to the kitchen and rifled through the freezer. Someone must have gone to the grocery store because there was fresh meat. The slab of meat hadn't frozen yet, so I put it in a pan and added seasoning. I watched the meat sizzle as it cooked, just as Zac watched me.

"It still baffles me that you know how to cook," he said.

"Just because I don't eat doesn't mean I can't smell when something's burning."

"Can you though? I mean, eat. Can you eat food or will it hurt you?"

"Yes, I can eat food."

"Why don't you?" He searched through the fridge for something.

"I don't need it as sustenance. So there's no point in ingesting it."

"You should try it some time. Food is awesome." He came back with a soda and popped the top before he chugged it.

I rolled my eyes. "That thing is full of stuff you don't need to get better."

"I know, but it tastes so good."

I snorted at that and put the meat on a plate. Zac watched as I slid the plate toward him and he took a grateful bite. Just watching him relish every bite of the steak I had cooked almost made me want to take a bite myself. Almost.

"Do you want to try a piece?" he asked.

"No, I'm not hungry. I had my fill earlier today as you know."

"You haven't had blood in weeks. Almost over a month. Shouldn't you need more than what you took from me?"

"Surprisingly, I don't. It must be the fact that you're immortal and your blood is stronger or something like that."

"I can't stop thinking about the way it felt when you drank from me. The drop you took before didn't even ready me for what it was actually going to feel like. Let me tell you, if I hadn't been so weak and we hadn't been fighting for our lives, things would have turned out a lot differently."

He put down the piece of steak he had been about to eat and kissed me. There was so much passion in his kiss and I knew he was thinking about what I had done to him. I wanted things to go further, but all I could think about was the pain, and I never wanted to feel that way with Zac. I pulled away from him, breathing hard, and leaned my forehead against his chest, my palms resting on either side of my head.

"I can't," I said.

"I know." He wrapped his arms around me, and kissed the top of my head. "I'm sorry."

Zac finished his steak, and then put the plate in the sink. He grabbed my hand and took me back upstairs and set me down on the bed. "Try and get some sleep. I'm going to get a shower and then I'll join you." He covered me with the blanket before turning out the light and strolling into the bathroom.

He left the door open when he turned the water on, and I stared at the empty doorway, watching the steam diffuse into the bedroom. My eyes slowly drifted closed, then cracked opened when the shower went off, and I heard the faint sound of Zac drying off with a towel. He came out of the bathroom smelling clean and his hair damp. He climbed into the bed and wrapped his arms around me, holding me close to his body. His scent washed over me, his heart beating against my back and his breath fanning across the back of my neck.

I rolled over in his arms so I was facing him, and snuggled against his chest. He touched my hair and kissed my forehead before settling down to go to sleep. This was what I wanted for the rest of my life. This was what my parents had and I didn't know what I had been so afraid of.

<Be safe, Schuyler,> the same unknown voice said. <It's not over.>

CHAPTER 27
FIGHT

The sun was shining and it looked like it was going to be a beautiful day. I stretched in Zac's embrace and he sighed before hugging me to him tighter, wrapping his leg around me to keep me in place.

"You know, we'll have to get out of the bed eventually," I said, and Zac chuckled.

"I don't want to. Besides, you make that sound like we should be doing something."

"Well I'm getting up. Sleep all day if you want."

Zac watched me as I walked to the bathroom to brush my teeth and hair. Once Zac was dressed, we went downstairs to the kitchen. I sat on the counter and watched him make breakfast. While he ate, Sarah and Caleb came down and got some breakfast of their own. They finished breakfast right before Aunt Lenore and Jared walked in from the back yard.

"We need to talk," Jared said.

The four of us followed Jared and Aunt Lenore into the living room. Caleb sat Indian style on the floor while Sarah, Aunt Lenore, and Jared occupied the couch. Zac pulled me down to sit on his lap in the overstuffed armchair.

"We need to figure out what we're going to do. Craven found where Lenore and Schuyler were living and it won't take long for his men to find all of your hiding places. We need to go somewhere new," Jared said.

"I know of this really great place in Canada we can go where we'd be left alone a majority of the time," Caleb said.

"No, I have a house in Canada that some in the pack know about," Aunt Lenore said.

They kept talking about different places we could go, but I knew it was all useless. They were going to chase us until they got what they wanted from me. That Cymbal guy was the one behind it all and, for some reason he wanted to know my talent. If killing me because I was an abomination wasn't why he was hunting me, then I had no clue what it could be. I just knew it would never stop.

"Maybe somewhere overseas would be best," Aunt Lenore said.

"No," I interrupted.

"What do you mean 'no', baby?" Zac asked.

"They'll never stop chasing me."

"We'll never stop protecting you," Sarah said.

"They'll never stop chasing me and you guys will never stop protecting me. Do we really want to run for the rest of our lives?"

None of them wanted to agree with me, but they knew I was right. Running was no way to live. It was time I took control of my future, and I wasn't going to do that by running.

"What do you want to do, Skye?" Zac asked.

"I want to find the one that's looking for me. I want to find him and kill him, so I don't have to look over my shoulder every day afraid that someone might kill me or someone I love. I say no more running. It's time we found out who's behind this."

Caleb appeared relieved to have some sort of fight plan. Sarah wanted to kick some butt for what they had done to us. Aunt Lenore looked weary and I knew she just wanted it to all be over, so she could be with Jared. Jared smiled and I knew he was looking forward to a fight. Then I turned to Zac. He looked at me and I saw the decision in his beautiful eyes that had always been there. He was with me no matter what.

"So we fight?" Zac asked.

"We fight," they said.

"We fight," I said, and smiled.

Game on.

ABOUT THE AUTHOR

M. E. Megahee lives in Lilburn, Georgia where she enjoys spending her time writing, watching movies, and hanging out with friends. She loves to act and sing and hopes that her writing will inspire others to achieve their own personal creativity.

30133889R00111

Made in the USA
Lexington, KY
20 February 2014